W9-CZO-137

New Mercies

**Center Point
Large Print**

**This Large Print Book carries the
Seal of Approval of N.A.V.H.**

New Mercies

SANDRA DALLAS

CENTER POINT PUBLISHING
THORNDIKE, MAINE

For Harriett Dallas
1912–2001
One daughter's greatest mercy

This Center Point Large Print edition
is published in the year 2005 by arrangement with
St. Martin's Press.

The text of this Large Print edition is unabridged. In other
aspects, this book may vary from the original edition. Printed in
Thailand. Set in 16-point Times New Roman type.

ISBN 1-58547-618-8

Library of Congress Cataloging-in-Publication Data

Dallas, Sandra.
    New mercies / Sandra Dallas.--Center Point large print ed.
       p. cm.
    ISBN 1-58547-618-8 (lib. bdg. : alk. paper)
       1. Widows--Fiction. 2. Inheritance and succession--Fiction. 3. Aunts--Crimes
against--Fiction. 4. Loss (Psychology)--Fiction. 5. Natchez (Miss.)--Fiction. 6. Home
ownership--Fiction. 7. Large type books. I. Title.

PS3554.A434N49 2005b
813'.54--dc22
                                                                        2005001148

Acknowledgments

I first heard of Natchez's infamous murder on a trip there in 2002 with my daughter Dana. While touring Auburn, one of Natchez's splendid mansions, I picked up a booklet entitled *The Goat Castle Murder*. The idea for *New Mercies* came from that booklet. Both the real victim and my victim, Amalia Bondurant, were reclusive widows, murdered in their mansions in the 1930s, and an elderly neighbor was the primary suspect. Beyond that, the stories diverge, and *New Mercies* is entirely fiction.

Natchez people are gracious to interlopers, and I'm grateful to many Natchezians for sharing their history. Mimi Miller at the Historic Natchez Foundation, Delores Mullins and Janet Minor at the Natchez Library, and Ron Brumfield, general manager of the Natchez Eola Hotel, helped me with local fact and folklore. Clarence and George Eyrich and Patricia Clark, whose family owned the Eola for many years, shared hotel stories. Don Estes supplied information on Civil War firearms.

Denver and Carl Mullican explained Southern history and attitudes and gave me the best lines in the book. Philip Atchison researched architectural details. My Georgetown friend Nell Tomasi shared her collage technique.

My longtime agent, Jane Jordan Browne, to whom I owe an incredible debt, read the first draft just before her death in 2003, and made helpful suggestions. Scott Mendel helped shape the book in its early stages. Danielle Egan-Miller, who ably took over for Jane, and Joanna Topor at Brown & Miller Literary Associates shepherded the book through its final drafts, and my editor, Jennifer Enderlin, and copy editor, Carol Edwards, at St. Martin's made final improvements. *New Mercies* wouldn't have worked without all of you.

Thanks to Arnie Grossman for sharing the highs and lows of writing and even more, for being my friend. And thank you, Bob, Dana, Kendal, Lloyd, and Forrest. You are proof that new mercies come every day.

It is of the Lord's mercies that we are not consumed, because his compassions fail not. They are new every morning: great is thy faithfulness.

—*Lamentations 3:22–23*

Chapter One

IN THE ODD CITRON LIGHT of dusk, the house appeared grand and elegantly proportioned. Four fluted pillars equally spaced across the front of the old place rose two stories, setting off porches on each floor—galleries, I later learned to call them. The pillars were optical illusions, tapering slightly just above their midpoint to give an exaggerated sense of their height and sending the house soaring into the Mississippi sky. Avoca must have been one of the grandest houses ever built in Natchez. Of course, that was years ago. This was 1933, so the house was seventy-five or eighty years old at least, built before the Civil War.

Peering through the window of the taxicab, I could tell that, while grand, Avoca also was in peril of falling down. The house was set back two hundred feet or more from the dirt road, and looking across the expanse of weeds and rubble that passed for a front yard, I saw that the paint was gone, leaving weathered and splintered boards, many of them lying on the ground. Six chimneys jutted out of the roof; two of them had crumbled to almost nothing. Windows were broken, and there was a hole in the center gable of the attic. The railing on the second-floor gallery had crumbled, and a ladder was propped against the porch floor, replacing wide stone steps, which were now broken and scattered.

Branches from a low-spreading tree that was heavy

9

with Spanish moss hung over the roof, softening the decay but, at the same time, giving the sullen house a slightly sinister, almost funereal, appearance. The air was heavy with moisture, and the lush foliage that surrounded the house was wet, overripe. It had rained earlier, and from time to time, beads of moisture the color of lemon drops ran off the leaves, splashing onto the ground and adding to the smell of rot. But the overwhelming feeling of the place was of misery and great sadness.

"Will you wait?" I asked the driver.

The man shrugged. He'd said earlier that he had taken others to Avoca, and I knew he probably thought of me as just another morbid tourist. But he was agreeable. "I ain't got nothing to do but die and stay black." He gave me a sideways look. "Folks don't go inside. They just want to see where the goat lady lived, where they found them shackly bodies. You sure you want to get out?"

"I'm expected." I wasn't so sure of that now. The old house wrapped in moldering foliage was not inviting.

"Ma'am? You what?"

"I may be spending the night." The driver continued to stare at me, his eyes wide, so I added, "Or not." The day was slipping away, and the house had become gloomier in the time the two of us had sat there. "Would you like to come inside with me?"

The driver looked at me as if he'd been invited to enter a tomb. He muttered something about "hants."

"What?"

"Hants, you know, raw head and bloody bones."

Haunts, I thought. Ghosts. "Wait, then."

He got out of the cab and opened the door for me, and I started along what had once been a brick driveway. Wide enough for two carriages to pass, it curved in front of the house before returning to the road. The drive was broken through and uneven where tree roots had forced themselves under the bricks and pushed them up, a good twelve inches in places. Weeds and briers as high as my knees grew in the cracks. I should have worn sensible shoes instead of my good slippers, but I'd a notion—a ludicrous one, as it turned out—that I should arrive properly dressed. After all, I had wanted to make a good impression—but on whom, on the haunts that flitted behind the broken windows? A brick crumbled under my foot, and I stumbled, righting myself and glancing back at the taxicab driver.

He was slouched against the car, arms folded, watching, and he waved me on. "Room over there on the right. That's where they found 'em. She was murdered cemetery-dead." He seemed to be amused at me, but whether that was because his passenger was a white woman or a northerner or a fool wasn't clear. I'd encountered Negro porters and draymen all my life, but I'd never known any colored men personally, never thought about them really until today, when I'd arrived in Mississippi in the wake of my aunt's murder and seen so many black faces. I'd never thought about Mississippi, either, until a week ago, when the telegram arrived summoning me from Denver to settle the estate of an aunt I had not known existed. There was a time when getting away unexpectedly would have meant canceling a dozen social engagements, but that was before my divorce six months ago. Now I was at loose ends, ignored by former friends and with only a few business responsibilities.

I continued down the pathway and climbed the ladder to the porch, then tried the massive front door—it did not occur to me to knock at that crumbling house—but the door did not open; it was locked or boarded shut. I'd read once that southern mansions did not have keys to the front door because guests were welcome day and night. Besides, there was always a servant, or slave, to answer a knock. Avoca was not one of them, not now, at any rate. There was no way to force the door; a cannonball would not have broken it down, although something had broken the fanlight overhead, as well as the leaded-glass sidelights that flanked the door. The openings were not large enough for me to slip through, which was a relief.

There were enormous French doors on either side of the main entrance, each set centered between two pillars. The doors that led to the room on the right were open slightly; a tattered drapery had caught in them and prevented them from being closed securely. With some reluctance, for I felt like an intruder, although I had as much right to be there as anyone—more, in fact—I walked across the porch. I tiptoed, but the sounds of my shoes reverberated on the boards, which gave a little, making me wonder if they would hold my weight or break, sending me through the floor into the foundation.

But they held, and I reached the room without mishap, pushed open the door, and peered into the darkness, wishing for a torch or even a candle. Of course, I hadn't thought of either, since I had expected the house to be habitable, with someone there to welcome me. Perhaps it was just as well there was no light, because I did not care to explore the old house at night—nor by day either, at least not alone. It wasn't that I was fearful. David had remarked on it once, saying, "I'd bet a four-dollar dog you're the bravest girl in Colorado." Of course, that wasn't true. Nonetheless, I didn't frighten easily.

Still, I was not foolhardy and thus knew it would be best to return tomorrow with someone besides a cabdriver. One thing was certain: I would not be spending the night at Avoca, even if someone had received the telegram with my arrival date and was expecting me.

Emboldened by the thought of leaving momentarily, I took a step into the room, which was cluttered with black shapes—furniture.

"You git."

The voice came from nowhere, and it was deep and soft and filled with loathing.

I put one hand on the door, touching the drapery, which was velvet. Thick and very expensive, it was worn and probably covered with dirt. I should have retreated then from that murderous place, with the smell of damp and decay that clung to it. The man inside might have been a tramp or an intruder set on robbery and rape. It was doubtful the cabdriver would hear my cries.

But I was more surprised than scared. Besides, the man did not seem to want anything except for me to leave.

The disembodied voice spoke again. "Git for home. You got no right to step by here, dishonoring the dead."

Just then, there was movement, and an animal wandered into the center of the room. It was the size of a large dog, but it bleated softly; the animal was one of her goats. For an instant, it seemed that the voice had come from the goat. But I was not much for apparitions —no believer in haunts, except for those that I had brought along with me—so I looked into the depths of the room for the man.

He emerged slowly and went to the goat instead of to me, pushing the animal toward the French doors. The goat took a few steps and stopped to nuzzle me, then went outside, its hooves clicking on the porch before it bounded off onto the ground. The room gave off a smell that was more than just rot, a fetid animal odor. The goats must have wandered through the house at will, I realized. The strangeness of the place and its stench, more than the man, tempted me to back out, but I feared that might make whoever was in there think that he had frightened me. And I still was not really frightened, for this was only a man in a dark room who wanted me to leave. Besides, the scene was so surreal that being there was a little like watching a picture show, one of those old movies back before talkies, when everything was exaggerated.

"What you want?" the man asked when it was clear that I would stand my ground. He moved toward me. He was an old man, and in the darkness, it was unclear whether he was black or white.

"Who are you?"

"Ezra, Miss Amalia's old boy. I take care of things. You got no business here."

"I do."

He waited for an explanation, and when none came, he asked, "You come looking for treasure? Or maybe you another one of them newspaper peoples, mislaying the truth?"

I shook my head, then realized he couldn't see the gesture in the dark. "No," I said.

"Then what?" He took another step or two toward me, and up close, he gave off a smell that was not of goats, but a piney scent.

"This is Avoca, the Bondurant place?"

"You know 'tis."

I straightened my back. "My name is Nora Bondurant." I nearly added Tate, which had been my name for ten years but wasn't anymore.

The man was still for a long time, making me wonder if he had not heard me. But of course he had, so I did not repeat myself.

"You Mr. Winship's girl." It was a statement, not a question.

The name seemed wrong. Whenever she spoke of

him, which was not often, Mother called my father Wink, which seemed to me now like his given name, Wink Bondurant. But of course it was Winship Bondurant.

"Yes."

"Your name ain't Bondurant no more. It something else."

I was astonished that he knew of my marriage. "It's Bondurant now—again, that is."

"What you doing here? Why you come around too late, after all these years?"

"There was a telegram from a lawyer. It said that my aunt Amalia—that is, Miss Amalia Bondurant—was dead, that I was her heiress. There was something in the newspaper at home about her murder, but I don't really know what happened, only that a neighbor shot her, then killed himself." I stopped, a little annoyed at having to explain my presence to a caretaker, who, if he thought about it, worked for me now.

"So you come for the leavings."

"I came because I was summoned by an attorney."

Ezra snorted. "Where was you when Miss Amalia have need of you, when you can ease her years?" He came close and looked into my face. His skin was pale, and his nose aquiline; he was a white man. "You thirty-three years old. You should be here long time since."

I did not remark on the extraordinary fact that he knew my age; instead, I said, "Not that it's anyone's business, but I'd never heard of Amalia Bondurant until a few days ago. And I don't know a thing about her now except for what was in the newspapers." The stories had caught my eye because the woman and I had the same last name. Of course, there was no reason at the time I read them to think that we were related.

"You never heard of her?" There was sadness in his voice.

"We didn't know my father came from Natchez or even Mississippi, only that he was born somewhere in the South." In fact, my mother said, Father really wasn't southern at all, because he'd gone to boarding school in the North, probably had never lived in the South for more than a few months at a time. "Until the telegram came, we didn't know he still had family," I added, annoyed with myself for telling the man something that was none of his affair. "I'm all in and need to find a hotel. It's clear this place is uninhabitable."

"Not for Miss Amalia. This her bedroom."

"That's fine, but I don't intend to sleep with goats." I was a little ashamed of the remark, so I added lamely, "I mean, you weren't expecting me. I'll find a place to stay and come back in daylight."

While it had grown dark outside, there was a little light from the moon now, and as the man followed me out onto the porch, his face became clear. It was devoid of expression. "I'll come back in a day or so." Impulsively, I held out my hand. After a moment, he took it. His hand was rough and calloused, moist and warm— and limp. Perhaps women in the South didn't shake hands with retainers.

"You do that. I be out back, me and Aunt Polly."

"*Aunt* Polly? You mean Aunt Amalia had a sister?"

He laughed, although there did not seem to be humor in the sound. "White folks call old colored ladies 'aunt.' You ask them why."

For some reason, I felt relieved for this unknown Aunt Amalia that a woman had lived nearby. Not that in the end it had helped her.

As I walked back across the bricks to the taxi, the rankness of the house faded, replaced by the scent of some night-blooming flower. The air, so heavy with humidity that I did not know why it had not turned to rain, was oppressive with its sweet smells, different from the clean, dry air of Colorado, which always seemed cleansing. The southern air was like a blanket, heavy around me, slowing me down.

The driver still leaned against the taxi, one foot on the running board. He had not moved, and he waited until I reached the vehicle before he straightened up, unfolded his arms, and opened the door for me. When he got into the driver's seat, he said expectantly, "Well now."

The familiarity was unwelcome, but perhaps he realized that he had me at his mercy. After all, he could leave me there to find my own way back into town. I could wander off the road into the thicket of foliage, perhaps fall and hit my head and die, then decay before anybody came looking for me. Nobody else but Ezra would ever know I'd been here. I was not morbid, however, and the idea of my flesh rotting into the damp

Mississippi earth almost amused me.

The more immediate problem was finding a hotel room, since I knew nothing about Natchez. "I won't be spending the night at Avoca. No sir." I shook my head. "Is there a place in town to stay?"

"We got two, three hotels and some guest houses, too, nice places where old ladies put out signs saying 'Rooms to Let.'"

The idea of encountering another old house, even one in decent shape, did not appeal to me, so I told the driver to take me to a good hotel. If the accommodations were not to my liking, I would ask the lawyer who had contacted me to recommend a better place.

The driver turned the car around and started back toward town at a leisurely pace. "Look like you got in that house without no mishap," he said, inviting me to tell him about what had transpired inside.

"Yes." I did not relate the details.

"You meet old Ezra, I reckon."

"The caretaker. He was there."

"Ezra's always there. He's full-blooded Natchez ever since he was born on the place in slavery times, stayed on after freedom come, him and Aunt Polly. Now that Miss Amalia's dead, I guess their last string's been loosened."

"Sir?"

"They got no more ties to the place, them two. I wonder where they'll go, mebbe just stay on. Ain't nobody going to live in that house now."

"He was a slave?" Of course there were men and

women still living who'd been bought and sold, but the sudden knowledge that my own family had owned them revolted me. "He couldn't have been a slave. He's white." And then I remembered that the newspaper articles about Amalia's death had mentioned a Negro servant who lived on Avoca. That must have been Ezra, and Aunt Polly was his wife.

"Ezra's black as me, leastways he is inside. I don't know where it is you come from, mist'es, but round here, folks say if you got the leastest drop of colored blood in you, you're a colored."

That struck me as ludicrous, but then, what constituted a colored man? What if this purply black man in front of me had one drop of white blood? Why wouldn't that classify him as white? But unfamiliar with the relationships of black and white in the South, I kept my musings on race to myself.

The driver took me to the Eola Hotel, which was new and efficient and clean, and he carried in my suitcase, setting it down in front of the registration desk. A clerk in a rumpled suit, his hair parted in the middle and lying in damp curls about his face, greeted me in a soft voice. Everybody I'd encountered in Mississippi had a soft voice.

"Welcome to Natchez, Mrs. . . . ." He dragged out the words, another Mississippi trait.

He waited for me to state my name, but, hoping to avoid a conversation about the Bondurant family, I simply corrected him. "It's Miss, and I will be staying

20

one or two nights, maybe three."

When he looked at me as if I were new money in town, I added quickly, "Price is a consideration. I would like a reasonable room."

"I think you will find our prices quite satisfactory." He asked if three dollars would be acceptable, and I nodded my approval, quite pleased, for the rate was cheap.

"With private bath?" I asked.

"Course. All our rooms have private bathrooms." He picked up a pen and dipped it into an inkwell. "May I inquire if you are vacationing in our city?"

His smile bordered on a smirk, and he seemed over-friendly. Then it hit me that perhaps the man thought that as a female alone, I was a woman of unsavory character, and his job was to spot such creatures and keep them out of the hotel. Or perhaps I was just being thin-skinned.

Still, my appearance was not in my favor. My white gloves, which lay beside my pocketbook on the registration desk, were crushed and filthy. My stockings had runs from where they had caught on the weeds at Avoca, and my shoes were dirty. My navy blue suit, which had looked so smart in Denver when I boarded the train, was as wrinkled as tissue paper and stained from the dust that had blown in through the open window of my compartment. My hair, stylishly straight at home, had crinkled into a nest in the dampness, and grime covered my face. "I'm here on business. In the morning, perhaps someone will direct me to Mr. Satterfield's office. He is a lawyer. Do you know him?"

The clerk straightened, his smile slipped a little, and he tore up the card on which he'd written the room rate. "I think you will find our prices quite satisfactory indeed." He wrote "$2.50" on the second card and turned it around for me to fill in. I took out my own fountain pen, the green marbleized one that David had given me four years ago for my twenty-ninth birthday, and wrote my name and address, then handed the card back to the desk clerk. He took a key from a cubbyhole behind him and summoned the bellboy. "Clyde, take Miss—" He glanced at my name on the card, then turned to me quickly. "Miss Bondurant?"

I nodded.

The clerk looked at the cabdriver, who stared at me as if I were the haunt now. He had been as ignorant of my name as the clerk.

"Well, it is a pleasure to welcome you, Miss Bondurant." He crossed out the room number on the card and wrote in another, then exchanged the first key for a second. "Take Miss Bondurant to room three twenty-two." It wasn't clear if room 322 was a better or poorer room than the first one.

The bellboy didn't look at me as I followed him into the elevator, and he closed the cage door and took me to the third floor. He left the elevator doors open as he carried my suitcase to the room and set it on a rack. Then he made a great show of opening the window, switching on the ceiling fan, and checking about the room to make sure that everything was in order. "You got your circulating ice water in here. It's real nice to drink on a hot day." He turned on a tap over the bathroom sink and filled a glass with water. Then he gave me a bold look. "The goat lady that was murdered, she your kin?"

The question made me shiver, since I'd never known anyone who'd been the victim of a crime, even robbery. Now I was to be identified by my relationship to a murdered woman. The boy's nosiness also offended me, and I wondered what Aunt Amalia's life had been like in this place, which, from my brief acquaintance with it, appeared to have atrophied since the Civil War. The Bondurant name certainly accounted for something, but was it respect or ridicule? The bellboy waited for my answer, one that would be repeated to the desk clerk. "I don't know any goat lady," I replied coolly, considering whether to forget his tip as punishment for his cheekiness. Or perhaps I should overtip, I thought, to make up for my disdainful reply. But there was no reason for my tip, too, to become cause for comment, so I gave him a quarter, which was the standard gratuity for carrying one's suitcase in Denver. He seemed surprised and pleased, flipped the coin into the air, caught it, and closed the door. A dime would have been adequate.

Unpacking my suitcase, I hung up the few clothes I'd brought with me, then took off my suit, brushed it, and put it on a hanger. I rolled down my ruined stockings and threw them into the wastepaper basket, then massaged my thighs where the garters had left a ring. Next, I sudsed out my undies in the bathroom sink. I put on the soiled white gloves and washed them with a bar of soap, as if washing my hands. At last, I ran a bath and soaked in it until I was almost asleep. Toweling myself off, I took a thin nightgown from a silk bag and put it on, turned down the bed, and slipped between the sheets, the damp air in the room pressing down on me like a quilt.

To my surprise, I slept until eight o'clock the next morning, which was not so late, only seven at home, but it was the first time in many weeks that I had awakened feeling rested and almost peaceful, instead of weighted down with failure and guilt. But the demons that were my constant companions would return as the day wore on, intruding when least expected. In the past, they had come at unguarded moments, when I was admiring a hat in the window of Gano-Downs on Sixteenth Street and one evening as I walked past the Shirley-Savoy Hotel and heard a dance orchestra play "They Didn't Believe Me." That had been our song. Another time, I was looking out at the park from my apartment window, and the sense of remorse was so engulfing that it almost took away my breath. Perhaps being away from Denver, even on this strange mission to settle the estate of a crazy old lady, would give me a respite. I doubted it, however.

I leaned out the hotel window and looked toward the river. A white man across the street, his foot on a shoe-shine box, talked loudly to the Negro who was using a rag to apply polish to the man's shoe. The slap of the rag punctuated the words, and a breeze carried the smell of the polish to my room. The air smelled of rain, but maybe that was just the everyday humidity in Mississippi. Rain in Natchez probably did not clear up the air, just added to the oppressiveness. I would look for a drugstore to purchase talcum powder, although it probably would not help much in keeping me dry. I bathed again, dressed, and put cologne on my wrists and the tips of my ears, stopping to view my short dark hair in the mirror over the bathroom sink. The dampness made it kinky, so instead of combing it into its usual straight, cropped look, I tried squeezing it into curls, rather liking the effect. The waves softened my too-large brown eyes and rounded my face, which was long. The rest of me was too long, as well—too tall, too thin. I had become even thinner in the months since my divorce and then David's death.

Although it was still the coolness of the morning, the air was oppressive, stifling me in my wool suit. But there was nothing else to wear, since I had wanted to look businesslike for the meeting with the lawyer. Thinking the trip would be no more than a day or two, I had traveled light, bringing only an overnight case and a suitcase, which contained a second suit, two blouses, and a severe black wool dress, proper for a funeral, for surely there would be a service. Staying on in Natchez would require me to shop for something more suitable to wear in this heat. I considered the hat from the day before, a navy blue cloche that matched the suit, but the idea of the wool close around my face was too much, and I left it behind. Besides, the hat would smash my newly discovered curly hair.

Whether my outfit was proper for breakfast was unclear, since I was the only woman in the dining room. There was a hush when I walked into the coffee shop, either because I was a woman or because the word had gotten around that I was the goat lady's niece. Instead of taking a stool at the counter, where someone might start a conversation, I asked for a table. But no sooner had I been seated and given the menu than a man dressed in rumpled white linen pants and white shirt, carrying a wrinkled seersucker jacket, got up from one of the tables, where he was breakfasting with several other men in crumpled clothing, and approached me. Did women in Natchez iron?

"Miss Nora Bondurant?" He had blond hair that was almost white and a mustache of the same color, and he held a white Panama hat in one hand. His face was pink, either from the heat or his age, which appeared to be in the mid-sixties.

I raised an eyebrow. For all I knew, he was selling cemetery plots, and perhaps I needed to purchase one. "What is it?" I chided myself for being so prickly. It seemed as if the least little thing offended me these days.

The man ignored my disdainful manner and pulled out a chair. "Of course you are. The hotel sent word you'd got here. I hope your trip was a pleasant one. I am Samuel Satterfield." He pronounced his first name "Sam'l."

"Oh, of course, Mr. Satterfield." I held out my hand. He took the tips of my fingers and pressed them lightly, and I reminded myself not to offer my hand again to a southern man.

"You go ahead and order you your breakfast." Mr. Satterfield sat down. "I hope there is something that satisfies. We Natchezians pride ourselves on our hospitality and our food. It's mighty good, I can tell you."

It was also mighty heavy. The menu included biscuits and gravy, hotcakes and ham, scrambled eggs and brains, and squab—squab for breakfast? I ordered a bowl of Shredded Wheat and coffee. Mr. Satterfield, who had left an unfinished breakfast behind, told the waiter, "Boy, you bring me another plate of ham and eggs, eggs over easy now, not too hard. And the lady'll want a basket of beaten biscuits. I expect she'll like them." After the waiter left, Mr. Satterfield raised his eyes to the ceiling and said, "That bakery way upstairs, they beat the dough with a rolling pin till it blisters, beat it thirty, forty, fifty minutes. That's your beaten biscuit, and you can't find it nowhere better, South or North, than at the Eola."

I didn't argue. Nobody I knew in the North would spend the better part of an hour pounding biscuit dough.

The waiter poured coffee for us, and Mr. Satterfield added a generous amount of cream and sugar to his, then stirred the liquid and took a sip, holding the cup by

27

the bowl instead of the handle. He added more sugar and sipped again, satisfied. "I had coffee in one of your Yankee cities, and it tasted like Borax. They brought it to me in a mug. No saucer, no place to set your spoon, excepting the tablecloth." He shook his head at such a breach of good manners. "You'll like our coffee."

I tried mine, and I did.

"There's talk you went out to Avoca last night." He chuckled. "Lordy, Miss Nora! I apprise you it's no place for a young lady in the daytime, and purely dangerous after dark, with all those trees and bushes. It bears down on a person some days. You could have broke your neck on that porch, or maybe stepped on a nail and got yourself a good case of the lockjaw." He gave me a chiding look, as if I were a child.

"From your telegram, I'd assumed I would stay there."

"You did?" His face fell. "Then I most certainly did you a wrong. I ask you to excuse it. If I'd known you were arriving yesterday, I would have made arrangements myself for you to stay here at the hotel. I am delighted you found it on your own. The Eola's a real nice place, rightly priced. I see they gave you the rate for a traveling man."

This did not seem much of a town for secrets. He probably knew I'd thrown away my stockings, too.

When the waiter set down our breakfasts, Mr. Satterfield passed me the basket of biscuits, which were the size of silver dollars. "Here's you your beaten biscuit. Taste it and tell me if you've never had better."

After chewing the biscuit, which tasted like a thick cracker, I admitted that I hadn't tasted better, because I'd never tasted beaten biscuits before—and hoped never to again. Uneeda, the cracker company, didn't have to worry about southern competition.

Mr. Satterfield looked at my meager breakfast and shook his head but didn't comment. Instead, he poured syrup on his ham and eggs and on top of a white mass that he told me was grits, then began to eat. "The will is dull business, and we can commence to discuss the particulars at my office. Right now, you and me ought to get acquainted."

"You knew my aunt."

"Oh my, yes. A lovely lady. Tragic end. Just tragic." He pursed his lips together. "I blame myself for not seeing this coming."

"Were you friends?"

He considered the question while he cut into an egg and let the yoke spread into the grits. "All the old families in Natchez are friends. Breeding wouldn't let 'em be otherwise."

"Even if they lived with goats."

"Ma'am?" Mr. Satterfield jerked up his head and looked at me, decided that was a joke, and laughed. "Miss Nora, we have our peculiarities here in Natchez. And Miss Amalia had as many as anyone, more than most, I'd say. We tried to help her. That's the truth. But she was mighty proud, wouldn't allow anybody about the place except for Ezra and Aunt Polly. They did for her, but at the end, they did not do a very good job of it. Course, it wasn't their fault. Course it wasn't. They thought Miss Amalia could protect herself. Many's the time she run off somebody with a shotgun. She knew how to use it, yes. She could shoot like a man, ride like one, too, once upon a time." He shook his head. "She wasn't always queer, mind you. Why, after the War, she was thought to be the most desirable young woman in Natchez. I thought so myself."

I frowned, wondering how old a woman had to be in Natchez before people stopped referring to her as "young." "The war ended in 1918. My aunt must have been nearly sixty by then."

Mr. Satterfield wiped his mouth with the bottom of the napkin he had tucked into his shirt front, and he looked at me as if I were pulling his leg. "Why, you Yankees! I don't mean the Great War. When we talk about the War, we mean the War Between the States."

"The Civil War?"

"We say the War of Northern Aggression, or, as the ladies prefer to call it, the Unpleasantness. It's you Yankees who think of it as the Civil War."

Actually, I did not think of it as much of anything. The Civil War was not a great topic of conversation in the West, and when we did talk about that war, it was a given in my family—among everyone we knew, for that matter—that the South had been wrong. My information about the war came from my grandfather Bullock, my mother's father. He'd been a union soldier, was captured and sent to a southern prison camp. He went home to Iowa when the war ended, but after a couple of years, he sold his farm and moved to Colorado to recover his health. I thought it would be prudent not to mention that my grandfather had fought for the North or that Grandmother had once known Mrs. Ulysses S. Grant in Galena, Illinois.

"Captain Bondurant was a cavalry officer."

"Who?" I reached for another beaten biscuit. Perhaps I could develop a taste for them. I bit into it and decided that was unlikely.

"Captain Bondurant, your grandfather. In my growing-up time, there wasn't a boy in Natchez who didn't want to be Captain Bondurant. Why even old Jeb Stuart couldn't shake a stick at him."

I shrugged. "I don't know anything about my father's family. You see, he died—"

"In nineteen and three," declared Mr. Satterfield, finishing for me. "Oh, yes, I know. Struck down in the prime of life by an Oldsmobile autocar."

"Yes." I pushed my dish away, wondering how people could eat when it was so hot.

Mr. Satterfield, too, had finished his breakfast and now looked longingly at the beaten biscuits. "If you're not going to eat them . . ."

"Help yourself."

"I do hate to see good food go to waste." He put several biscuits onto his plate. "It's a pity you didn't know Miss Amalia better."

I sighed. "I thought it was clear that I didn't know her at all, had not the least idea she was a relative until your telegram arrived."

Mr. Satterfield moved his plate to the side and leaned back. He took out a silver cigarette case, then glanced at me, and I told him it was all right to smoke. In fact, I would have liked a cigarette myself, but I wasn't sure it was proper for women in Natchez to smoke in public. He lighted it, leaned back in his chair, and blew smoke out of the side of his mouth. "You were a poor father-less girl."

"Not at all. My stepfather is as fine a father as a girl could have. Mother remarried when I was five."

Mr. Satterfield nodded, making it clear that he knew she had.

"After that, she almost never mentioned my father. When your telegram came, Mother wasn't sure who Amalia Bondurant was. She told me Father never said much about his family, but she did remember that he thought they blamed him for his mother's death. You must know that his mother died just after he was born, from the effects of childbirth, I would guess."

Mr. Satterfield looked away, as if childbirth were not a fit subject for the breakfast table. "In her last years, Miss Emilie, your grandmother, enjoyed poor health," he said.

"Father was sent to New York to live with relatives. When he was old enough, he was shunted off to boarding schools. Mother met him just after he gradu-ated from college. Father was an engineer and had gotten a job in Colorado. Apparently, he never went back to the South. Mother told me he didn't even have a southern accent."

"Now that's a pity. But you can't blame the Bondurants for sending him off. Those were hard times. Miss Emilie kept that family together after the War. When she passed, why it caused the awfulest grief. The captain solaced himself at the fleshpots at Natchez Under-the-Hill."

"Under what hill?"

Mr. Satterfield cleared his throat and added quickly, "He put your daddy with his sister Rose up north because he didn't know what to do with a baby. After Rose died, young Winship went to military school."

"He seemed to have been shipped here and there, like a trunk without a label. Why didn't his sister raise him here in Natchez?"

"Oh, the malaria was bad then, and Miss Amalia was not the sort of woman to raise a baby." Before I could ask what sort that was, he added, "The Bondurants did what they thought was best for him. There it is."

It didn't appear to be the best way to me, but I hadn't come to Natchez to discuss my father's upbringing.

Mr. Satterfield snubbed out his cigarette and took out the silver case again. I did not want to listen to gossip about dead relations, so I put my napkin on the table as a sign that breakfast was over. "Forgive me for keeping you from your friends," I said, gesturing to the waiter. Mr. Satterfield intercepted the check, and I did not protest, familiar enough with lawyers to know it would be buried in the legal bill for settling the estate.

We agreed to meet in the afternoon, and Mr. Satterfield walked me to the door of the dining room. "Enjoy your time among us. As even Yankees know, Natchez in its day had more millionaires than anyplace in America outside New Orleans, and you will not see finer homes anywhere in the country. These days, there is still wild excitement here about the houses, but not much about business." He bowed a little as we parted. Having learned my lesson, I did not offer him my hand.

Not everyone knew Natchez had once been an affluent city. Before I received Mr. Satterfield's telegram, I did not know there was a Natchez. Other Yankees didn't, either. The ticket agent at Union Station in Denver had told me there was no such place as *Matches,* Mississippi.

"Natchez," I said, correcting him, as I pulled out the Western Union envelope.

He examined it. "Oh, never heard of it."

Since I'd seen little of Natchez on the taxi ride the day before, I decided to walk around and take in some of those finer homes. It certainly would be more interesting than sitting under a fan in my hotel room.

The Mississippi sky was a cool blue, but it was hot outside nonetheless. The humidity wrapped around me like a damp coat as soon as I went through the front door of the hotel, reminding me that I would have to find something more comfortable to wear. Turning east, I walked up Main Street through the business district, looking into the store windows. The dresses displayed in the first shop were chiffon and linen, printed with gaudy flowers—not my style. All the stores seemed to carry the same brightly colored clothes, however, so I went inside a shop whose windows were filled with headless, armless mannequins. I asked the clerk if she had a tailored summer dress. After some looking, she found a plain short-sleeve rayon frock that fit me. I purchased it, along with two cotton skirts and blouses, and a pair of canvas shoes, which would be more suitable than my good slippers for poking around Avoca.

"You will take an out-of-town check, won't you? I'm staying at the Eola," I said, and the saleswoman nodded.

After paying, I picked up my dress boxes by their little string handles and started to walk away. I had almost reached the door, when the clerk called, "Wait! Wait!" She pronounced the word as if it had two syllables—"Weigh-it! Weigh-it!" She waved my check in the air. "Slow down! Halt!" she added, although the first outburst had stopped me. The clerk rushed through curtains hung in a doorway in the back of the store and returned with a woman who appeared to be the owner. Holding the check in front of her mouth, the clerk whispered frantically. The only word that I understood was *goat*. When she lowered the check, the clerk was biting her cheeks to keep from smiling. My aunt must have been ill-served in places like this. Then I realized that Amalia Bondurant probably had not been inside a dress shop in years—perhaps ever. In her more affluent time, she would have summoned a dressmaker to Avoca.

"You're from out of town?" the owner asked. She stood in front of a corset in a glass display case.

"Yes."

"And you're here . . ." She waited for me to complete the sentence.

"Yes. I'm here."

"Oh." When she realized that she was unlikely to get more information, the woman took the check from the clerk and examined it, then said, "If you don't mind my asking, are you kin to Miss Amalia?"

"Is there something wrong with the check?" I set down the boxes. "Because if you're concerned that it might not be good, I wouldn't dream of taking these things." Natchez, like the rest of the country, surely was suffering from the Depression, and my purchase might be the best sale the shop would make all day, possibly all week.

The owner looked me up and down, taking in my suit, which was expensive, and said, "Oh, no, ma'm. It's fine. You come back and see us."

That was unlikely. "Thank you."

Back at the hotel, where I had gone to deposit my purchases, a man in shirtsleeves, smoking a cigarette, rose as I crossed the lobby and accosted me. "You Nora Bondurant?"

Instead of answering, I waited for him to identify himself.

"Bill Kilpack, *New York Herald.* I've been covering the Bondurant murder. And I was just about to leave town, when I heard you were here. I'm glad I didn't go, you betcha, because I've got a couple of questions for you. You haven't talked to anybody else, have you?"

"No, and I'm not interested in talking with you." I tried to get around the man, but he blocked my way.

"You're her closest relative. How come you let her live like she did?" He took a final drag on his cigarette, then put it out in the sand of a standing ashtray next to him.

"I didn't know her."

He took out a pencil and wrote a few words in a notebook.

Annoyed with myself that he had tricked me into saying something he could quote, I said, "There's nothing more to say to you. Please let me pass."

"You think she has money hidden out there in that big old place. What's it called, Avoca?"

He knew perfectly well what it was called.

"What's 'Avoca' mean, anyway?"

It meant a shady, restful place filled with friends. The name had been in a book that was among Father's things, which Mother had shown to me just before I left Denver. "I wouldn't know."

"What about that Lott woman? You going to help her out?"

"Please get out of my way."

Mr. Kilpack chewed his pencil, which was pitted with bite marks. He was short and square, and his forehead was moist. There were rings of sweat under his arms; I was glad to see that the heat and humidity made him as uncomfortable as it did me. "Don't be so short with me, lady. I wouldn't let my worst enemy live in a pigsty like that."

"Goats." I could not help myself. "She lived with goats, not pigs."

"You southerners got no heart, if you ask me."

"Did someone ask?" Would I have to knock down the man to get to my room? Just then, a woman interrupted.

"My dear, shame on you for being late. And they say we southern girls think we're on time if we're only an hour behind!" The woman, with Titian hair and dressed like one of the mannequins in the shop windows, only with head and limbs, put her arm through mine and drew me away. "You'll excuse us, won't you?" she said to the reporter, and without waiting for his reply, she yanked me down a long hall with peacocks on the wallpaper, past potted palms, to the restaurant, where she took one of my parcels from my hand. "Oh, you found Miss Sabra's store. She has the yummiest clothes, just precious. I trade there myself." The reporter followed a few steps behind.

The woman held on to me until we reached a table in the corner farthest from the door. Then she turned back to the reporter, and with a dismissive wave of her hand, she called, "Be going about your business. Don't you disturb us, you." There was a hint of iron in her voice, and the man went back to the lobby. We watched as he picked up a cardboard suitcase covered with hotel stickers and started for the door. The woman said, "That horrid little man is not a gentleman." She smiled at me. "Honestly, you must think I'm fuzzed-up for grabbing you up like that, but I had to rescue you. I just hate those disagreeable reporters. They're such tartars, asking their nasty questions, writing queer things about us. I'd like to break their bones. From what they print in the newspapers, you'd think we spend our Saturday evenings hunting up old ladies so that we can chop off their heads with our little axes. Or guns. Miss Amalia was killed with a gun. And, of course, her head was let be."

A waiter came to the table, and the woman ordered a "New gray ape." "Two?" she asked, looking at me. It took me a minute to realize she had asked for a Nu-Grape.

"A Coke."

"A new gray ape and a Coke-Cola," she told the waiter. She took off her gloves and adjusted her hat, which was straw and had a brim, making me wish I'd stopped in a millinery as well as a dress shop. "You are dying to know who I am, I know, and why I have kidnapped you. I'm Pickett Long. I was on my way into the hotel when I saw that man accost you, and I thought you needed a friend. I hope you don't think I'm too bold."

"No, of course not. I'm grateful you did." In fact, I was delighted Pickett Long had taken me in hand.

"I already know who you are."

"Is there anybody in Natchez who doesn't?"

"Oh, now don't be too critical of us. We are a small town, and it is nice to know that we look out for one

39

another, although in Miss Amalia's case, we were purely derelict in our duty." She paused while the waiter set down our drinks. "But I have a reason to know you. I'm Sam Satterfield's niece. He told me you had gone out to Avoca last night, thinking you'd be staying there. They could most likely eat you at Avoca, but they surely could not sleep you out there." She stopped talking long enough to roll her eyes. "I hope you don't try that again very soon. I told Mr. Sam, 'You don't know a thing about ladies and never did, and that is why you have been a bachelor all your life.' Oh course, that's not the only reason." She raised her Nu-Grape and said, "Welcome to Natchez," then took a sip. "Avoca must have been a terrible surprise for you."

"Something like that. Deserted except for the caretaker."

"Ma'am?"

"Ezra, the caretaker."

"The servant, you mean. He belongs to the place."

When my eyes narrowed, she added quickly, "Oh cake! You know what I mean. We don't have slavery any longer. You Yankees took care of that, although it was only a matter of time before we would have ended the institution ourselves. What I mean is, Ezra was born on Avoca, and he'll die there. That made him Miss Amalia's responsibility. We don't throw our servants aside when they grow old, and that's the pure-d truth." She gave me a stern look, as if over the years I had thrown scads of family retainers onto the dole.

"Miss Amalia couldn't have gotten along without Ezra. He helped her care for those goats, raised them, drove her into town, where she sold the milk. It gave her a modest competence." She laughed. "That is what the Old South has come to, dear old ladies in hoop-skirts selling goat's milk out of the back of REO cars—and with style, you see. Miss Amalia always wore white gloves." She glanced at my hands, which were bare, since the gloves I'd washed hadn't dried overnight. "She didn't really wear hoopskirts, not on the streets leastways. Who knows how she dressed at Avoca, although I could tell you . . ." Her voice trailed off.

My Coke seemed sweeter than what I was used to, but everything in Natchez was sweeter—the air, the clothes, the talk. Even the dining room smelled sweet from the rose in a tiny vase pinned to Pickett Long's dress.

"Miss Long," I said, but she interrupted.

"It's Mrs., but you call me Pickett, and I'll call you Nora."

"Pickett." The name did not come easily.

"Half the girls in the South are named after dead Confederate generals, as if we needed another reason to keep the Unpleasantness alive, and the other half are named for dead relatives. Pickett's better than my first name."

"Which is?"

"Mosby—after John Mosby, of course. Everybody knows him."

41

"Oh, yes, I think Pickett is better than Mosby." John Mosby must have been another Confederate officer, I thought.

"Everybody does."

Pickett finished her soda pop and caught the waiter's eye, making a circling gesture over the glass with her finger, and he brought her another one. "Mr. Sam thinks you ought to see more of Natchez than that rickety old Avoca and the inside of the Eola hotel. So I was on my way to offer my services as tour guide when I spotted you in the lobby." She leaned forward. "I won't try to pry any information out of you, but if you have questions about Miss Amalia, I will surely try to answer them. Mr. Sam thought you would be more comfortable talking about her with another lady, although he is the worst gossip that ever lived. He said you'd never met Miss Amalia. I did used to think not knowing one's relatives was a pity, but Yankees just might be smart to go about their business. There is something to be said for money over tradition."

She looked at her watch and got up. "Here I am, just piddling about, and I have a million things to do. You'll come for dinner at the Buzzard's Nest this evening, won't you? That's our little place."

"How nice of you."

Pickett added, "It's just a teensy to-do, with Mr. Sam and one or two old Natchezians. Natchez society antedates the Christian era, you know. Mr. Sam will call for you at six." She had finished her second drink and was shaking the ice cubes in the glass. "We'll have something southern. Mr. Sam must have his beaten biscuits."

Pickett got up in a swirl of chiffon. "Have you had them, beaten biscuits?"

"For breakfast."

"There's nothing like them in the world," she added, then made a face. "Thank God for that little thing."

My appointment with Mr. Satterfield was for four o'clock. In the lobby, where there was no sign of the reporter, I collected my key, then went to my room, where I changed into the new dress and powdered my nose, which was not only shiny but beaded with perspiration. Then I went back outside and walked up Pearl Street, which ran along the side of the hotel. A few cars were parked in the shade. A mule hitched to an ancient buggy was tied to a fence post, and from inside the buggy came the sound of a Jew's harp. Two white boys slapped mosquitoes as they sat on the veranda of a white frame house that towered above the street. A few doors farther on, a Negro boy pushed a mower back and forth across a yard, the blades clacking slowly. Nearby, a little girl in a sunsuit perched on the steps of a brick house, braiding a clover chain. The houses were in various states, some beautifully maintained, others run down, although none was as dilapidated as Avoca. From one of the houses came the sound of "Red Wing" on the Victrola. It ground to a stop; then the machine was rewound and, with a *whoosh,* the song started up again.

Three blocks from the hotel, at the corner of High Street, was a mansion larger than any I had ever seen. Surrounded by an elaborate iron fence, its grounds covered an entire city block. The house itself was a massive white structure, two stories high, with a belvedere on top and dozens of green shutters framing long windows. The house looked solid but shabby, although it was clear that it was occupied. Perhaps the Bondurants had once been welcomed through the front door of that imposing home.

I walked past the mansion and crossed the street to where a stout woman in a housedress was deadheading rosebushes with a pair of scissors. "I have to search real sharp to find those dried-up roses," she said, wiping her damp face with her arm. She wore elbow-length white gloves that had gone through at the tips of her fingers, not a bad use for worn-out evening gloves.

"I expect you're visitin'?" she said.

I nodded.

"That's Stanton Hall you was looking at. You should see it in the spring, when the jonquils are in bloom— just like sunshine spilled out on the ground." She pointed with the scissors at the mansion, shuffled along a few steps, and reached deep into the rose hedge. She wore a man's laceless brogans and old stockings, held up by garters, which showed when she raised her arms. The woman might have been a servant in that house, or maybe she was the owner. "Natchez was abloom with them houses back before the War—Dunleith, Magnolia Hall, D'Evereux,

44

Avoca. I guess you heard of Avoca, where that goat lady got killed."

"Yes."

The woman made a clicking sound with her mouth, pushing out her right cheek as she did so. "Everybody has." She eyed a bush and reached in to clip a dead rose, catching her glove on a thorn. "You know all about it, I suppose."

"More than I care to." My reply was sharper than it should have been.

"Well, kiss my foot!" The woman's expletive was not due to my rudeness. She ignored me as she inspected a tiny spot of blood spreading across the white fabric of her glove where a thorn had pushed through into her flesh. She mopped her face with her arm again, trying to recall what we had been talking about. Before she could do so, I waved my fingers at her and started on my way. But she remembered what she had been saying and called after me. "All I can say, missus, is there's lots in the goat lady's story besides the truth."

Chapter Two

MY FATHER, WHO HAD DIED at the age of twenty-five, when I was three, was a dreamy presence in my life. His sepia photograph, in a silver frame engraved with the initials W.T.B., had stood on the mantelpiece until I was five and Mother married Henry Varian. Then the photograph was moved to my bedroom, where, in later years, it shared space with pictures of my favorite male moving-picture stars. Father seemed to be in the same category as the actors: a person to be admired from afar, someone who was not quite real. In his photograph, Father was young and handsome, a dark-eyed man with curly dark hair, his smile a little lopsided. He seemed tall, although the photograph showed him only from the shoulders up. He probably had been tall, however, because I am five eight. Mother was just over five feet, as was her mother, so my height probably came from Father's side of the family. After awhile, the picture became like the lamp or the black Van Briggle vase, a stationary object in my room, one that did not intrude into my consciousness but which left an empty space if it were moved. The photograph went into a drawer when I married, but I missed it, not because it showed my father, but because it was a familiar and comforting presence. So I put it on my dressing table, where it has sat to this day.

It undoubtedly would shock people in Natchez that, over the years, Father was not much in my thoughts. Mother rarely mentioned him. Perhaps his death had been so painful that she could not talk about him. She probably did not want me to feel the loss of him, and in those days, people believed if you didn't talk about a thing, you would forget it. Mother and Henry had always had a good marriage, and Henry had been a wonderful parent to me, which was another reason I did not miss Father. Henry always seemed to be my real father, and perhaps I believed it would be disloyal to him to ask about Wink Bondurant.

After he and Mother had been married two years, Henry adopted me. "You'll be Nora Varian," Mother told me.

"No, I'm not. I'm Nora Bondurant." Mother probably thought my objection to taking Henry's name had something to do with my loyalty to Father, so she did not insist. But the real reason was that Bondurant was higher up in the alphabet. I had started school and knew that things were done alphabetically, and those at the end of the alphabet did not fare as well as those at the beginning. That same rationale came to mind fifteen years later, when I married David Tate, although the real reason I did not want to take David's name was that Tate seemed like a borrowed name (which, in fact, it turned out to be). It would identify me from then on as a wife, rather than as a person. Of course, I never told David that. It was unheard of and probably not even legal for a woman to keep her maiden name when she married. When, after ten years of marriage, David and I were divorced, the society editoress of the *Rocky Mountain News* referred to me as Mrs. Bondurant Tate, which would have been my proper name as a divorced woman—my maiden name followed by my married name. So I went to court and restored my own name, becoming Nora Bondurant once again. Bearing David's name seemed a sham, and being called Mrs. Tate, as I was by those who didn't know I'd dropped his name, made me relive those wretched times that I had tried to bury in a dark place inside myself.

Henry was a man of great character. When he married Mother, he insisted that Father's money be put into a trust for me, which he managed even after I came of age. A lawyer and a banker, he was a shrewd investor. Shortly before the 1929 Wall Street crash, he sat down with me and said, "Snooks, my secretary told me this morning about a stock tip she heard on the Colfax trolley, and she went right down to the lobby, took out her savings, and put it all into those shares. She even recommended that I buy the stock. The market is full of fools who have no business investing. There's bound to be a fall. I'm getting out while the getting's good, and I advise you to do the same."

"And what do you advise me to do with the money, Henry, put it under the mattress?"

"That's probably a safer place than the market. Myself, I'm taking your Grandfather Bullock's advice and investing in land. He said if things go bad, you can always farm it."

So the two of us cashed in most of our stocks in the spring of 1929 and invested in real estate. I bought the Cardwell, the three-unit apartment building on Humboldt Street where David and I lived and which continued to be my home after he moved out, and two other buildings, just across Cheesman Park. After the divorce, I used the buildings as an excuse to give up the Junior League and other volunteer organizations, as well as golf and tennis outings. "I'm not a gay creature anymore. I'm just a working stiff now," I told my friends. And they, knowing that so many in our set were experiencing financial difficulties, did not insist. I also began declining social invitations, although it became obvious after David moved out that the world operated on twos, and that as a single woman, I was not as welcome at social events as I once had been.

Even with the rental market off in Denver because of the Depression, my apartments, in a fashionable section of town, had few vacancies. So I never had to follow Grandfather Bullock's advice and plant crops in the yard.

Although Mother would have preferred that I find another husband, she supported me in my work, probably thinking that being caught up in real estate would keep me from thinking too much about David. "And it's a good excuse to avoid those gossipy little lunches at Baur's and the Daniels & Fisher tearoom," she'd told me once with a little too much enthusiasm.

"Yes, I can't bear them. You can guess who's the favorite topic of conversation. If I'm there, people are bound to bring up David's name, or, even worse, they'll scrupulously avoid mentioning him. Still, it's only fair, since I've done my share of gossiping over the years."

"Nora dear, you're overreacting. You do have good friends. Caroline is a real stalwart."

Caroline Bancroft, my friend since childhood, indeed had stood by me, suggesting when I left for Reno to get the divorce, "When you're rid of the old boy, let's the two of us take a steamer to the Orient." We had not because Caroline had to work to support her mother. And I was in no mood for foreign travel.

"Name one besides Caroline," I told Mother.

"Oh, I'm sure there are many." She changed the subject. "I am proud of you, you know. You're carrying on an independent tradition among the women of our family." Indeed, after Father died and before she met Henry, Mother opened a millinery shop to support the two of us, rather than live off her parents. And her mother and grandmother had run a farm when my grandfather went off to fight for the Union in the War of Northern Aggression, as I had just learned to call it.

"That's the stuff," I replied cheerfully, although we both knew that my divorce was not in the family tradition.

I first read of Amalia Bondurant in the *Denver Post.* Handy Dan, who did odd jobs for me, had spent the day helping me clean out the flower beds and plant lilac bushes at the Cardwell. Since my divorce, I had become quite the gardener. The physical work felt good, and there was something soothing about watching my plants flourish. I'd even written a few articles on gardening that were published in the *Denver Post*, thanks to Caroline Bancroft, who was a reporter there.

At noon, the workman went to his rickety truck, with HANDY DAN—NO JOB TO SMALL on the driver's door— the word *too* misspelled—and brought out a battered dinner bucket with a boiled potato and a chunk of hard bread inside.

I couldn't let him eat such a pitiful lunch, so I said, "Why, Handy, I have the fixings for your lunch upstairs."

"Oh, you don't have to do that, Miss Nora." He put the food back into the pail.

"You'll hurt my feelings if you don't eat it." I hurried upstairs to my apartment and fixed sandwiches, and on impulse, I took two bottles of bootleg beer out of the icebox, opened them, and carried them down with the sandwiches and some cookies. I handed him a beer. "Here's to you, Handy."

"And right back at you, Miss Nora."

We sat in the front yard, eating egg-salad sandwiches and drinking beer, and when the bottles were empty, we drank two more. It was strong stuff, and I got a little high. The afternoon was pleasant, since the gardener was not listening for hidden meanings in my talk. In fact, I had as good a time drinking beer with Handy Dan and talking about the best kind of manure to mix with soil as I'd ever had dishing the dirt over cocktails with my girlfriends at one of Denver's speakeasies.

When Handy Dan left, I went upstairs, dirty and tired, took a shower, and swallowed a couple of aspirin for my sore muscles. Then I mixed myself an Orange Blossom, heavy on the orange juice, light on the gin, because of the two beers; I didn't want to wake up with a hangover, which had happened more often than it should have since my marriage fell apart. I carried the drink and the newspaper from the kitchen to the dining room and then into the little sunroom that looks out over the park. The *Post*, Denver's yellow journal, always had screaming headlines and stories on crime and human oddities played up on the front page. I subscribed partly because it was lively and partly because the owner, Frederick Bonfils, an acquaintance of my parents, had lived in a mansion just up the block from me on Humboldt Street. It had always seemed odd that no story was too vulgar for him to print, and yet he himself had been a gentleman with impeccable manners. When he had passed me walking in the park, he had never failed to remove his hat and say, "Good day, my dear Miss Bondurant. And how is your lovely mother?"

The *Post* had run a story about David's death, under a banner headline, but the piece included few particulars. At first, it seemed that Mr. Bonfils, who was ill at the time and then died not long afterward, had held back in deference to Mother and Henry and me. But Henry dismissed that idea, snorting, "Even on his deathbed, old Bonfils would destroy his own mother's reputation to sell newspapers." So Mr. Bonfils had not known about David and me. Neither had Henry, for that matter.

The *Post* was delivered at home of an evening, and that was another reason for my having taken out a subscription to it. The paper filled up the most difficult hour of the day. Early evenings were the time David and I had liked best, when we would sit together over a drink and talk about our day. We would wheel a tea cart containing crystal decanters and glasses and a silver dish of nuts or crackers, caviar on special occasions, into the living room and sit on the sofa, where we could just see the mountains over the treetops. "It's cozy up here, like our own little tree house," David had said more than once.

When the air outside had not been too hot or too cold, we'd preferred the sunroom, where we would open the casement windows to let the breezes come through. We'd listen to the shouts of children playing in the park, dogs barking. Once, a bagpiper had walked all the way across the slope of lawn from the pavilion to Franklin Street, casting a long shadow on the grass. "Do you think they play the pipes on the streets in Scottish towns, or do they do it just on special occasions?" I'd asked David that evening.

"Why don't we go there and find out."

"Go to Scotland?"

"And England. Wouldn't it be swell, Muggs? Let's do it."

We wrote away for hotel and steamship brochures, but then Wall Street crashed, so we put off the trip, and by the time we felt we could go, it was too late.

I spread the newspaper on the sunroom table and then looked over the headlines, which were mostly about President Roosevelt and the people he had appointed to get the country moving again. Eleanor Roosevelt had gone off to visit poor folks somewhere in the South. The government was urging us to look for the NRA eagle. A circus elephant had crushed a man in Ohio; unusual human deaths involving large animals were a *Post* favorite. Below the fold was the headline RECLUSE MURDERED IN LOVE NEST. I was a sucker for such stories and chuckled when I read the subhead: "Southern Belle Bondurant Called Goat Lady." Imagine my sharing a name with such a creature!

The story was indeed worthy of the *Post*. The body of Amalia Bondurant, who was seventy-five, had been found in bed in her ancient mansion by a Negro servant. Near the dead woman was the body of her neighbor, Bayard Lott. After an investigation, the sheriff concluded that Lott had shot the woman, then turned the gun on himself. While the sheriff didn't speculate on the reason for the shootings, the reporter suggested it had something to do with love gone bad, albeit more than fifty years later. Magdalene Lott, who lived on in her husband's family home next door to Amalia Bondurant and who was referred to repeatedly as "Lott's wife," had told him that when they were young, Amalia and Bayard had planned to be married. For a reason that Magdalene didn't specify, Bayard had asked to be released from the engagement.

"Amalia was purely hating Mr. Lott for sixty years," Lott's wife was quoted as saying. Although they knew each other their entire lives, the dead pair never spoke, she claimed. Instead, they conveyed their complaints through her or other intermediaries. The sheriff revealed that Lott had filed complaints about Amalia's goats, which regularly trespassed on his property, and that could have set him off, although the sheriff couldn't say for sure. "She loved those goats like I love divinity candy," the sheriff told the reporter. But no dead goat had been found. The reporter hinted, too, that Lott's wife was not entirely in the clear, since it was apparent to him that she was jealous of Amalia. But the sheriff said the gun that killed the two was found in Bayard's hand. It was a derringer manufactured before the Civil War, and the bullets were handmade. The servant who lived on Avoca, the Bondurant estate, claimed Bayard had threatened Amalia. But the servant was a Negro, whose word in court was only half as good as a white person's, the sheriff said.

The article went on to state that Amalia had been a noted belle in her day, and had been presented at the Court of St. James's, but she had never married. Her fortune had once included several plantations, but they were all gone now. In later years, she'd supported herself by raising goats and selling their milk. Bayard, too, had come from an old Natchez family, but as a gentleman, he did not work. "He lived in reduced circumstances. I got no idea where his money come from, but that ain't unusual in Natchez," the sheriff said. Then he asked, "How 'bout where you come from?" The reporter must have been tickled by the question, because he included it in the story. Then the sheriff said that things were so dull in Natchez that people supported themselves by taking in one another's washing.

I felt a certain connection with poor dead Amalia.

Although Bondurant was not a common name, it was not unknown, either. I searched for further references to the goat lady in the following days' papers. Once, the *Post* printed a grainy snapshot of the woman, taken with her goats, but it was so out of focus that I couldn't make out her features. After three or four days, there was no more mention in the *Post* of Amalia Bondurant. The story of the murder-suicide in Mississippi had been replaced by that of a forty-three-year-old farm woman in Kansas who had run off with a hired hand half her age. She had cleaned out the family savings of thirty-five dollars, taken the hams hanging in the smokehouse, and gone off in her husband's Model T. The husband was left with a nickel and a dime and two Jersey cows that his wife left behind because they didn't fit into the auto. According to the article, the farmer told the reporter, "I don't care so much about the wife, but I sure would like my flivver back."

Amalia Bondurant had slipped from my mind by the time the telegram arrived a week after her death, and I thought the wire probably was a request for me to attend a fund-raiser for the Junior League House or the Preventorium at the National Jewish Sanatorium, both charities that I had supported in the past. Since it was sent to me at the Marion Street address, where Mother and Henry lived, I thought it had come from someone who believed I had moved back home after the divorce. "I'll take it with me on my walk around the park, about teatime," Mother said when she called to tell me about the wire. Mother, knowing the early evenings were especially difficult for me, frequently stopped by at that time of day.

While waiting for her, I fixed tea, cut up a lemon, and took a coconut cake out of the icebox. Cakes had delighted David, so I'd loved baking them. Whether it was red velvet, Lady Baltimore, or a devil's food cake, David always said, "Muggs, you dearest thing, you know it's my favorite." For some reason, I found it comforting now to bake cakes. No matter that they went stale and had to be thrown into the garbage pail before they were eaten. The cake was fresh that morning, made with a real grated coconut and ground almonds mixed into the batter. The three layers were put together with a coconut marshmallow frosting, which was swirled on top of the cake like drifts of snow.

I transferred the cake to a cut-glass stand, warmed the silver teapot, and set out translucent white china plates, cups, and saucers on a pure white bridge cloth. The tablecloth with the Scottie dogs embroidered on it was put away. It reminded me too much of David, how he'd loved to see the table set with our best things, and I could not stand that.

After the two of us separated, I had set about making the apartment mine, getting rid of the dramatic touches that David had liked. The brown walls were painted white now, and the gold velvet drapes that had darkened the living room were gone. The sunroom's sheer curtains, which I'd had to starch and shape on curtain stretchers every six months, went to the Community

Chest drive, and the windows were now bare. David had taken most of the art objects that we had collected over the years—after all, he was the one who had purchased them—so that my rooms were simple and stark and orderly, everything black or white, with touches of chrome and silver and glass. The only color in the entire apartment was the green Chinese rug in the living room, which had silver-gray half circles and diagonal lines on it, and the pillows I'd made from antique velvet and scraps of lace. My rooms were too austere for most people, harsh even. "They're dramatic, but not very inviting," Mother had said, "but I believe they suit you." She was right, for I, too, had locked up the soft things in my life. My life was lived in black and white and shades of gray.

Mother arrived, dressed in tweeds and stout shoes, smelling of lily of the valley cologne, and presented me with a bouquet of purple asters from her yard. They looked smart, arranged in the black vase, set on the glass table in the sunroom. Then we sat down, and mother poured tea while I cut the cake, thinking how pure the white layers looked on the white plates, beside the silver dish of lemon slices. "Antiseptic," I said, nodding my head at the table.

"Oh, but very pretty. You simply can't have white things with a man around. Every married woman must envy you."

We were on the second cup of tea when Mother remembered the telegram and put down her cigarette in a heavy crystal ashtray. She smoked only a little and only at my apartment, believing that Henry would not approve of the habit. In fact, Henry knew that she smoked, but gentleman that he was, he let her have her little secret. She fished in her pocket for the envelope and handed it to me.

"Probably a party invitation," I said. "People think you'll pay more attention if they send it by wire instead of mailing it."

"I hope that's what it is." Mother was cheerful. "It will do you good to circulate a little more. You have been too solitary since David . . ." She let the end of the sentence hang in the air. I was glad she did not mention that it might also be an opportunity for me to meet men, although she must have been thinking that, too. Perhaps if she'd known the details of my divorce, she would have understood that I did not care to marry again, would not risk another betrayal, did not want to hold another man's life in my hands. But I had not told the particulars to anyone, not even to the lawyer. Mother and Henry suspected something—everyone did—but they did not suspect the truth.

"This isn't from anybody I know, or it would have been sent to the apartment, so it can't be important. Still, a telegram is not a thing to be ignored." I slit the envelope with the tip of the cake knife, took out the folded page, and read the purple lines of type pasted onto the yellow foolscap: AMALIA BONDURANT DEAD YOU ONLY RELATIVE HEIR TO AVOCA COME NATCHEZ IMMEDIATELY. It was signed SAMUEL SATTERFIELD, ESQUIRE.

I read the telegram again, trying to make sense of the revelation that I was related to that absurd goat woman in the newspaper. Mother took the telegram from me, read it, and frowned. "Amalia Bondurant?"

"She was written up in the *Post*, some crazy woman in Natchez who was murdered. They called her 'the goat lady.' Do you have any idea who she is?"

Mother shook her head. "Some relative of your father's. She'd have to be. I didn't know there was money in the family."

"Judging from the articles, there can't be much of it—just an old house, probably encumbered, and a herd of goats. Did Father ever mention her?"

"It was so long ago." Mother tasted the cake, then mashed a little of it with her fork to make it look as if she'd eaten more. She set down the fork. I'd forgotten that she didn't like coconut.

"Could she be my grandmother?"

Mother bit her lip. "Your grandmother died when your Father was born. I remember that much. Maybe Amalia was your father's sister. After he died, I looked through his things to see if there was anyone I should notify, and I came across a name. It was a woman's, and I remember thinking the name was pretty. But Amalia?"

She got up and stood looking out over the park. "Your father wasn't close to his family. He didn't talk to me about them. He never wrote to them, and he didn't get any letters. Whoever I sent the notice to telling of his death didn't reply. Wink said once he

60

might as well have been an orphan, for all the affection he got as a child. It seemed to me there was some kind of secret in that family, something he wouldn't talk about. I didn't pry, thinking that one day he would tell me." She shrugged. "He did think they blamed him for his mother's death. After you were born, Wink said he wanted to make sure you never felt abandoned. I thought that was so sad. He adored you. You don't remember that, do you?"

"No." I wished then that I did remember Father.

"I put Wink's things into a box when Henry and I were married, thinking you might want them one day. I'd forgotten all about them. The box must be in the basement." Mother picked up a slice of lemon and squeezed it into her cup, although she had drunk the tea. For an instant, the citrus scent hung in the air like a ray of sunshine. Mother ate a bite of cake and placed her fork, tines down, on her plate; then, picking up her silver teaspoon, she removed a lemon seed from her cup and set it on the saucer. "It's sad, isn't it? All that's left of a man's life is in one small cardboard box." She put her hand on mine.

"There's me. He left me." Because she looked downcast, I added, "Me and the goat lady."

I sent a Western Union to Mr. Satterfield, asking him to clarify my relationship with Amalia Bondurant and saying it would be impossible for me to leave for several days. That would give me time to go through Father's things and find out about the family. But as it turned out, the box contained little. Father's college diploma from the University of Denver was there; his middle name was Tobias, not Thomas, as Mother had believed. Father's death certificate was in the box, along with a copy of his will and an article from a society page about his marriage to Mother. There were several books—one of poems, a grammar-school text, and two novels, James Fenimore Cooper's *Leather-stocking Tales* and *The Gem of the Season (1850)*. Leafing through the poetry book, I found a flower pressed between the pages of a Thomas Moore poem, "The Vale of Avoca." One of the *Post* articles had reported that Amalia Bondurant's house was called Avoca, and from the telegram, it appeared that the mansion had been left to me. I did not know people who named their houses—except for mountain cabins, and then they chose silly names, such as "Wit's End" and "Bide-a-wee"—and was curious about where Amalia's family had gotten the estate's name. Two lines of the poem were underlined:

Sweet vale of Avoca! How calm could I rest
In thy bosom of shade, with the friends I love best

Had Father highlighted the lines? Perhaps his father or grandfather, whoever had built the house, had done so. Maybe Amalia Bondurant had picked the name and the book had been hers.

A small leather box with AB on the lid contained father's jewelry—a stickpin with a diamond in it, collar studs, a red amber cross on a gold chain—which Mother did not remember—a gold pocket watch, engraved EWB. When Mother wound it, the watch began to tick, and a slender second hand made its way around the face. There was the head of a walking stick, a carved silver knob engraved with initials, a large *B* in the center, but the smaller letters on either side were worn off. The Bondurants seemed partial to monograms.

"The name of the woman I notified when your father died isn't here," Mother said, a little put out with herself. Nor was there anything else in the box that identified the members of the Bondurant family—no letters, no family tree. "You'd think he'd at least have had a Bible with his family's names written in it," she said as we spread the contents across the table. "He must have felt so alone." Her voice cracked, and I put my hand on her arm, but she shook it off. Mother was of a generation that believed you cried only in the bathroom, with the tap open.

The last thing in the carton was a glove box filled with photographs held together with a black ribbon. Mother must have tied them into their little bundle, because on top was a picture of her with Father. It had been taken in the mountains. Mother wore a shirtwaist and long skirt and leaned against a boulder, while Father, in high-laced boots, stood beside her, towering over her. "He was tall," I said.

"Oh yes." Mother's face was very white in the picture, and the curls that peeked out from under her hat looked white-blond. My coloring came from Father, whose olive skin in the photograph was even darker than usual, Mother said, because he worked outdoors. He had been a mining engineer, employed by a company that owned mines at Leadville, Colorado. Father had his hand on Mother's arm, and they were smiling at each other. It was such an intimate photograph that I felt like an intruder viewing it.

Mother took the photograph from me and studied it for a long time. Then she got up from her dining room table, where we had placed the box, and went into the kitchen. There was the sound of water running in the sink. Perhaps Mother had turned on the faucet because she was crying, or maybe she was just getting a drink of water. Mother and Henry had always seemed so romantic to me. I was the only one in my set who had lost a parent, and consequently, I was the only one whose mother had been courted. Henry had brought her bouquets of tulips, which were Mother's and Grandmother's favorite flower—and mine, too—and boxes of bonbons from Mrs. Stover's Bungalow.

Once, Henry gave her a bottle of perfume, but she told him sternly, "Mr. Varian, you know I cannot accept anything from you of such a personal nature." That little bit of propriety had remained a joke between them, and Henry always gave Mother perfume on their anniversary. Had my father wooed her just the way Henry had? Like David and me, they must have shared intimate looks, little jokes. Perhaps the picture of the two of them brought back intense feelings, ones that

Mother had long ago put behind her. She would have put away the photograph so as not to be reminded of a happy time with Father, just as I had hidden—no, destroyed—the photographs of David and me.

When Mother returned, we spread out the other pictures that were in the bundle. They were formal portraits, five of them, about the size of playing cards. One showed an older woman, her hair parted in the center, wearing a severe dress with a high collar and long sleeves. The second was of a much younger woman. "They must be the same person," Mother said, sitting down at the table. She picked up the photos and held them side by side. "No, they're posing in front of the same background. And look at the dresses, Nora, especially the one on the younger woman. It's quite fashionable. That was the style after the Civil War, and it cost a pretty penny. My guess is they are mother and daughter. They were quite the pair, weren't they?" She handed the photos to me.

The younger woman, tall, her hair parted in the center, but with a braid across her head and the rest of her tresses gathered at the nape of her neck, wore a long, full skirt with a train. Her hand rested on an urn to show off her flowing sleeve, which was adorned with ruffles and lace. She was not girlishly pretty, but she was striking—handsome. While the older woman looked into the camera as if posing were irksome to her and she was anxious to be done with it, the younger woman appeared serene, a bit condescending, as if she was used to being admired, either by gentlemen or a camera lens. "Father's mother and sister?"

"That would be my guess."

The third photograph was a full-length portrait of a man, a riding crop held against one leg. He was clean-shaven but had elaborate sideburns. His hair was hidden under a top hat, and he had moved while the shutter was open, because his features were blurred. Three generations later, the face of my grandfather—because if the two women were Father's mother and sister, then the man was surely my grandfather—was lost to posterity. I ran my fingernail over the crop. "Did Father ride?"

"Oh yes. He was quite good. He rode like a gentleman, not a cowboy. He taught me."

"You rode?"

She blushed. "Not only rode but sat astride. You must promise not to tell Henry."

The next photograph showed just a man's head. About the age of Father's sister, the man was uncommonly handsome, with deep-set, intelligent eyes and a pleasant countenance. His hair was parted just off center, and he sported a large mustache with pointed ends. "Did Father have a brother?"

"He might have. I'm embarrassed to say that I don't know for sure. He never talked about . . ." She shrugged.

The last picture was of a child—a little boy in a wool jacket with big oyster-shell buttons and a white collar so large that he appeared to have no neck. A bow of grosgrain ribbon was tied at his throat. His head was turned to the side and he was frowning. It was not a picture of joyous boyhood, but a solemn, strangely disembodied portrait of head and shoulders surrounded by mist. "Father?" I asked, looking for a resemblance to the man whose portrait was on my dressing table.

Mother nodded.

"He looks like a perplexed and solitary child."

"Well, he certainly did not grow up to be a perplexed and solitary man," Mother said a bit defensively.

"Or you wouldn't have married him."

I turned the photographs facedown. None of the persons in the pictures was identified, but the photographer's name and address were on the back of the first four: "A. McFarland, Photographer. Main Street, Natchez, Mississippi. Negatives preserved." There was neither a photographer's name nor city on the back of the baby's picture, no guarantee that a negative remained.

Putting aside the portraits, I gathered up the remains of Father's life and repacked it in the carton. "If this is all there is to go through, I might as well leave for Natchez tomorrow. There's no reason to delay."

"You must send a wire to the lawyer so he'll know you'll be there sooner than you'd expected. I could call him for you, if you'd like."

"No. I'll wire Avoca. That way, whoever's in charge will have a room ready for me." But apparently the name of the house was not a sufficient address, and the telegram never got there. Or perhaps the Negroes living at Avoca could not read, because, of course, I arrived unexpected.

I placed the photograph of Mother and Father in a silver frame that had once held a picture of David and me, then set it on my dresser, next to Father's picture. The five tiny portraits went into an envelope in my purse. Then because it already had snowed in Denver, I packed warm clothing for the trip, along with two books to read. Reading filled my vacant hours and kept me from thinking. Books were kept beside my bed, in the living room, even in my car. Hell was being someplace without a book, someplace where my mind could wander.

In the morning, Mother drove me to the depot, but she did not go in. She gave me a searching look as she stopped the Packard, then said she had not slept well the night before, worrying about whether it was a good idea for me to go. "Sometimes it's best not to know too much about a thing," she said.

"What thing?"

She gave a little laugh. "Well, I don't know."

"Do you want to go?" I asked suddenly. "We can go back and pack your things and take a later train."

Mother was not surprised at the invitation, which made me wonder if she already had considered accompanying me. "No. The Bondurants aren't my business anymore. They're yours. Besides, Henry's feelings might be hurt. He wouldn't approve of my going off in search of Wink's family." Henry approved of everything Mother did, but if she wanted to use him as an excuse, that was all right. Going through Father's things had loosed too many old memories. I understood that.

Instead of purchasing a Pullman ticket, I impulsively treated myself to a private compartment. Since the divorce, I hadn't slept well, and I was sure that the nocturnal sounds of strangers—the snoring, the whispers behind bed curtains, the hushed footsteps up and down the aisles, the murmured talk between porter and passengers—would keep me awake. Besides, talking to other passengers did not appeal to me. They would ask my destination, the reason for the trip, then offer unwanted sympathy for the death of my relative or try to satisfy their curiosity when they learned she was unknown to me. If they found out she had been murdered, they would be relentless in their prying—just as even our closest friends had tried to pry from me the reason that David and I had ended our marriage. On the train, I put off meals until a late hour, when the dining car was all but empty and I could have a table to myself. When a gentleman sitting across from me in the diner held up a flask and asked, "Girlie, are you a drinking woman?" I sent him a withering glance and fled to my compartment, got out a deck of cards, and played solitaire.

Mr. Satterfield's building was just a block from the Eola. The elevator in his lobby was empty, the mesh cage closed, and no sign of an operator, so I climbed the stairs to the second floor.

"You are mighty prompt," Mr. Satterfield said as I walked into his office just as his wall clock with the big pendulum finished its fourth strike. He glanced at the clock, then took out an ancient timepiece and studied it. He looked at the clock again. Pickett Long had said a woman in Natchez was on time if she were only an hour late. Perhaps that applied to all appointments, business as well as social.

At any rate, it was clear that Mr. Satterfield had not expected me to be there at four o'clock on the dot, because he was sitting at his desk in shirtsleeves and suspenders, his necktie loosened, shelling peanuts onto a newspaper. "Would you have one?" he asked. When I declined, he shoved the peanuts to one side, then wadded up the newspaper and shells and dropped the whole business into a wastepaper basket. He stood up and put on his jacket, saying, "There now" as he sat down again and rearranged the piles of paper on top of his desk. When he had cleared a space in the center, he looked around until he found a large brown envelope, then emptied it onto the small ink blotter on his desk and began sorting through the contents. The ceiling fan ruffled the papers as he spread them out, and he picked up a revolver and placed it on top of half a dozen newspaper clippings about to blow onto the floor. Henry had showed me how to use a gun and taught me something about firearms, but this was an ancient piece, a curiosity that probably went back to the Civil War.

As Mr. Satterfield busied himself with what was in

the envelope, I glanced around the room, which was on the second floor of an old stone building on Main Street. Curtainless Palladian windows looked out over the street. Law books, pamphlets, and old leather-bound novels, similar to the two in the cardboard box of Father's things, were piled on the wide windowsill. Three caned chairs sat in front of Mr. Satterfield's desk, and six matching chairs, one with its seat broken through, were lined up against the wall. A walnut bookcase with glass doors held more leather-bound books as well as the flotsam that Mr. Satterfield had accumulated over the years. Much of it, like the firearm, appeared to be remnants of the Civil War—a gray forage cap, a canteen, a sword and belt, small framed portraits like the ones I had found among Father's possessions. Perhaps they had been taken by A. McFarland and the negatives were still preserved. Above the bookcase, two crossed pistols were mounted on the wall.

"Does everybody in Natchez decorate with weapons?" I asked.

"Ma'm?" He glanced up at me. But he had heard what I said, and replied, "You never can tell when we'll be invaded by the Yankees again. Best to be prepared."

Mr. Satterfield continued to sort through the items on his desk while I returned to my inspection of the room. Mr. Satterfield's desk, what was called a partners desk, was made for two men to sit facing each other. The flat top of the desk was inlaid with leather, which was scratched and worn and cut through, as if it had been sliced with a knife.

71

Mr. Satterfield glanced up at me again, surprised to see me standing. He half-rose. "Sit, sit. Pick you a chair." He gestured at the three chairs. I sat down in the center one and pulled it forward, so that my knees fit inside the kneehole on my side of the desk. I folded my gloved hands in my lap.

"So, you didn't know Miss Amalia?" he asked, still arranging the papers.

He knew perfectly well that I did not, and the question was tiresome. "No, so I can hardly be blamed for not getting in touch with her. As she knew about me, perhaps the fault for the estrangement was hers." I hoped my remark didn't sound quite as pompous to Mr. Satterfield as it did to me.

Mr. Satterfield looked up, amused. "Oh, you don't know Natchez women. They do not unduly care to contact outsiders. But you got that right when you said she knew about you. She surely did. Knew you got a divorce. But she didn't know why. She had me to look into it, but I never got around to it." He gave me a questioning look.

"It's too late now, isn't it?" I stared the man down.

"Miss Amalia did used to think it was her business, but it's not mine. No, it ain't. I don't care a continental about other folks's private affairs."

That did not strike me as the truth, but I said nothing, waiting for Mr. Satterfield to find what he was looking for. Finally, he held up several legal-size pages of paper in a blue wrapper. "Miss Amalia's will. It is an imperfect document, but it will suffice."

He studied me for a reaction, but there was none, so he handed the will to me. I smoothed it out and looked at the last page, the signature. "Amalia Bondurant" was written in a faint hand, in purple. "She signed in pencil?"

"Indelible pencil. My fountain pen ran dry. I took the papers to her at Avoca. She didn't have but one pencil, and it was a stub. Had to sharpen it myself with a penknife before it showed enough lead to write with. I guess it's not lead when it's purple."

I chuckled, liking Mr. Satterfield.

"It's perfectly legal, no matter what she used. Why, it's legal even if you sign it in blood. Thank the Lord, that wasn't necessary." He cleared his throat. "I expect you'd like to know what it says."

"I would like to know about Amalia Bondurant." That caught him off guard, for he had expected me to ask first about what was coming to me. "Why did she die, and will there be a service? I'll pay for it, of course."

Mr. Satterfield waved his hand. "Done it already, two days ago. You can't wait too long in this heat, and you telegraphed you wouldn't be here for a while." He looked at me reproachfully. "There was a likely crowd in attendance, worthy of a Bondurant. Of course, some came out of curiosity. That's not worth denying. Folks were mighty nosy about Miss Amalia, always had been, 'cause nobody but me and Ezra and Aunt Polly had been inside Avoca for twenty, thirty years. Us and maybe Maggie Lott. Bayard Lott, too. Who's to say?

After all, he was there at the end. Anybody else come calling, Miss Amalia'd turn them away, tell them she was in the middle of spring housecleaning. Didn't matter if it was spring, summer, fall, or winter. She wouldn't accept invitations, either. Miss Amalia had her reasons. People said she was too proud. Myself, I think she didn't need other folks. No, you do not know Natchez women."

"And she made her living selling goat's milk?"

Mr. Satterfield leaned back in his swivel chair and folded his hands under his chin. "That's what people think, and yes indeed, she sold milk. But Miss Amalia had a tidy little sum in the bank. She did not unduly care to have Natchezians know about it."

"Then why—"

Mr. Satterfield waved off the question. He seemed about to tell me a third time about not understanding Natchez women, so I interrupted. "Tell me about her murder. It was in the newspaper, but there weren't many details."

Mr. Satterfield took out a handkerchief and mopped his face. He lifted the pistol and pushed the newspaper clippings across the desk to me. "Here's you the newspapers. I saved them for you." He opened the gun and removed a handmade bullet, which he tossed from hand to hand. "Shot dead by Bayard Lott, the old rascal," he said, setting down the bullet in order to push the top clipping to me with the gun. "And when Bayard saw what he done, he turned the gun on himself. Did I tell you he used an Odell derringer, made right here in

Natchez." He held out the revolver to me.

"That one?"

"No, ma'am. One just like it. This one was my daddy's. He carried it in the War, along with a rifle, a bowie knife, and a pistol. The captain had an Odell, too. I believe Bayard used his to shoot one of Miss Amalia's goats. There's some who say that is what caused this tragedy." Mr. Satterfield put the gun back on his desk, and I pushed the barrel aside with my finger so that it did not point at me. "Oh, it don't hold but one bullet," he said. "Now when you think about it, that means Bayard shot Miss Amalia; then he reloaded in order to shoot himself. Bayard must have done some heavy thinking while he did that. He killed himself a'purpose."

"One of the stories in the Denver paper reported the sheriff didn't find a dead goat."

"Oh, it did, did it? Well, maybe Ezra hauled it off and him and Aunt Polly cut it up. Had you thought of that?"

"No." I wondered if Mr. Satterfield had, or if the words had just come out of his mouth. Shifting in the chair, which wobbled a little, I asked, "Was it murder-suicide?"

"You could call it that. I don't know what else you could call it."

"Is that what the sheriff called it?"

"It is. Like I said, Bayard shot Miss Amalia, then reloaded and shot himself. We know how he done it, but we don't know why. I guess we never will."

I asked about Mrs. Lott, since one of the stories speculated that she might have killed them both.

Mr. Satterfield sat up straight and slapped his knee. "Magdalene Lott? She was a beauty in her time, and in Natchez, that counts for something—more than something, in fact, although not as much as money. But it was enough to make up for the fact that she was never quite as bright as day. Why, in a million years, she couldn't have shot Miss Amalia, reloaded, killed Bayard, and then have put a gun in his hand. And old Bayard would not have stood there while she did it. Poor old soul. I guess she lived in the shadow of Miss Amalia all her life. They were engaged to be married, you know, Bayard and Miss Amalia. Bayard was besotted with Amalia Bondurant. But Miss Amalia called it off."

"Mrs. Lott claimed in the paper that *he* broke the engagement."

"You can believe that if you want to, but nobody in Natchez does. Ask anyone who knows whether Bayard Lott was the same after Miss Amalia left out. She broke off with him about the time Emilie Bondurant went off to New Orleans to have your daddy. Miss Emilie could hardly walk. She was too old to be in that condition. She had to be pushed around in a roller chair, and Miss Amalia went with her as nurse-companion. There's some said that was why Miss Amalia broke the engagement, but don't you believe it. I think Bayard done something she couldn't tolerate, and it estranged those two for fifty-five years."

He leaned back precariously in his chair. "That and

then her mama dying was all too much. Miss Amalia wasn't never the same person." He shook his head. "There was some of us young men thought maybe we had a chance with Miss Amalia with Bayard out of the picture, but she never was interested in men after she broke with Bayard. I asked Miss Amalia once what Bayard did to her. She didn't care for the question and asked me, 'Do you need to know that?' I guess she only tolerated me asking because I was her lawyer. But I said, 'No, I just ask because I'm curious.' She wouldn't tell me."

"Then Mrs. Lott was wrong about how the engagement ended."

"Oh my, yes. Ever since she married—and that's been more than two score years and ten—Miss Maggie had been in an eternal tug-of-war over Bayard Lott, only Miss Amalia wasn't tugging. Whatever it was Bayard done, Miss Amalia didn't want a thing to do with him after that. Myself, I was at Avoca once when Bayard came into the yard, and Miss Amalia picked up a shotgun and said, 'Stand back a distance, or I'll shoot you.' She was as cool as a fresh cake of ice, and I didn't have a doubt in the world that she'd do what she said. Neither did Bayard, because he scurried back over to Shadowland. That's his place."

"Why do *you* think he shot my aunt and killed himself?"

Mr. Satterfield rocked back and forth in his chair as he thought over the question. "The second part's easy. When he saw what he'd done, Bayard didn't want to live anymore. The first part, I don't hardly know. My guess is Miss Amalia provoked him. She could be a provoking woman. Of course, Bayard wasn't always right in his mind. He never worked a day in his life, but then, he's not the only southern gentleman who hasn't—'genteel poverty,' we call it. Worthless, some say, and I wouldn't disagree. Bayard was the nearest thing to nothing that I ever saw. Now, you want to know what's in this will?" He picked up spectacles that were hanging from a ribbon and set them on his nose. The ribbon, normally attached to his coat, had been unpinned, and it swung back and forth with the lazy motion of the ceiling fan.

Mr. Satterfield cleared his throat, leaned forward in his chair, and peered through dirty lenses at me. "Except for providing for Ezra and Aunt Polly, Miss Amalia left everything to you. You get Avoca and what she had in the bank. I can't say what Avoca's worth, but the account has somewhat more than ten thousand dollars in it. She kept it in a bank in New Orleans so folks wouldn't know she had it. She was very private about that money. And you get anything you want that's left in Miss Amalia's house. It wouldn't surprise me if folks are trying to sneak into it now, thinking there's valuables hid away. Ezra'll keep them out, but he's old and a Negro, so I advise you to go out there soon to collect what you want."

"Are you sure there aren't any other relatives?"

"Natchez people always have relatives, but Miss Amalia didn't like hers, except for you, and as far as I know, the others are gone anyway. She had me to write it down that she was disinheriting anybody who made a claim. She didn't speak to her brother for years—her brother Frederick, that is. He passed on sometime back. He didn't have but one child, and I don't know what's become of her. Dead is my guess. Miss Amalia was always partial to you, even subscribed to one of the Denver newspapers because she liked to read about you and your social doings. She didn't approve of a lady being in the newspaper, of course, but she liked to read about you just the same."

The idea of this strange old lady peering into my life perplexed me. "Why me? Why leave her fortune to someone she'd never met? She and the rest of Father's family treated him as if he didn't exist."

"I couldn't say exactly. It might be she felt bad about that. Maybe she thought she should have raised him, been a mother to him after his own precious mother, Miss Emilie, died. But how could she? The captain had took to drink, and Miss Amalia had her hands full with him. Your daddy was better off up north. Still, I know it never felt right to Miss Amalia, letting him grow up the way he did. And it set real hard with her when she got that letter from your mama saying young Winship'd died."

"Then why didn't she reply?"

"Miss Amalia wrote an infrequent letter." Mr. Satterfield took out his pocket watch again and flipped open the lid. Then he cleared his throat and said, "Since we are due at the Buzzard's Nest in an hour, we can talk about the details tomorrow. I'll draw up the papers for you to sign; it'll take a little time to get the money, but if you're in need, I can arrange for a part of it." He glanced up, and I shook my head. "I'll take you out to Avoca myself, so's you can see if there's anything you want for a keepsake."

I stood then and, before remembering the limp hand-shakes, almost put out my hand. Instead, I straightened my gloves and moved my pocketbook from one hand to another, silly gestures women make to stall for time. But there was no reason not to ask my question, so I removed the envelope with photos I'd taken from Mother's house and lined up the portraits on the desk so that they faced Mr. Satterfield. "These were my father's. Who are these people?"

Mr. Satterfield, who had risen, sat down again and looked at the photographs one at a time. "Bondurants mostly," he replied. He pushed the picture of the old woman toward me. "Miss Emilie, your grandmother." He moved the photograph of the old man next to the one of Emilie. "Captain Bondurant, your grandfather." He picked up the picture of the young woman and looked at it closely. "This is Miss Amalia. In her last years, she grew littler all the time, and you forgot how tall she was in her prime. And see that hair? She was famous for it. It reached most nearly to her knees." He held the picture closer to his spectacles. "You can't tell from the likeness, but she had the whitest skin I ever saw, like cream—goat's milk, I guess you could say." He chuckled at his little joke and placed the photograph beside those of Amalia's parents, but he continued to look at it. "She was as pretty as candied cherries. Did you know she was presented at the Court of St. James's?"

"Yes."

"And I expect this one is your father. He looks some like a Bondurant." He pushed the baby picture forward.

"So the last one must be of Father's brother," I said.

Mr. Satterfield picked it up and studied it, slowly shaking his head back and forth. Then he snorted and flung the photograph onto the desk. "Why, bless me, no, dear heart. He's not a Bondurant." He paused, then said, "Now why would your daddy have had a picture of Bayard Lott?"

Chapter Three

T HE BUZZARD'S NEST WAS NAMED Fair Haven until a Union officer who was quartered there during the Civil War walked into the library, where illiterate Northern soldiers had ripped out the pages of books for toilet paper, then strewn the books across the floor. He declared the room looked worse than a buzzard's nest. Pickett's grandfather renamed his mansion to remind his descendants of the infamy of his unwanted Yankee guests.

Mr. Satterfield told me the story as we drove up to the sprawling neoclassical home in his Ford automobile (which he called a "Fode"). When he turned off the motor, there was the sound of a fountain splashing. The fountain was behind the house, he explained, and we would see it when we walked in the gardens after dinner. Pickett's grandfather had installed it a hundred years before, and when Pickett and her husband restored the fountain, they had searched in vain for water pipes. Then an old retainer told them that slaves had carried buckets of water up a ladder hidden in the shrubbery and poured it down a chute into a trough that led to the fountain. Natchez seemed to be about stories, and I hoped that some of the ones I heard tonight would be about Amalia. When I accepted Pickett's invitation, I had expected nothing more than a pleasant diversion from the ominous duty of settling my aunt's estate. But for some reason, probably curiosity, although perhaps something more, I had gotten caught up in Amalia's death—and in her life—and I hoped to find out more about her over the course of the evening. I was beginning to feel a kinship with her.

A Negro butler opened the door before Mr. Satterfield could lift the heavy knocker, and he ushered us into a large central hallway. "Lookit here," Mr. Satterfield said, tapping the head of his walking stick on the top of a table that was inlaid with a marble mosaic of birds and flowers. "Shipped here from France and boated up the Mississippi. Now see that?" He tapped one of the birds. "The eyes are gone. Every last bird had its eye scratched out by the Yankees. They must have used their knives. Yes, I'll be good and damned if they didn't."

He sent me an accusing glance, as if I were responsible for blinding the birds. "Well, 'twasn't your fault." He thought a moment. "Miss Amalia never minded the Yankees so much, maybe because your daddy turned into one." He asked the butler, "York, where's Miss Pickett?"

"They in the East Room, sir. You the last." Since we were right on time, I wondered about Pickett's remark concerning the South's lack of punctuality. It was likely that the others had gathered ahead of time to discuss me. Well, why shouldn't they? After all, I intended to discuss Amalia.

York led us across the marble floor, past a library where shelves were filled with old volumes, so either the books had been replaced after the Civil War or not all of them had fallen victim to Yankee sanitary habits. He took us into a princely room filled with rosewood furniture, ornate and old and very sharp, with cushions like boards. It might have been the most uncomfortable-looking room in the world. Modern chintz draperies kept it from feeling like a museum, but they added an incongruous touch of informality.

"Well, Sam darling, how's things?" As Pickett greeted her uncle, the conversation in the room came to a stop. He kissed her cheek and said things were okay. She turned to me, and warmly welcomed me to the Buzzard's Nest, making me glad I'd come. "Were you cooped up with Mr. Sam all afternoon, or did you see anything of our town?"

"I walked about a little this afternoon. There is an

enormous white mansion not far from the—"

"Yes, that would be Stanton Hall," she said, interrupting me, probably in an attempt to forestall a story from Mr. Satterfield about the house.

Taking my hand, she led me across the room as two men rose from one of the sofas adorned with filigreed wood. Two women sat in hard-backed little chairs with caned seats. They all stared at me so hard that Pickett laughed. "You must excuse us. We are all of us curious."

"To see if I brought the goats?" When they did not respond, I bit my tongue. *They* might make fun of Miss Amalia, but they would not put up with jokes from an outsider.

But after a few seconds, one of the men chuckled, and then he guffawed. "That's a good one."

A woman wearing a fussy black dress and a necklace with a diamond pendant as faceted as a prune whispered loudly behind her hand, "What did she say? Yankees are so hard to understand."

"She said she didn't bring any of Miss Amalia's goats with her."

"Why, whatever would she do that for?" The woman drew back and looked at me in astonishment. Then she realized I was joking, and she, too, began to laugh, her face turning almost the color of the rouge spots on her cheeks. The spots were round and the size of half-dollars. "I will say to you Miss Amalia's goats produced the best milk I ever tasted," she said. She asked if I were going to sell milk.

"Odalie, dear thing!" Pickett turned to me, explaining they weren't quite sure how to take me.

"And I bet she doesn't know how to take *us,* either," said the man who had laughed first. He had a military bearing and looked something like the formal portraits of Southern officers. He introduced himself as Stephen Shields. "And this charming woman," he said, reaching over and patting the shoulder of the woman who had thought me a milkmaid, "is my wife, Odalie."

"And you are the Yankee," Odalie said. She held a lace handkerchief in her hand and touched it to her temples. Although the French doors were open and the blades of a black metal fan clicked from across the room, the air was stifling.

"Oh, honey, she's not a Yankee. She's Miss Amalia's niece," said the other woman, who was somewhat younger and wore a silk pongee dress with a flowered pattern. It looked as if it had come from one of the store windows I'd seen earlier. "That makes you next to royalty here in Natchez. Even if Miss Amalia did give up entertaining before the invention of the motorcar, we still hoped for an invitation to Avoca. Miss Amalia was a very superior lady."

"Now, Parthena, northerners don't care about pedigree," said her husband, a jolly, balding man who introduced himself as Merrill Carter.

"That's because they don't have any," Parthena replied with a disarming smile that made me think she was not insulting me as much as stating a fact.

The remaining person in the room was a sandy-haired man in his mid-forties, leaning against a marble fireplace—Buckland Long, Pickett's husband. He snuffed out his cigarette, threw the butt into the fireplace, and walked to a table where a heavy silver tray held an ornate tea set—a large urn on a stand, a teapot, creamer, sugar bowl, and waste bowl. Bottles, an ice bucket, and glasses were crowded onto another tray. I was transfixed by the tea set because it was exactly like one I'd given to David just last Christmas.

A few years earlier, David had helped a wealthy client fight a provision in her husband's will—he had left a stipend to his mistress. The widow won, and in gratitude, she presented David with a silver tea set that had been in her family for generations. The lovely set was put into use whenever we had tea parties. When the woman died last year, however, David gave the set to her daughter. I was so touched by my husband's kindness and sensitivity that I contacted an antiques dealer in New York and asked him to find a replacement. It was the last present I ever gave David. "You are such a swell girl, and I am the luckiest boy in the world," he'd said. I let myself remember how my heart had once filled with love for him, then forced my thoughts to the present to avoid the bitterness that always followed those memories of David.

Buckland Long was staring at me, waiting for me to reply to some question he had asked. When I looked at him blankly, he said, "Oh, you do drink, don't you?"

"Of course she does," Merrill told him. "Colorado

86

just voted for repeal. Sensible people. Join me in a Rob Roy, Miss Nora."

I said a Rob Roy would be fine, then sat down in an uncomfortable rosewood chair.

For a minute, everyone stared at me, and there was an awkward pause, but after my remark about the goat, I didn't intend to risk another attempt at humor.

At last, Pickett said, "You must have been admiring the tea things. That's an old family set, dented, as you can see. Grandmother buried it to keep the Yankees from stealing it. One of the servants must have hit it with a shovel when he dug it up after the War. I could have it repaired, but in the South, we take such relics seriously."

"Weren't you the lucky one to have had honest servants," Odalie said. "We never got our silver back." She picked up her glass. It had left a wet ring on the table, which she ignored. "Our family is quite old, you know. My great-grandmother opened a ball with General Lafayette."

"Didn't they all?" said Pickett, cutting her off and thus winning my gratitude for what I was sure would have been a recitation of Odalie's pedigree. "Miss Amalia had splendid silver."

"Which she sold, I'm sure," I said.

"Why would she do that?" Odalie asked.

"I assumed . . . ," I began, then fell silent.

After another pause, Parthena said to me, "I'm just so strongly reminded of Miss Amalia when I look at you. You favor her, you know, only you're younger."

"I hope so."

"Cleaner, too," Odalie added. Her husband touched her gently on the arm. "Now don't fuss with me for being indelicate. I am just honest."

"And we love you for it," Buckland said. He rolled his eyes as he handed me my drink.

It was very strong, and I set it down after one sip. Then I asked what Aunt Amalia looked like. Besides the picture in the newspaper, I had seen only one photograph of her.

"She was sizable, tall as a man, just like you. It's odd, because it's said that when she was born, her father displayed her in a silver cake basket, just like she was a bundt cake," Parthena said.

"Miss Amalia was presented at court, you know," Buckland interjected.

Pickett turned to me. "We buried her in her presentation dress. It was white satin, very elegant, with hundreds of little pearls stitched onto it." She took a sip of a martini. "Not so long ago, I was driving past Avoca and saw her wearing the dress. I stopped because there was a light flickering in one of the rooms, and I thought it might be fire. That's a terrible problem in these old houses. But the light went from the library into the great hall and then on into the front parlor, so I assumed someone was wandering through the house holding a lighted candelabra. Then I saw that it was Miss Amalia, and she was wearing that court dress." Pickett looked at me before she added, "She was dancing. There wasn't any music, not even a Victrola, but Miss Amalia was dancing all the same, and she was as graceful as anything I ever saw. It seemed like she had a partner. Then the moon disappeared, and I didn't want to move closer, for fear she'd hear me. She would have died from embarrassment."

"You, too, if you'd been caught snooping," Odalie said. "What in the world do you think she was doing?"

"Waltzing with ghosts." Pickett gave a little smile. "The gown was water-stained and there were mildew spots, and the pearls were dull, but we arranged the dress in the coffin so that you couldn't see how badly damaged it was." She squeezed my hand in a gesture of sympathy, and I was touched at her kindness in making Amalia presentable in death.

"Miss Amalia herself was a little water-stained," Odalie said, lifting her shoulders and giving me a naughty grin.

"Odalie—" Pickett said disapprovingly.

But I interrupted and said, "Indeed she was."

"Oh," Odalie replied, disappointed that she hadn't offended me. "I was just baiting you. I adore to do it."

"Well, you did not get my goat this time."

They all laughed. "She got you there, dearest," Stephen said. "You ought not to go after her like you do."

"Then please kindly forgive me," Odalie said. I decided she was nuts.

Then Mr. Satterfield told them that I had never met Amalia, and they nodded, so it was obvious that they had indeed discussed me earlier.

89

"You didn't miss much. She was a queer one," Buckland said.

"That's because you didn't know her when she was young, Bucky," Mr. Satterfield interjected. He was standing beside the tea table, where he had spent a great deal of time bruising mint, adding an inch or so of sugar and bourbon whiskey to a silver cup, then tasting and stirring and adding more liquor. "Very fine." He dusted the drink with a grating of nutmeg. "I'd have married her in a minute."

"You were twenty years too young for her," Pickett told him.

"Ten," Mr. Satterfield said. "Nonetheless."

"And not solely for the money, either, you opportunistic old thing, although the Bondurants had a great deal of it, didn't they, Mr. Sam?" Stephen asked.

Mr. Sam raised his eyebrows but didn't reply.

"What happened to it?" I wriggled a little in the chair to find a comfortable position. The chair was very low, and my legs were cramped. The others, clearly embarrassed at the question, looked at one another instead of at me, and it occurred to me then that perhaps there were things about Amalia they did not want to talk about.

"Bucky, would you be so kind," Stephen said, holding up his glass.

Buckland, who was sitting on the bench in front of a grand piano, took the glass and poured a healthy slug from a bottle whose silver label identified it as bourbon. He added neither water nor seltzer and handed back the drink. "What happened to the Bondurant money happened to most of the fortunes in Natchez," Buckland explained. "Most of us pretend we haven't lost them. Some of us live as if we haven't." He glanced at Odalie, but it was impossible to tell from the look whether he was referring to her or just waiting for her to speak.

"Some of these old places may look like they're held up by wisteria vines, but they are the homes of the first families of Natchez," Pickett said. "The houses may not have indoor plumbing and the gasoliers have not been electrified, but the owners still throw the most desirable parties in Natchez."

"It's harder to get an invitation to a Natchez party than to Mrs. Roosevelt's White House," Pickett said.

"Well, of course. Who'd want to dine with the Roosevelts?" Odalie asked. I laughed, although I was not sure she was joking.

"Mostly what we do is sit around counting ancestors. It's perfectly mortifying," Pickett said. "Still, Natchezians do put on the dog—cut-glass goblets, silver cutlery made by hand. Why, one family still has a thousand-piece set of Old Paris china. Natchez people would sooner go to the poorhouse than part with their finery. Your Aunt Amalia was one of them," she added. "Oh yes, she kept her silver. You'll probably find that cake basket somewhere."

"Too poor to paint, too proud to whitewash," Buckland said.

"Too poor to pay their taxes, too. Bayard Lott was at

the treasurer's office last year, fussing about his taxes. The bill was eighty-eight dollars and two bits," Stephen told us. "He said, 'I've got all of it except for the eighty-eight dollars. The county will just have to be content with two dimes and a nickel.'"

"Funny thing is, the county must have been, because Bayard never lost the house," Buckland said.

"Who would want it?" Stephen asked. "I know for a fact he had a little something stashed away, although it's anybody's guess where he got it." When the others looked at him inquiringly, he added, "I am president of the bank, after all." Now I knew why Amalia had kept her account in New Orleans.

I suggested that the war must have wiped out just about everyone in Natchez, but the others shook their heads. Mr. Satterfield explained that Natchez had avoided the shelling, which devastated Vicksburg and other cities, and many Natchez families came through the war quite nicely. "The Bondurants kept all four of their plantations, as well as Avoca, and lived almost as well as they always had. Miss Amalia and her father went on a tour of the Continent, and Miss Amelia had her a season in New York, where she danced with President Grant at a ball, not that we thought so highly of that." Stephen pinched his nostrils together in distaste.

Pickett said, "Captain Bondurant not only got his plantations up and making money during slack-water times but he went into the lumber business, too. The captain ran the plantations. Frederick was in charge of the lumber company."

"You mean Amalia's brother?" I asked.

"Yes, that would be your uncle," Mr. Satterfield said, leaning forward. "He suffered from the southern infirmity of alcoholism. I never saw him when he wasn't squiffy. Miss Amalia hated that about him—and other things." Mr. Satterfield drained his silver cup and started to get up, then, perhaps in light of what he had just said, thought better of it and set the cup on the table beside him. The room was very hot and close, and I wondered how people could drink heavy liquor in that atmosphere. I had taken only one sip of my Rob Roy.

"Then my aunt and uncle weren't close?"

Pickett exchanged glances with the rest of the guests. "You could say they were purely hating each other, and if you did, we wouldn't argue with you. Miss Amalia hated Frederick as much as she did Bayard Lott."

I asked why.

"Partly the drinking, but mostly . . . there was some secret between them. Frederick made her as nervous as a bug on a hot stove," Mr. Satterfield said.

He looked uncomfortable, and Pickett came to his rescue with a nervous laugh. "The Old South is all about secrets, isn't it? We pretend to have secrets even when we don't. There was a secret between Bayard and Miss Amalia, but God knows what that was."

Mr. Satterfield explained that things between my aunt and uncle were so contentious that the captain was afraid Frederick would turn out Amalia if he were left the Bondurant properties. So the captain left the plantations to Amalia and the lumber business to Frederick.

Mr. Satterfield had said nothing to me earlier about the plantations being part of Amalia's estate, so I asked what had happened to them.

The boll weevil wiped them out, Buckland explained. The boll weevil had come in twenty-five years earlier, and many of the planters couldn't make a crop, he said. "It wiped us out so bad, we didn't even notice Mr. Hoover's Depression when it came along in nineteen and twenty-nine." He added that Amalia had sold off the properties one by one to pay taxes and upkeep on the remaining plantations, and in the end, she lost them all.

"What about my father? After all, he was Captain Bondurant's son, too. Wasn't he left anything?"

The silence lasted a long time. "Apparently not," Mr. Satterfield said, looking at the others and not at me. After another pause, he added, "By the time your father came of age, there wasn't much of anything left to give. After Miss Emilie passed, the captain lost his grip. Miss Amalia tried mightily to save the plantations, but it was too much for her, even before the boll weevil. Course, Frederick ran the lumber company into the ground, and he died of alcohol poisoning. His family moved way up north to Virginia, and they're all gone now, I expect, just like the Bondurant money."

I caught Mr. Satterfield's eye, since we both knew that a little of the fortune remained, but he looked at me blankly.

"The captain and Frederick were the last of the Bondurants, except for Miss Amalia and your father. We all thought it was a good thing your daddy went out west," Buckland said.

"Winship was the pick," Mr. Satterfield said, and the others nodded.

I was not willing to let the subject rest, so I remarked that Mother believed Father's family blamed him for his mother's death. "Is that the real reason the captain didn't leave him anything?" I asked.

There was another awkward pause before Stephen said, "Might be."

They moved around a little on the hard furniture and studied their drinks. The room was so silent that I could hear the fountain splashing outside and the scat sound of bugs as they came in through the French doors. Pickett turned up the fan, which made the room noisier but did not relieve the heat. I thought back to what her guests had said about secrets and wondered if they all shared some secret that by common consent was being kept from me. Then I thought that southerners were not the only ones who kept secrets.

"Can I freshen anyone's drink?" asked Buckland as he went to the tea table. He lifted the whiskey bottle and looked at Stephen, who put his hand over his glass. Buckland pointed at my glass, but I shook my head. No one else wanted a drink, so Buckland sat down again. Then Pickett opened a cigarette box and offered it around. Stephen took one, and so did Mr. Satterfield. She did not offer the box to Odalie or Parthena but looked inquiringly at me, and I took one, figuring that it must be all right for a woman to smoke in Natchez,

95

at least in a private home. Odalie looked at me in surprise. Then she reached over and snatched a cigarette and put it into her mouth. Her husband removed it and set it in the ashtray. Odalie pouted. The others ignored them.

I was sorry then for taking the cigarette, although not because of Odalie's silly little scene. It was much too hot to smoke. Still, having caused Odalie's funk, I felt obliged, so I accepted a light from Buckland and inhaled. Then I set the cigarette in an ashtray, where it smoldered, adding to the closeness in the room.

As if to punish me for smoking, Odalie gave me a coy glance and asked, "Have you a sweetheart?"

Pickett, who had been sipping her drink, choked, and Parthena sucked in her breath. Mr. Satterfield took a linen handkerchief out of his pocket and patted his forehead. Buckland gave Odalie a disapproving glance, which she ignored, and Stephen said, "Take care, my dearest. People might think you have no regard for propriety."

"Aren't we all dying to know, and you, too?" she asked, looking at Stephen.

Pickett opened her mouth, but before she could speak, Odalie asked quickly, "Well, have you? Or maybe you're a career girl."

Pickett shook her head in disapproval, although she could not know how the question was a blow to my heart. I tried hard to keep my voice steady as I replied, "I'm divorced." There was no reason to tell them that David was dead.

"Yes, we know you are, and we do not think highly of that. You are lucky you are a Bondurant, or you would not be taken into Natchez society."

"Oh, and have I been?" My voice was chilly.

"Well, who do you think *we* are?" Odalie asked. Her husband had tightened his hand on her arm, but she shook it off. The others looked appalled, but they seemed not to know what to say.

Pickett glared at Odalie, who was only emboldened by the look. "Well, do you have a sweetheart?" Odalie was not just off her trolley but mean-spirited, too.

"No, I do not." I looked her in the eye. "Do you?"

Pickett shot me a look of triumph, and Stephen chuckled and said, "My golly, she got you there." The others laughed, perhaps relieved that I had not taken offense.

Odalie was not willing to give me the last word, however. "Just my old fellow," she said, looking at her husband. "I ask because we intend to introduce you to a gentleman—Holland Brown. He's a Yankee and divorced, like you. I only mention it out of kindness. You should have invited him for dinner, Pickett."

The room was very quiet again, and Pickett said bluntly, "Shame on you, Odalie. Nora is here on an errand of mercy. Not all women are lost without a man." She might have winked at me, but I didn't know for sure, because she stood up and said, "We must all of us be famished, I'm sure. Dinner is waiting." Turning to me, she added, "It's just a poor little supper, not like in the old days, when we never served fewer than two hot breads and two or three desserts. But it won't kill you."

There was a clinking of glasses and rustle of clothing as the guests finished their drinks and stood up. Odalie, her body as lumpy as a cotton stocking over an old leg, took Stephen's arm and left the East Room, limping a little. As Parthena and Merrill followed, Pickett took my hand and held me still, and we let Buckland and Mr. Satterfield precede us.

When the others were out of earshot, Pickett squeezed my hand. "Odalie has a mighty high kick for a low cow. Don't think poorly of the rest of us, because I want you to be my friend. We're not all so ill-mannered as Odalie. She takes a grain of morphine every so often, you know. I blame that. She can be entertaining, which is something you do not see much of in Natchez society. That's why we tolerate her. I'd hoped she would amuse you, since you are here under such grim circumstances, but tonight she is past redemption. By the way, she did not come from one of the old Natchez families, although she pretends she did." Pickett sniffed.

"But she said her great-grandmother danced with Lafayette."

"There's a cottage industry of women who danced with him." Pickett waved her hand dismissively. "Odalie reached her position by marrying well, and she is afraid we have not forgotten it."

"And have you?"

"Have we what, dearie?"

"Forgotten Odalie married up."

"No, of course not." Pickett leaned toward me and whispered, "We know her family never had any silver to bury, and as for turning out slaves after the War, her family never had them to turn out. Her grandfather was a plantation overseer, and he got into a fight on a Mississippi riverboat and fell off. The body was caught in the paddle wheel, poor old fellow. He bloodied the Mississippi for half a mile."

I laughed, impulsively putting my arm around Pickett's waist as we went into the dining room. She was frank and kind and witty, but she was nobody's fool, and I had begun to think of her as my friend, too.

Pickett quickly assigned us places around the mahogany dining room table, which was big enough to seat twelve and no doubt could have been expanded to accommodate another dozen. Two large pyramids of fruit were spaced between lighted tapers in tall silver candlesticks along the center of the table. Like the East Room, the dining room was fifteen feet high, with tall French doors that were open, but no air came through. Unfolding my napkin, I discretely used it to rub my sweating palms while making a show of looking around the room.

Hanging above the center of the table and attached to the ceiling was a heavily carved wooden apparatus, a little like an outsize breadboard, which appeared to be some sort of chandelier. But neither candles nor light-bulbs were attached to it, and immediately we were seated—I between Buckland, at the head of the table, and Merrill Carter and as far away from Odalie as possible—a little black boy came into the room and began pulling an attached cord, which caused the thing to swing back and forth. "A punkah," Mr. Satterfield explained when he caught me staring at it. "A shoofly. When your Ezra was a boy, he had the charge of the fly brush at Avoca."

Pickett rang the little bell beside her plate, and York entered the room and went to a sideboard, where he ladled soup from an enormous tureen—part of the china set stored in the cupboard—into soup plates and set them before us.

"Hot soup always cools me," Parthena said.

That was an absurd contradiction, but the others agreed, and Stephen even had a second helping, so perhaps there was something to what Parthena said. After York cleared away the soup plates, he brought in an enormous ham—a Virginia ham, Pickett said, not that I could tell the difference between that and the garden variety; it was ham, which is to say it was heavy and salty. There was, as well, a cornmeal soufflé, called spoon bread, butter beans, sliced tomatoes, deep-fried potato balls that Pickett said were potato croquettes, and Mr. Satterfield's favorite, beaten biscuits. I was not so sure Pickett was right when she said the meal wouldn't kill us. This was a "little supper" like Diamond Jim Brady gave little suppers, and I was glad I had not been invited to a *large* supper. The Confederacy must have lost the war after dinner, when the soldiers were snoozing off a big meal.

No one seemed willing to start a real conversation over the dinner table, perhaps for fear of what Odalie would say. So instead they made little sounds of approval about the dinner. "Southern cooking makes the world a better place in which to live," remarked Stephen. The others nodded in agreement. I ate a beaten biscuit, which was tasteless, and when the bread basket was passed to me a second time, I took another, broke it, and put both halves onto my plate, one overlapping the other, so that it appeared partially eaten. Pickett caught me and winked, and to make up for my little act of deception, I told her the tomatoes, which were sprinkled with a tiny bit of sugar, were the best I had ever tasted.

She replied that she grew them herself and then asked if I gardened.

Handy Dan and I had worked in the garden the day Mr. Satterfield's telegram arrived, but spading manure did not seem like the sort of thing southern ladies would discuss at dinner parties. "A little. Sometimes, I write gardening articles for the newspaper at home."

"A newspaper woman!" cried Parthena. "Oh, how exciting. You must meet our editor, my neighbor. He is a gardener himself."

Since I had intended to visit the newspaper office to find out about my aunt's death, I said I would like that, and Parthena offered to make the introduction.

"We are passionate about gardening," Pickett said, and she and Mr. Satterfield launched into a discussion of what made the best compost. Parthena announced that she used chicken manure in hers, and Odalie threw in that her gardener thought the best manure in all of Natchez came from Miss Amalia's goats. So apparently I was wrong about southern dinner-party conversation.

"Ezra tried to keep up Miss Amalia's gardens best he could," Mr. Satterfield said. "But he couldn't." Then he gave a nod of acknowledgment to Odalie and added, "Even with the goat manure."

"Oh, that Ezra," Odalie said. "He's nothing but a colored sport."

"He's Mr. Roosevelt's 'common man,'" her husband added with more than a hint of condescension.

Odalie licked a tiny bit of cornmeal off her upper lip. "What is this 'common man' business anyway?"

"You never saw Avoca's gardens in their heyday," Mr. Satterfield said, turning the conversation back to the safer subject of gardening. "The plantings covered ten acres. You had to take a carriage to gather the roses." Mr. Satterfield piled up beaten biscuits on his plate. When he saw how many he had taken, he said, "I am overhungry tonight." He patted his paunch. "I am overhungry most nights."

"Well, I say Ezra's a slowpoke, like all of your Negroes. There was never a darky did a lick of work when he didn't have to. They were a good deal better off under slavery." Odalie sent me a sly glance, and the others cleared their throats and stared into their plates.

Odalie was baiting me again, of course, and I had no intention of responding. If Odalie's family had had silver and slaves to bury it, the slaves would have dug it up and kept it.

When I did not reply, Parthena said, "Oh, Odalie, don't be tiresome. You know the sun never rose on Ezra in bed. He is a worker."

But Odalie thrived on being tiresome. "Ezra is not to be trusted. He was always there to make sure Miss Amalia gave you not so much as one drop more of milk than you'd paid for. Whenever I called at Avoca, he told me Miss Amalia was busy with spring cleaning and was not receiving. Who was he to say she didn't want guests? You'd not hardly have allowed a servant to do that in the old days."

That was a point in Ezra's favor. Surely, my strange old aunt, who evidently had enjoyed few people, would not have relished a visit from Odalie.

"Did you expect him not to answer the door?" Pickett asked.

"Oh, you know what I mean." Odalie, who was buttering a biscuit, waved her knife in the air, sending a yellow dollop onto the Oriental rug. York quietly wiped it up. "He didn't know his place. A white woman taking orders from a servant—it is too much to consider."

Pickett glanced around the table and, seeing that we were finished eating, nodded at York, who began removing the plates. "Ezra took wonderously good care of her, he and Aunt Polly," Pickett remarked.

"So they say. But Ezra knew too much about what went on at Avoca," said Odalie, turning to me. "I advise you to turn them out."

"Now, Odalie, you know that's not our way," Mr. Satterfield said.

"What was there for Ezra to know?" I asked.

"Oh, this and that." Odalie looked up at the punkah instead of at me. I did not push the subject, knowing that she wished me to do so. Besides, I believed that Odalie would not be stopped if she intended to tell something, and in a minute, she looked at me coquettishly. "Maybe he knew about Miss Amalia's murder. Maybe he saw it." Looking around the table to make sure she had all of our attention, she said, "Or maybe he did it."

While the others looked at her in astonishment, I caught York's eye. He had just entered the room with a huge china bowl in his arms, and his eyes widened in surprise. He stopped in midstep and stared at me, shaking his head slightly.

"Why Stephan ought to whip you all the way home for saying that," Buckland told her.

"Don't believe it if you don't want to." Odalie leaned so far across the table toward me that the diamond on a chain around her neck clinked against her plate. "People here cannot bear the thought that their servants would turn against them, but it happens." She shrugged and looked around the table. "Ezra will not bear close inspection. I have a mind that figures out these things. That's the way I am, although I never cared to brag about it."

Not bragging did not seem to be in Odalie's character, but that was not the point, and I did not challenge her.

The servant still stood rooted beside the doorway with the china bowl in his hands, and Pickett told him sternly, "York, be dishing up the pudding now."

"Yes'm." He turned to the sideboard and spooned berries into dishes. He covered the berries with custard from the bowl he'd been carrying, then topped each serving with whipped cream. Holding a silver grater above each dish, he ran a nutmeg across it. Then he put the dishes onto plates and set them before us.

"Oh, your wonderful custard!" Parthena explained to me that Pickett made it herself from an old family recipe. "She won't share it. Isn't she the mean thing?" The others grunted their approval of the dessert and began eating, while Pickett insisted she couldn't give out the recipe because she herself didn't know how it was made, just a little of this and that. Even her cook, who had prepared the rest of the dinner, couldn't make custard to Pickett's satisfaction.

The conversation was a great deal of bother about a dish as ordinary as custard, but everyone seemed eager to talk about something besides Ezra—everyone but me, since I was curious to know why he disliked me. I told them that Ezra all but ran me off Avoca. Someone groaned at the mention of Ezra's name again.

It surely was not Odalie, who gave me a surprised look and opened her mouth. Before she could speak, Merrill said, "Well, wouldn't you if you'd been born on the place and had never spent a day away from it?"

"Not a single day?"

Merrill waved his hand at me. "Oh, you know what I

105

mean. He's never had another home. The poor old fellow's probably scared to death that as a northerner, you'll turn him out, and then where would he go?"

It seemed they expected me to reassure them that Ezra would be taken care of, but I had no idea what would become of Avoca. Instead of responding, I picked up my spoon and tasted the dessert, and although it was rich, I ate most of it. If I had trouble sleeping that night, it would be nice to blame the heavy dinner and not what really might have caused my sleeplessness.

"Why would Ezra have killed his mistress, Odalie?" As I asked the question, York, who had poured coffee from a set nearly as elaborate as the one in the East Room, set a full cup and saucer beside my plate. His hand shook a little, and a drop of coffee spilled over the side of the cup. York started to remove it, but as the others were looking at Odalie now and had not seen the spill, I touched the back of his hand with my little finger, and he left the cup alone.

Put on the spot, Odalie began to hem and haw. "Did I say he did? I just supposed about it. And, of course, you'd not hardly think a Negro could be smart enough to shoot them both, then lay the blame on Bayard?"

"We all know Bayard did it," Mr. Satterfield insisted. The others nodded while Odalie played with her dessert spoon. "My guess is that Bayard sneaked up on her." Mr. Satterfield smiled as he seemed to remember something, then turned to me. "Miss Amalia had a temper. There's a statue of her in the Great Hall at

Avoca, covered with a sheet now. It was made when she was sixteen. She was dressed in a riding outfit and had a crop in her hand and a dog beside her. She hated posing for that thing. One day, she just announced she was done with it. When her father objected, she took her crop and whacked off the tail of the dog in the statue, and that was the end of her posing."

"I didn't know that," Stephen said. "It sure was one funny-looking dog. You know, I had a hunting dog that—"

"We all think Bayard did it," said Merrill, interrupting him, so as to keep the conversation on the subject of the murder. "We'd all like to know why, but we have as much chance of finding out why as I have of roller-skating to heaven on a sunbeam."

"Why didn't she ever leave, move to another city?" I asked.

"Leave Natchez?" Parthena was incredulous.

It did not seem so far-fetched to me. Any number of Natchezians must have left over the years. I ventured that Amalia could have sold Avoca when it was in decent shape and moved elsewhere, taken a job.

"Doing what?" Stephen asked.

I shrugged, realizing how different these people were from my mother's side of the family.

"Stephen's right. Miss Amalia couldn't have done a thing but sell goat's milk," Pickett said. "She never had an education. Women of her day weren't brought up to get jobs. They expected to be taken care of. We still do." She smiled at Buckland, although I thought

107

Pickett could easily take care of herself. "Miss Amalia was not raised in the automobile age, when you can get into a car and drive all the way to Jackson. Besides, leaving Avoca would have been a heresy. These old families didn't let go of their homes. The women stayed on and on as an act of loyalty. I believe Miss Amalia wanted to preserve the Bondurant heritage."

"Why?" I asked. "She was the last Bondurant."

The others were still. Finally Buckland spoke up. "*You* are the last Bondurant."

Yes, and as the last Bondurant, I found the idea of my aunt staying on in that moldy old house for my sake demented. If Amalia had wanted to pass along anything to me, she should have contacted me while she was alive. "She surely would have been happier if she hadn't had to live there," I said.

"Happier?" Mr. Satterfield asked. "Why would you say that?"

I was foolish to talk about something I didn't know about, so I only shrugged.

"There never was a person happier than Miss Amalia. Queer as she was, Miss Amalia was loved by every-body, except for Frederick and the Lotts, and to tell you the truth, I think Bayard did love her," Mr. Satterfield said.

"You never met a person so sweet-natured," Parthena said. "Oh yes, she was happy."

"Right well content," Mr. Satterfield muttered. The others nodded, while I tried not to show how shocked I was to think that this strange old woman who had lived in a decrepit house with goats might actually have been content with her life, might have preferred it to any other.

Mr. Satterfield, apparently done with the conversation, announced that he had promised to show me the gardens.

Pickett rose, saying she would take the ladies outside, while Buckland and the men retired to the library for cigars and brandy. Parthena and Odalie led the way into the hall. Pickett lagged behind with me. "Mr. Sam is right about Miss Amalia being happy. The time I told you about when she was dancing, she was smiling. I swear I could see she was. She might even have been laughing. Miss Amalia never spoke a cross word to anyone except for Bayard, and she didn't speak to him at all. Of course, she liked her privacy, but when you did encounter her, she was all goodness. I should have taken better care of her"—she waved off my protest—"of course I should have, but Miss Amalia's happiness was so golden. I think if I had taken her over, I would have tarnished it. Perhaps one day you will understand."

"I think I do."

"No, you do not. Not yet," she said.

Odalie had opened the rear door, revealing an iron fountain framed by the doorway, water cascading over the edge into a small pool. There was no sign of the chute the slaves had used to activate the workings of the fountain, so I assumed the water must be forced through pipes by a motor these days. The terrace was paved with stones, and on either side of the steps beyond the fountain was a stone balustrade. Iron urns filled with tuberoses stood on the railings. Ferns and other shade plants, some the size and shape of elephant ears, were thick in the garden and gave a feeling of dampness, and there was the strong scent of overripe flowers. The air was yet hot, and the lighted torches scattered about made the evening sultry, which made me homesick for the cool, clear summer nights of the Colorado mountains. David and I had spent summer weekends in the little house in Georgetown that had belonged to Grandmother's brother. We'd throw an old quilt on the ground in the backyard and lie under the stars, listening to the mountain noises—the wind in the pines, the stream near the house, the whistle of the train. The nights were so cool that even in midsummer we slept under blankets. And except for mosquitoes, I thought as I slapped something that bit my leg, there were few insects in Colorado.

Pickett led us down the steps along a walk that was bordered with foliage. She pointed out sweet olive trees, japonica, and cape jasmine. An enormous tree hovered above us, its outstretched branches, which were almost parallel to the ground, covered with wispy moss, like a ragged lace shawl. "A live oak," Pickett told me. "Sometimes the Spanish moss looks like ghosts swinging in the trees like monkeys. You should see the azaleas in the spring—pink and white and cerise. The yellow jasmine are like chains, and the wild dogwood blossoms look as if they're suspended in air. You must come back then."

"Come back?" Parthena asked. "She's the mistress of Avoca now. Why would she leave?"

"That makes her one of us, doesn't it?" said Odalie. In a single evening, I had gone from Yankee outsider to a member of Natchez society.

"Unless she already has a small fortune to fix it up, how could she live at Avoca?" Pickett asked.

"Do you?" Odalie asked, stopping on the walk in front of me. The Spanish moss behind her blew softly in the breeze, framing her with its torn gray and giving her a Madonna-like look that was out of character. She picked a flower and waved it in the air, spreading its perfume.

"Do I what?"

"Have a small fortune."

"Odalie, you are a snoop," Pickett told her. But like Odalie, she and Parthena waited for me to answer.

"You have all suggested that Miss Amalia was penniless," I told them, having no intention of discussing my finances. "Perhaps the lumberyard could be revived."

"Oh, that was sold years ago." When Odalie was sure she had my attention, she added with a touch of spite, "To Pickett's family. That's where all this comes from." She waved both hands to indicate the garden. "That and the Nu-Grape franchise. And they've been selling leases on their plantations to oil companies."

"Odalie! You really do talk too much," Pickett said. She explained to me that the lumberyard sale had been

111

quite legal. No one else had wanted the business, and Pickett's father had paid Frederick more than it was worth. She continued down the walkway to a pair of stone benches under the tree and sat down.

The benches were damp-looking and green with moss. Nonetheless, the rest of us joined her and sat listening to the fountain and the movement of some creature in the bushes. Perhaps there were snakes and rats in the underbrush, but if odious things lurked nearby, the others would know it and not sit there so languidly. The greater danger was Odalie's tongue, a serpent in its own right.

Odalie spread out her ringed hands in her lap, palms down, and studied a large diamond that sent off glints of light in the glare of the torches. Looking up, she told me, "It's just a little ole antebellum diamond." When I did not respond, she said, "I misspoke about Ezra."

That did not sound like an apology, and I prepared myself for another tasteless observation. Pickett must have been wary, too, because she tried to turn the conversation to something else. "We've talked enough about poor old Ezra. Would you like to see the conservatory, Nora?"

"Pickett is crazy about orchids. She has all kinds," Parthena added.

Pickett grasped my hand and pulled me up with her, but Odalie remained seated, moving her hands back and forth to let the diamond catch the light. "I misspoke when I said he killed Miss Amalia. Why would a person wipe out the gravy train?"

"What do you mean?" Parthena asked against her will, it seemed.

"He was blackmailing Miss Amalia."

Pickett and Parthena laughed, relieved that Odalie's revelation was so ridiculous. "You mean he was dunning her for the goat's milk money?" Pickett asked. "Oh, Odalie, you have gone too far this time."

But Odalie cut her off. "Who's to say Miss Amalia didn't have a little something more stashed away?"

Since Mr. Satterfield had been scrupulous about not mentioning my aunt's bank account in New Orleans, Odalie might have been smarter than she seemed. Perhaps her mind did indeed work in some uncanny way.

"Even if she did, what could he possibly blackmail her about?" Parthena glanced at me, caught between curiosity and politeness. I bet on curiosity.

"Really, Odalie!" Pickett admonished her.

"I've been studying on it." Odalie paused dramatically, waiting for one of us to ask her to go on. When no one did, she continued anyway. "It's like this. Miss Amalia and her mother went to New Orleans. Her mother died, and Miss Amalia came back with a baby."

The other two women exchanged glances, as if they knew what Odalie was about to say, and Pickett, her hand in mine, took a step down the path. "You really must see the conservatory." Then she muttered to me, "This is all because Odalie was not invited inside Avoca. Her wrath is like the Lord's."

But I withdrew my hand as I waited for Odalie to finish.

She ignored us for a minute, watching a firefly as it flitted near her. Slowly, she closed her hands around it, and when she opened them, the insect lay dead on her left palm. She flicked it into the bushes. "What if Ezra knew it was Miss Amalia and not her mother who'd had the baby?" Odalie gave me a smug look, and as if I had not understood exactly what she was saying, she added, "What if Ezra knew your father was the illegal child of Miss Amalia, and no mistake?"

Chapter Four

ALTHOUGH IT WAS ONLY A little after seven o'clock when I left the hotel the following morning, the air already was too hot for comfort. Fall mornings in Natchez did not seem to be the beginning of a fresh new day, but only a slight letting up of the previous day's heat. Perhaps southerners were not as torpid as they seemed; they were merely conserving energy. Of course, they might have been stupid from overeating. I had slept poorly.

Since my only sight of the Mississippi had come from the train window, I walked along Main Street to the edge of a high bluff and looked down two hundred feet or more to the water, surprised at the river's immensity. The Mississippi was nearly a mile wide, and the quantity of water stunned me. It did not rush on its way to the ocean, but moved sluggishly along, as if it, too, were too hot to hurry.

A road led down from the bluff—Silver Street. The cliff shaded it from the thick yellow sunshine, so I followed it down to a single street at the bottom, which was lined with very old buildings. This must be Mr. Satterfield's Natchez Under-the-Hill, I thought.

The buildings were mostly two-story structures of soft red brick, a few with makeshift porches and fanciful iron balconies, and they had long windows and French doors to catch the breezes coming off the river. Many were boarded up. Others, which appeared to be speakeasies or stores, were not yet open. An Orange Crush sign hung from the window of a grocery store that looked as if it had been closed for some time. The building's broken shutter doors were tightly closed, and what had been a wooden sidewalk was all but gone, leaving only dirt and weeds. A thermometer was inserted in a tin bottle-shape Coca-Cola sign nailed to the porch post of a general store but the glass tube was broken, so I had no way of knowing the exact temperature. That was just as well.

Steamboats would have once docked at Natchez Under-the-Hill, and perhaps they still did. In the old days, the crews got drunk in the saloons, then visited the whores in the upper floors, which were now boarded up. Mr. Satterfield had thought to protect me from the knowledge of such goings-on, but I was well aware of the underside of frontier life. David and I had once tramped the mountains around Breckenridge, an old Colorado mining town, where in exploring the buildings along the river, we had come upon the Blue Goose. We knew that it was a whore-house and still in operation, but we were surprised at the homey scene around the little cottage. A woman hung washing on the line. Another sat on the porch, shelling peas. We waved and exchanged pleasantries and continued on.

I sat down and looked out at a ferry that was making its way from the Mississippi side of the river to Louisiana. The river, the color of dirty dishwater, was low along its banks, but it was a massive force nonethe-less. Branches and trash, a broken oar and a wooden crate, all were swept along in the flow. Far out in the river, an uprooted tree moved with the current. I leaned over and scooped up a handful of the water, which felt silty as it ran out through my fingers.

Leaving the silent river, I walked back up to Silver Street, nodding to a large white-haired Negro woman who had come out of the building with the broken ther-mometer and was sweeping the wooden sidewalk. When I asked if the store was open, she nodded, saying nothing, and held the screen door for me. Inside, the room was gloomy and damp and smelled of garlic and kerosene and rotted wood. Strings of dried herbs hung from the ceiling, along with bunches of bananas that had turned the color of the woman's skin. Muslin bags of sugar and flour filled the shelves. Packs of Old Golds, Fatimas, and Lucky Strikes, little bags of tobacco fastened with gold strings, and packets of cig-arette papers rested on the counter. Tootsie Rolls and Milky Ways in faded water-stained wrappers were piled inside a case whose rounded glass front was scratched and cracked. The woman caught me eyeing the case and said, "Puttin' the sweetnings in there keeps 'em from being thieved."

She did not walk so much as undulate from side to side on legs that were angled from rickets. With the rhythmic gait, she made her way to a wooden chair behind the counter and eased herself onto a pillow. I selected a bottle of Coca-Cola from a tub filled with tepid water and handed her a nickel, which she put into a drawer under the counter. She took the bottle from me and opened it, and while I sipped the cola, she pried up the cork that lined the bottle cap, placed it inside the bosom of her wash dress, then put the metal cap on top of it and pushed the cork into place so that the cap was affixed to the dress like a brooch. "First one today. This how I keep track." Her dress was dimpled from where she had attached bottle caps on previous days.

The smells inside the store were unpleasant, so I started for the door.

"Two cents deposit for the bottle if you want to take it round and about."

"I'll bring it back." I went outside and sat on the edge of the porch and drank the Coke. Below the store, a driver unloaded crates from a wagon hitched to two red mules. There was the rattle of glass as he set a box on the ground, and I thought the man was a bootlegger making deliveries to a speakeasy.

Two little girls in dresses made from flour sacks

played jacks in front of a building where a broken iron balcony hung precariously over the street. White chickens pecked at the ginger-colored dirt beside them. One girl dropped the ball, which rolled down the street toward me. I scooped it up and rolled it back, and the girl called, "Why bless your black heart." Her friend whispered something, and the girl shaded her eyes to look at me, snickering when she discovered I was not a Negro.

I finished the Coke and went back inside. After the glare of the street, my eyes took a minute to adjust to the dark, since the woman had switched on a fan but not a light. She remained seated, listening to a soap opera on a large wooden radio behind her as she squinted at a book in her lap. I set the bottle in a box filled with empties and was almost to the door when she said, "You get heatstroke, you don't cover your head." She reached up to a shelf above her and took down a braided straw hat. "Two bits is all. It'll keep your white skin from turning red as a turkey wattle. I got a pretty certain demand for 'em. These days, I ain't no good for nothing but plaiting straw hats and reading a Sears & Roebuck's Bible. That's what I do while I wait for the old ship *Zion* to take me away."

I felt a little intimidated by this large black lump of a woman and a little sorry for anyone consigned to the ill-smelling store day after day, and I did need a hat, so I gave her a quarter.

"What you doing down here, you don't mind me askin'?"

118

"Visiting."

"Ah-huh. You the one visiting at the goat lady's house?"

Ignoring my frown, she waved her hand and said, "The taximan that taken you's my boy, Strotter. I lost his daddy, and he's dead, but I don't miss him. His soul was empty as his pocketbook. Strotter was just like him till he confessed religion and give up the gin place. Now he's a Baptist from head to foot and a taxi driver. You can't ask for better, 'cept he believe in spooks. Strotter say you kin to Missy 'Malia."

"That's right." I could not tell if the woman was bored and making conversation or if perhaps she was getting at something.

"You fixin' to study on her murder." It was a statement, not a question.

"Yes."

"Maybe there's things you don't want to know. You thought about that?"

"What things?"

She snorted, then patted her open Bible with a hand the size of a skinned chicken breast. "Things." She shrugged. "I know Missy 'Malia from the time I first know myself, bred at the place on yeller cornmeal and sorghum molasses."

After sorting through her words to make sense of them, I asked, "Do you mean you lived at Avoca?"

She nodded. "I got to be the house girl. I was never no good at chopping cotton, but I was a terror with a broom." Her whole body shook when she laughed. "I live there before that place go down, till I commenced to be prosperous and took on this store. My feets has been in this place forty years." She picked up a crochet hook and worked it back and forth, using yellow strings from tobacco bags.

I moved back along the counter toward her. "You must have been at Avoca when my father was there— Winship Bondurant."

"Oh, yes indeed. I 'member when Missy 'Malia brung him home. His borning was in New Orleans. She come home with that baby in a basket on her arm and her mama in a box. She walked off the boat right outside this door." The heavy flesh on the underside of the woman's arm flapped as she pointed with the crochet hook. "Mr. Bayard's right there when she get off the boat, too, his boots polished, his coat brushed, and all such as that."

I found myself holding my breath as I waited for her to continue.

She lowered her massive arm and pushed her lower lip up under her top lip, then rolled her lips around in a circle, as if savoring her story. "Missy 'Malia, her face turn midnight dark when she seen him. She wasn't craving for him and didn't say nothing but 'Get out the way.'"

"And did he?"

"Ma'am?"

"Did he get out of her way?"

"Oh, no, ma'am. Not that day. Not ever. Later and shortly, Mr. Bayard was hanging around the place."

"I've been told the two of them were engaged, but she broke it off, and they never spoke after that."

"He's sweet on her when he's a young bull, yes, ma'am. I seen him after she come home, watching her when she go out in the day like she's a piece of molasses taffy. But white mens got foolishments. Maybe his nighttime feelings wasn't the same as his daytime feelings. No, ma'am, they wasn't, 'cause he sure did kill her. No doubt about that."

"Why did he do it?"

The woman looked at me with hard yellow eyes then, making me uneasy with her intensity. "Ain't for me to say. I know no more 'bout white folks' doings than nothing." She leaned back and closed her eyes, and the room was silent except for a Rinso jingle on the radio. But she wasn't finished. "You meet Ezra." It was a statement, not a question. She knew I had; her son would have told her, so I did not reply.

The woman nodded. "Without Ezra, Missy 'Malia go down long before this. He works suitable. You had rather treat him right. Reasons you know. Reasons you don't know."

"What reasons?"

"You got to find them out for yourself." The woman set aside her crocheting and turned up the radio. She closed her eyes, her chin on her chest. With her white hair and that dark room, she looked like a Kodak negative. For a time, she rubbed her hand back and forth across the open Bible. The hand stopped, and she began to snore.

The two little girls had given up their game of jacks and were playing with a tin horn. One snatched it away from the other and blew it at me—a long, scratchy toot—as I passed. Near them, on a balcony, a man sat in his underwear, chewing tobacco. Every now and then, he leaned forward and spit into the street. A woman wearing only a slip came out and said something, and he waved her away. Walking back up the shadeless road, which now was bleached an acrid yellow by the sun, I panted a little, for the day had turned hot. Trapped between the blistering heat beating down from above and the heat that rose from the burning earth, I wondered why I was so caught up in Amalia's murder. It was clear to me that I had grown bored with my solitary life at home and that coming to Natchez was an adventure, a diversion. But there was more to it than that. I was curious about these people, of course. Who was Amalia, and why had she never contacted me? Who was my father, and who was I, for that matter? But beyond those reasons, Natchez and Amalia seemed to offer me something, although I could not say what it was. I knew I might go back to Denver the following week and remember Natchez only as a strange interlude. But there was a feeling I could not shake that my journey here had a purpose. Perhaps finding out about Amalia's demons would help me face my own.

Mr. Satterfield was seated at a table in the hotel dining room with his cronies, so I did not go in. Driving me home after Pickett's dinner party, he had offered again to take me to Avoca, and I had agreed, but after lying awake much of the night wondering whether my father was illegitimate, as Odalie had claimed—and as I already had suspected—I had made up my mind to go to Avoca alone. There was prying to do, and Mr. Satterfield might get in the way.

I asked for my key at the front desk and checked for messages, not expecting any. Mother knew from my wire that I had arrived safely and was staying at the Eola, but it was too soon to expect a letter from her. Caroline didn't know I was gone, and I was sorry that I hadn't told her, because after months of keeping my feelings to myself, I suddenly wanted to confide in a friend. I wondered if Pickett were someone I could talk to. Not yet, but in time, she might become my confidante.

There was just one message, and it was from Mr. Satterfield. "I await your call," he had written in a precise hand. Perhaps Mr. Satterfield knew best—that it would be safer if he accompanied me to Avoca—and for a moment I thought about changing my mind. But if I felt so strongly about doing this, then that was what was best for me. David had said those very words to one of the dowagers whose estates he'd handled. She had called him at home to complain that her children were pressuring her to sell her large house and move into the Brown Palace Hotel, but she wanted to stay where she was, and so she asked David what to do. "If you feel that strongly about it, then that is what is best for you,"

David had told her. Perhaps one day, I would be one of those lonely old women with a small fortune, too insecure to make my own decisions.

As I pondered that, a tall bear of a man walked through the lobby and nodded at the desk clerk, who said, "Hot enough for you, Mr. Brown?"

"Hot enough to melt a grindstone," he replied, then went into the dining room and sat down at Mr. Satterfield's table.

I wondered if this were Odalie's Mr. Brown, but I did not much care, as I had no desire to meet an eligible man. Besides, I had made up my mind to go to Avoca. I handed the key back to the desk clerk. There was no taxi starter outside the hotel, so I headed for the depot. As I passed a bank that looked like a Greek temple, a woman's voice called, "Yoo-hoo." Odalie waved a gloved hand at me from under the portico.

Remembering she was lame, I crossed the street.

"My old fellow said I was shameful last night. I ask you to excuse it," she said without the slightest hint of an apology in her voice.

"That's all right," I replied, determined not to let the same bee sting me twice. "I had not realized that southerners were so interested in other people's business."

"In Natchez, we call that 'being truthful.' If the devil doesn't get you, the truth will."

"How interesting." I wondered if Odalie had ever faced the truth that she was a graceless old busybody. "Then will you tell me the truth about something I've come here to find out?"

She dipped her head, looking self-important as she touched the corner of her lip with her finger, getting a tiny red smudge on her white glove.

"First, do you really believe Ezra killed Miss Amalia, or was it Bayard Lott?"

Odalie crimped her mouth as she thought. "I don't trust Ezra, but I suppose Bayard's my pick."

"Then why? If they lived next door to each other all those years, why did he kill her now?"

"I need to think about that a minute to give me a better start in my mind." Odalie studied the lipstick smudge on her glove. "It wasn't over any goats." She paused again, thinking. "Shadowland has gone to rack and ruin, you know. Never did I see a house in such rottendy shape, or folks so rackady, either. I called once out of the kindness of my heart to see how is Miss Maggie doing." Odalie put her hand in front of her mouth and whispered, "Her mind has got feeble." She nodded for emphasis and continued. "Old Demon Bayard was not gentleman enough to invite me in. I was treated something terrible. But I saw what had happened to Shadowland. A misdemeanor was done to that place. I remember of its prime."

Thinking over what she'd said, Odalie corrected herself. "That is to say, I have *heard* of Shadowland in its prime." She patted the hair at the nape of her neck, a switch, I thought, because in the daylight, it did not match the rest of her hair, which was dyed a poisonous red. "There was a path from Shadowland to Avoca."

"A goat path?"

"Now, how should I know that?"

An old Negro man with a homemade crutch shuffled along the sidewalk, and I moved aside to let him pass. Odalie stayed where she was, forcing the man to go around her. She looked through him as she said, "Bayard Lott did not kill Miss Amalia over the goats. He had another reason. Like we said, there were secrets at Avoca, secrets at Shadowland."

"Secrets so terrible they caused murder?"

Odalie tilted her head and stared at me, the impish grin of the night before spreading across her face. She waved to a black man standing next to an automobile, and he opened the back door for her. "How should I know? It's not my business. I trust in God and hoe my row. I'm not one to gossip." She limped toward the car. "It's up to you to find out. They're your kin."

After Odalie's driver pulled away from the curb, I continued on my way to the depot, where I got into a cab and told the driver to take me to Avoca. "Maybe so you want me to come back for you?" he asked when we reached the old house. Avoca did not seem so far out of town in daylight, however, so I told him I would walk back.

In the bright sunlight, the house was even larger and more imposing than at night, although it was less mysterious now. The vegetation that covered the house appeared to have become a structural part of it. If I stand very long in one spot, I thought, the vines will begin to grow up my legs.

Walking across the brick drive, I studied the house with a more critical eye than on my first night. My years as a property owner had taught me a great deal about buildings, and this one appeared too far gone to be restored. The roof had not been repaired in years, and water had destroyed the eaves and much of the trim. Exterior boards had fallen away, leaving gaping holes in the walls. The Corinthian tops of the columns were so rotted, they would have to be replaced, and the columns themselves would have to go, unless they had been built of a decent brick that had not crumbled. Many of the windows were broken, and the foundation looked unstable. Restoring just the outside would take the entire ten thousand dollars that Amalia had left behind in her bank account, perhaps more, and the house wasn't worth that. Pickett had told me that Stanton Hall, the great white mansion near the hotel, could be bought for ten thousand dollars.

Ezra came from around a corner as I reached the house, and he stood silently by the ladder that had replaced the front steps, a hoe held loosely in his hand. He might have been working in the garden, or he could have grabbed the hoe as a weapon when he heard the cab stop. He did not respond to my wave, just stood there with the implement and let me approach him.

"We met the night before last," I said, not sure that he recognized me. "I'm Miss Bondurant."

He dipped his chin a little.

"Mr. Satterfield said he would bring me here, but you could show me the house just as easily, couldn't you? I want to learn more about my aunt." Ezra did not seem to notice my stumbling over the word *aunt*. Maybe he didn't know the circumstances of my father's birth. After all, why should he? Or perhaps Odalie was wrong, and Amalia Bondurant was indeed my father's sister.

Ezra laid the hoe on the ground and put his hand on my elbow to steady me as I went up the ladder. Looking over my shoulder to watch him follow me up the rungs, I decided he easily could be mistaken for a white man. His skin was the light brown of the Mississippi, and his gray hair was curly but not kinky, his nose narrow, and his lips thin. He was tall, and while he was stooped, he once had been a powerful man, perhaps still was. He would have been good protection for Amalia, or at least he had been until the end.

Ezra leaned his shoulder against the massive front door and pushed, lifting a little on the doorknob as he did so, and the door shuddered and opened heavily. He stepped aside and let me enter what Pickett had referred to as the great hall. A massive chandelier hung from the ceiling. The dust cloth draped over it had slipped, and I glimpsed crystal drops hanging from candleholders and imagined how the fixture must have sparkled in the candlelight.

Ezra looked up at the candelabra. "That ain't brass. That's gold. Old Marster sent away to Paris, France, for it." There was a touch of pride in his voice.

"Was Old Marster my grandfather?"

Ezra thought that over for a moment. "His daddy."

There were holes in the ceiling where the plaster and lath had fallen, but the debris had been swept away. At the end of the hall was a stairway, hidden in an alcove to one side. That was a pity, because the staircase was elegant, curving in a full circle as it rose gracefully to the second floor. I followed the staircase with my eyes, past the thick crown molding along the ceiling to the second-floor hallway. One could put a hand on the railing, climb the stairs, walk around the second-floor opening, and down the stairs again without ever removing a hand from the rail. In the curve of the staircase was an object as big as Ezra, covered by a dust cloth. I tugged at the cover, brushing the dirt out of the folds, until Ezra came over. Taking one end, he helped me remove it from the statue of Amalia and her dog— a dog with a cropped tail—which sat on a pedestal.

The marble image was nearly life-size, and I walked around it, studying the young woman, who had been half my current age when she posed. She was bold-looking, and there was that sense of impatience that Mr. Satterfield had described in her. She was tall, too. She had passed down her height to me.

"Is that really the way she appeared?" I asked Ezra.

"She was always looking fine as silk."

More like osnaburg in her last years, I wanted to tell him, although I did not.

Ezra stared at the statue for a time, then turned and looked at me. "You ever favor her."

"It's possible. After all, she was my *aunt*."

He did not react. "Yes'm."

"Did my father look like her?"

Ezra rubbed his hands across his face. "Can't say. I never saw him much. Bondurants mostly all look alike."

As the two of us covered up the statue with the cloth, I thought it would be nice to keep the piece, but what would it cost to ship it to Denver? And where in the world would I put a life-size marble statue? The floor in my apartment would not hold the weight.

As if reading my thoughts, Ezra said, "It ain't ever been moved from here. Never."

I turned away from his intense gaze and looked at the stairway, which was blocked off. "Is it safe to go up?"

Ezra moved between me and the staircase. "Not safe, no. Now I show you the parlor." He led me across the hall into double parlors, musty and shuttered, connected by pocket doors. With the doors open, as they were now, the rooms were the size of a ballroom. When Pickett had seen her waltzing through the parlors in her white gown, Amalia must have been replaying a scene from her youth. "Was my aunt a belle?"

Ezra smiled a little. "Oh, yes. They ain't no lady in Natchez so fine."

Chandeliers draped with dust cloths hung from the ceiling. Sheets covered large pieces of furniture. Dim mirrors in gilt frames hung on the walls, and tiny gold chairs with dusty velvet seats were stacked in the back parlor. Along the outside wall was a fireplace mantel constructed of a pretty pink-and-wine-streaked marble, but it was broken and badly water-stained. Nearby stood a grand piano, and I touched a key, then played a chord. The piano was badly out of tune. It was not covered with a dust cloth, and I asked, "Did my aunt play?"

"She have a talent for most things."

"Including the piano?"

"Miss Amalia play in the twilight. Almost can I see her now. She tell me when she play, she think about the days gone by and the life that's to come." He went over and touched a key, then another.

"Do you play?"

"I never has." He closed the lid over the keys before taking me into the dining room, which was dark because matted vines covered the windows—or where the windows had once been. The glass was gone, and boards that had been nailed over the window frame had fallen away, allowing the wind and rain to ravage the furniture. The table was cracked and warped, the chairs broken. The only piece of furniture that seemed intact was a huge breakfront on the wall across from the windows. It held even more china than I had seen in Pickett's dining room.

The glass in the breakfront was broken, so I reached in without opening the doors and took out a plate, then another, since the top plate was so filthy that I could not see its design. The second plate was rimmed in blue and edged in gold and had a tulip hand-painted in its center. I blew the dust off the first plate and saw the lily painted on it. The third plate, which was visible through the glassless door, had a rose in its center. There were no hallmarks on the backs of the plates.

"Old Paris. Capt'n Bondurant order 'em in France," Ezra said. "Old Mist'ess, she just beg and beg for them dishes." He smiled to himself. "He give her rows and rows of 'em."

"Old Mistress?"

"Miss Emilie," he replied formally. He took the plates from me and carefully set them in the cupboard, the dusty one on top. "Not one piece ever got broke."

"Imagine that."

"Yet," he added, looking at me as if I were a threat to the crockery.

"I'll do my best to continue the tradition." I raised my eyebrow a little, but Ezra did not find that amusing. So far, my sense of humor had not been very successful in Natchez.

"You wants to see Miss Amalia's room? That where she keep everything."

We went into the room I had stumbled into on my first night in Natchez. The French doors to the front porch were open, and the room seemed fresher than it had earlier. The smell had been mold and rotted wood, not goat filth, I realized, because the room was scrubbed clean, the furniture polished. The velvet drapes I had touched were not dirty, only old, the pile worn off in places. I was sure the room had not been cleaned just for me.

"In the captain's time, this the library," Ezra explained. But that was obvious because hundreds, perhaps thousands, of leather-bound books were stored inside bookcases. A wood-inlaid desk decorated with ormolu was littered with papers and boxes and odds and ends. I picked up a pocket watch set into a shell, touching a spring on the side. The workings had been removed and the inside lined with pale blue silk. Diamond earrings rested on the silk. Clicking the watch shut, I set it back on the table and picked up a silver card case. Ezra moved the watch a few inches, to where it had rested earlier.

Across from the desk was a massive half-tester bed with shredded and water-stained silk draperies hanging from a crown attached to the ceiling. Mosquito netting hung from the bedposts, and an umbrella was suspended from the ceiling.

"What?" I asked, looking at the umbrella.

"It keep the rain off. I willing to fix the roof, but Miss Amalia say stay off the toppen part of the house. She scared most to death I fall off, and then who's to look after her and Aunt Polly? She catch the water in these." He pointed to mason jars and tin pails scattered around the bed.

I put my hand on the top of the footboard, which looked a little like an oversize rolling pin. Ezra lifted the object from its resting place and rolled it back and forth over the bed. "This even out the feathers in the bed. Miss Amalia always was keeping feathers in the mattress, not moss. That mattress sleeps soft." I took one end of the rolling pin and, together, we set it back on the footboard. "It supposed to go on the top of the bed, but it fall off on Old Mist'ess one time, so I fix it to the bottom."

"Good idea."

"This bed made by Prudent Mallard."

The name meant nothing to me, but I was learning to keep my mouth shut in Natchez when I didn't know about a thing, so I did not comment.

A folded crazy quilt lay at the end of the bed, and I picked it up, studying the patches. Some were shredded, with the foundation showing through. The binding was frayed. But the pieces that were intact were exquisitely executed, with people and animals embroidered in the center and held together with a variety of "chicken scratch" stitches. Names and initials were embroidered on patches. In the center of the quilt were the initials AB entwined with a heart.

"Amalia Bondurant." I ran my hand over the initials, which were rendered in satin stitches and French knots.

Ezra said nothing, just took the spread from me and set it back on the bed. "All those things like that, those bedcovers, Miss Amalia make, her and Aunt Polly. Miss Amalia make this way back, after her growing-up time."

"She must have liked to quilt."

"Miss Amalia stitched a plenty of quilts. She put 'em together with them stitches she call 'railroad tracks.'"

"I should like to keep this."

"Miss Amalia say once she wonder if you quilt." He looked at me, waiting for me to reply.

"My Grandmother Bullock, my mother's mother,

quilted. She took the measure of a woman from her needlework. Women did that at one time."

Ezra nodded, as if he understood.

"She taught my mother to sew, and Mother taught me. I like to work with lace and old silks and velvet." I fashioned pillows for my friends from those materials and had made a cape of a beautiful piece of antique silk velvet, sewing it by hand because the fabric was so difficult to work with. And I'd once made a bedspread by stitching together bits of lace that had come from my grandmother's scrap bag, fitting the pieces to one another in the same puzzlelike way that Amalia had made this crazy quilt. Mostly what I did, however, was make little pictures from tiny scraps of fabric too small to be used for anything else. "But no, I don't quilt. I never cared to."

Ezra turned away, and I sat down at the desk and began opening the drawers. "Now is as good a time as any to start going through Miss Amalia's papers. I ought to get to work."

"You need you something?"

I shook my head. "You surely have other things to do." I did not want Ezra, any more than Mr. Satterfield, looking over my shoulder while I went through Amalia's things.

Ezra stood in the doorway a minute. "You planning to sleep here? I got to tell Aunt Polly."

"No," I said quickly. "That's very kind of you, of course. But I've made arrangements at the hotel to stay as long as necessary."

135

Ezra dipped his head, not looking at all disappointed.

I turned back to the desk and saw then a rose in a crystal vase. There was dew on the petals, so it had been placed there that morning. Ezra was staring at me from the doorway.

"I always pick the flower for Miss Amalia. We ain't got but roses now."

"That's very thoughtful. Thank you." When Ezra looked embarrassed, I added quickly, "Mr. Satterfield told me about the gardens at Avoca. He said they were so vast, you had to take a carriage to cut the roses."

"Dogcart. When Miss Amalia was a young lady, she take a dogcart. I harness it up. That my job."

"You took good care of her." I returned to the desk, then had a sudden thought and asked, "What about the goats? Are you taking care of them? Don't they have to be milked?"

"We taken care. Aunt Polly keep the money in the quarters for you. She put down the amount on a paper. It there in the drawer." He indicated the desk.

"Oh, I don't want the money." The words sounded arrogant. "That is to say, we will consider that part of your pay as caretakers. We can discuss that later. Right now, there is so much to attend to."

"I leave be," he said, and was gone.

I got up then and wandered around the room, taking a closer look at things without Ezra getting in my way. On the table beside the bed was a dresser set that included a silver mirror and matching brushes and a basket for hairpins. I wondered if that were the cake basket in which Amalia had been displayed as a baby. Straightening the brushes, I pondered how a girl who had been brought up in such splendor could have lived out her life in squalor. The house not only lacked the basic necessities, such as electricity and plumbing— kerosene lamps stood on the desk and bedside table, and I had spotted a chamber pot under the bed—it was uninhabitable for any normal person. And to think that Pickett and her guests had called Amalia Bondurant happy!

Returning to the desk, I opened drawers, not knowing what it was I was looking for—treasure, financial records, family history? Perhaps there were only curiosities.

The center drawer's contents were disappointing, more like the makings of a pack rat's nest—a pretty rock, half of a bluebird's egg, dried petals the color of the rose on top of the desk, things that Amalia must have picked up as she wandered about Avoca. There was a sort of quilt diary, with drawings of quilt patterns and scraps of fabric pinned to the pages. Underneath the journal was a book tied together with string, its cover worn down to the boards. "Receipt Book" was written in pencil in the front. The pages were loose. I opened the book to a handwritten recipe for drop cake: "1 cup Sugar 1/2 cup Butter 2 Eggs 2 Table spoons milk 1/2 tea spoon Soda Nutmeg Currants." There were no directions. Flipping through the book, I found recipes for Cora's indian pudding, queen of puddings, bird's nest pudding, and wine jelly. On other pages were instructions "To Keep the Hair from Falling Out" and "The Cure for Drunkenness." A clipping tucked inside the pages was titled "To Bring the Dead to Life." Not knowing when such household hints might come in handy, I put the book aside to be read in detail later.

In the back of the drawer was a packet of letters tied together with a faded ribbon. They were invitations, most of them handwritten, to balls and parties that had taken place half a century ago. The paper was foxed and dotted with spots of mildew. In one envelope were locks of hair. Another held pressed flowers that had crumbled almost to dust. Most of the contents of the drawer could be tossed into the dustbin. But throwing away Amalia's things might offend Ezra and Miss Polly, so I shut the drawer.

Opening another drawer, I found myself staring at my own face. On top of a pile of papers was a picture from the 1926 Junior League Follies booklet, folded open to show my friend Caroline and me, dressed in overalls and caps, standing in front of a Denver & Rio Grande Western locomotive. The caption identified us and said that D&RGW's Panoramic Special was the favorite train of Junior Leaguers going to Salt Lake City and the Pacific Northwest. I remembered posing for the picture. The other Junior Leaguers were shown in front of auto dealers or at the Bredan Butter castle, but Caroline and I had liked the idea of going down to the tracks in railroader uniforms. In a million years, I would never understand how Amalia had acquired that picture.

Under the booklet were scores of clippings with my name in them, arranged in a haphazard manner, as if Amalia had pulled one out at random from time to time, read it, and set it back on top of the pile. The papers went back sixteen years, beginning with a mention of me in the *Denver Post* society column, attending a Christmas party when I was seventeen. There were articles on my debut, my marriage, pictures of me at various social functions, and eventually the legal notice about the divorce. She must have subscribed to the *Post*, read it front to back every day, searching for my name.

Returning the clippings to the drawer, I mulled over why Amalia would have kept track of me, and only one answer made sense: She was obsessed with me because I was her granddaughter, not her niece. The clippings, every bit as much as Odalie's pronouncement, convinced me of the truth of my father's parentage.

If that were true, the question I now wanted answered was, Who was my grandfather? Perhaps there were clues somewhere in this desk, and I continued my search. But the only thing in the next drawer besides a bonnet brush, button hook, and glove darner that matched the silver dresser set was an account book, with rows showing dates and dollar amounts. The record started on July 7, 1921, when the amount set down was $1.10. The last entry was on September 14, 1933, the day before Amalia's body was found: $2.40. These must have been the days' goat's milk income, and while it was not a great deal for three people—

Amalia, Ezra, and Aunt Polly—to live on, there were other folks who got by on considerably less in these hard times. A piece of paper had been placed in the book, and written in a different hand were the dates following Amalia's death, along with amounts. Ezra must have sold milk this morning, I realized, because today's date was there, along with the figure $2.20. I flipped to the back of the book, but there was no list of expenses. Did one buy feed for goats or simply let them graze in the yard—or the neighbors' yards? I laughed out loud to think I had inherited a herd of animals and knew not one thing about them.

Just then, one of *my* goats jumped up onto the porch and wandered through the French doors. She bleated and took a few steps into the room. Amalia might have considered the goats house pets, but I did not, and so I got up and led the animal outside. Closing the French doors would make the room too stuffy, so I pulled shut the louvers that were on either side of the opening. The shutters let air into the room but kept out the animals.

They made the room darker, however, and I lighted the kerosene lamp on the desk with matches from my purse before opening the final drawer of the desk. It was filled with small boxes and a stack of photographs tied up in a silk ribbon. I lined up the pictures on the desk, nearly twenty of them, and they included copies of the portraits that I had brought with me, although Bayard Lott's likeness was not there. Several of the pictures were tintypes, much older than those in the box of Father's things. They might have been pictures of Amalia's parents. Mr. Satterfield would know, or Ezra. There were also tiny portraits of black people. One could have been Ezra as a young man.

After I examined the photographs, I took out one of the small boxes, red leather with gilt edging, thinking all of them were empty. Amalia would have had wonderful jewelry in her day, but she would have sold it over the years, just as she had sold the plantations. But she had not, I discovered when I opened the first box and found a diamond ring, a large champagne-colored stone on a gold band. The ring was very plain, to show off the brilliance of the diamond, which was much better than the ones Odalie had worn. The ring is mine now, I thought, and slipped it onto my finger, holding it up to the kerosene lamp.

There were a dozen boxes in the drawer, some of them empty, but others containing old pieces, very good ones—a dragonfly inset with rubies, a spray of flowers with blossoms made of diamonds, pearls in their centers. There was a strand of pearls with a bow-shape clasp of diamonds. Amalia must have worn the necklace often because the pearls were not faded like pearls that are closed up in boxes for long periods of time, but fresh and milky pink.

I returned the pearls to their velvet resting place and opened another box, which held pieces of hair jewelry, never a favorite of mine. They brought to mind women shearing locks from dead friends and relatives, then mournfully braiding and twisting the strands into shapes and preserving them in tiny glass windows to be displayed on their bosoms. Along with a hair brooch framed in gold, Amalia had a plaited bracelet and a watch chain.

"That be old Miss Emilie's hair, Miss Amalia's mama. When she die, Miss Amalia make them," Ezra said. He must have come from the back of the house, because the porch shutters were still closed. But I had not heard his footsteps.

"She was very talented."

Ezra snorted. "She don't pleasure herself none with the doing of it. She say you ought not wear pieces of the dead on yourself. But that what ladies did, and the captain, he favored the watch chain."

He came over to the desk. "Aunt Polly cook a pan of ginger bread and cut you a corner piece." He set down a tray and removed a starched napkin that covered a glass of milk—goat's milk, undoubtedly—and one of the Old Paris plates from the dining room with a piece of cake on it. A polished silver fork lay beside the plate. My dinner companions last night were right indeed when they said the remnants of Natchezian society lived in poverty but still used their finest china and silver. "Miss Amalia like to eat off the tray."

I thanked him and asked if he would share the ginger bread with me, but he looked startled and shook his head. In all the years they had lived together had those three, mistress and two servants, ever sat down to a meal together? Then Ezra straightened the tray on the desk with his powerful calloused hands.

"Aunt Polly say you step by the quarters come dinner-time. She fixing enough for you to join us, just like Miss Amalia. She taken her dinner at the quarters."

And I thought how I had been wrong about one more thing in this moldy old place.

Chapter Five

E ZRA HAD NOT TOLD ME where to find the quarters—servants' quarters, I thought at first, but, of course, they had been *slave* quarters.

So I followed a path from the gallery to the back of the house and through what must have been the formal rose gardens. There were remnants of shell-covered pathways beside rectangular plots that were outlined by ragged boxwood and filled with weeds and overgrown rosebushes. The bushes still bore bright flowers. Ezra had reached through their thorns to cut the rose for me.

Two wings extended straight back from the rear of the house. The space between them, once open back galleries on both first and second floors, was enclosed by shutters, the louvers broken. The steps were gone, and a board was propped up to serve as a staircase. It struck me that a ladder was used at the main entrance but a sloping piece of lumber was good enough for the servants' entrance.

Attached to the house was a conservatory, its glass panes shattered. And behind was a collection of dependencies that were rotting into the earth. Since there was no kitchen inside the house, meals must have been prepared in one of these outbuildings and carried to the dining room, either because of fear of fire or to keep the smells and the heat of the cooking out of the house. Other buildings would have been a carriage house, which now housed the REO; a washhouse; and perhaps a smokehouse and a dairy, where crocks of cream and milk and butter were cooled in springwater to keep them from souring. Or maybe those housekeeping functions had been performed at one of the plantations, with the milk and meats brought to Avoca. Pickett had told me the antebellum mansions in Natchez were town homes, occupied during the social season. The real work took place on the plantations. The Bondurants, she said, had owned a thousand slaves, but only twenty had worked at Avoca. Now just two were responsible for all the work. No wonder Avoca was falling down.

A few more steps down the path, past a curious tree that was hung with glass bottles—blue milk of magnesia containers, green Coke bottles, and clear glass canning jars—I spotted a long, narrow two-story building close to the far side of Amalia's house. It was constructed of brick. Smoke came from a chimney at one end. I knocked on the door frame, then stepped inside.

The room, calcimined an off-white, was a respite from the outside heat, despite the fire in the enormous brick fireplace, which was fitted with cranes and ovens. A black spider with a lid stood in the coals, and a pot hung from one of the iron bars. This was Avoca's kitchen. Shelves along the walls held gleaming copper pudding molds. Why would anyone take the time to polish them, when there was so much other work to be done on the estate? Neatly lined up on shelves were cake pans and pie plates and serving platters big enough to hold a roast suckling pig. Heavy iron spoons and ladles and meat forks hung from hooks on the wall.

A flour barrel stood on the floor, and above it on a shelf, tin canisters for condiments were lined up. One container the size of a shoe box, marked SUGAR, was fitted with a lock. Perhaps the sweetener was once so precious that the mistress of Avoca—Miss Emilie, it would have been—had unlocked the box and, using sugar nippers, had cut the day's allotment of sugar from a big cone and given it to the cook.

A woman moved from the end of a wooden table that stood along one wall. In the poor light, she appeared to be only a shade darker than Ezra. Her face was freckled, and her hair was red, streaked with white. I had expected Aunt Polly to be a yard broad and very black, with heavy features, like the jolly southern mammies in magazine advertisements. Instead, she was slender and bent over and of an indeterminate age.

"Afternoon, Miss Nora." Aunt Polly shuffled forward. "My feets on the drag. I got rusty ankles." She laughed, a pleasing low sound.

I went to her and took her hands and said we should both sit down, but she shook her head. "I won't sit just yet." She turned to a narrow stairway behind the door and called, "Ezra, young miss step by here." In a minute, Ezra came down the stairs into the room and stood looking at me. Aunt Polly told me, "Turn go my hands, and I'll dish up the dinner."

"Let me help you."

She gave me a quizzical look. "God from Glory! Miss Nora. You don't help. Ezra help." She shook her head at the absurdity of it. "You taken yourself to the chair. I tell Ezra bring a tray to you, but he say you best get out that old house and come on to the quarters for your dinner."

The two of us looked at each other for a long time, each pretending that Ezra actually had invited me. He'd probably told Aunt Polly that I could go into town and buy dinner for myself. Aunt Polly was the one who had wanted me to eat with them. My feelings for Ezra were unsure, but I liked Aunt Polly.

I pulled out a chair, but Ezra grunted and pointed to the end of the table where Aunt Polly had been arranging the cutlery. Two places along the side had been set with tin plates and spoons, but there was an Old Paris soup plate, a silver spoon and fork, and a white linen napkin at the end of the table.

"Ezra, you get that chair for Miss Nora," Aunt Polly said. When he hesitated a second, she added, "You heard me. You ain't blind," and Ezra went to the chair and seated me.

"Thank you."

Ezra took my plate to the fireplace and lifted the lid off a heavy iron kettle. Aunt Polly ladled something into the dish, and Ezra set it down in front of me. The stew was made of rice, tomatoes, and okra and some kind of meat. If it were a southern specialty—squirrel, blackbird, hog jowl—I hoped that Aunt Polly wouldn't tell me.

Aunt Polly removed the lid from the spider and lifted out a corn bread round and golden as the sun and set it directly on the wooden table, without benefit of plate.

When she and Ezra had taken their places, Aunt Polly bowed her head. "For thy many blessings, Lord, we thank thee," she said in King James English. My surprise must have shown, because Aunt Polly gave me an amused look. "The Presbyterians is our dear belief. We don't hold with singing and shouting on Sunday and raising the devil with your neighbor on Monday like the Baptists does. Presbyterians don't go down under the water for their baptisements, either. Course, black people ain't scared of God like white folks. You think we do hoodoo, all that tricking and trancing devilment?" She laughed, and even Ezra smiled at that, and the tension in the room disappeared.

Aunt Polly broke the corn bread into pieces and handed one to me. She and Ezra crumbled their corn bread into the stew, which they ate quickly with large tin spoons. When I finished the stew, Aunt Polly offered a second helping. "We got a plenty of it, although Ezra, he sure do murder groceries."

The stew was very good, and I thought to compliment Aunt Polly by asking for more. Then I considered that they had already spread their fare thin by sharing it with me. So I declined. Aunt Polly got up and, moving heavily, brought a pan of ginger bread to the table, then

147

cut large chunks with a butcher knife, giving me another corner piece. She and Ezra ate the cake with their hands, but as she had put a fork beside my plate, I set the ginger bread in the soup bowl and ate it with the utensil.

Aunt Polly turned her head to look at me, and I noticed then that she was blind in one eye. She caught me staring and said, "My old mist'ess—that was Mist'ess Emilie but one—she so fetched mean. I drop a potato on the floor one suppertime, and it roll under the table. When I goes to pick it up, she say, 'This learn you to be careless,' and she stick me in the eye with a fork. I'm still blind till now."

"She's six years old then," Ezra added.

"I'm so sorry."

"It ain't your fault. The Bondurants been nothing but good to me. Ezra, you get that coffee."

Ezra poured coffee from an enameled pot whose bottom was burned black, into three tin cups and set them in front of us, along with a sugar bowl and a pitcher of milk.

"You want sweetening?" Aunt Polly asked. "I mostly takes sugar, but the sweet tooth ain't craving it just now."

"Black."

She and Ezra doctored their coffee and tasted it, then sat looking at me expectantly. Finally, Aunt Polly asked, "What you going to do with the place?"

There was nothing to tell them, since I had not yet made a decision. But I did not want to leave them uneasy. "Ezra probably told you that inheriting Avoca was a surprise to me, and I don't know yet what to do with it. Mr. Satterfield . . ." I paused to see if they knew who he was, but of course they did. "Mr. Satterfield advised me to look through my aunt's things for keepsakes. I would like to keep the jewelry and the photographs, and there must be other things that ought to stay in the family." Then I added, "And the quilt that Miss Amalia made."

Aunt Polly nodded her approval. "She like that. It choice."

"Mr. Satterfield said that my aunt took care of you in her will. You won't have to worry."

"So she say," Aunt Polly said.

"Miss Amalia quality," Ezra added.

"And even if she hadn't, I would have made arrangements."

Now both of them stared at me, making me wish the remark had sounded less patronizing. But Aunt Polly, at least, was not offended, because she said, "You a Bondurant."

"I'm trying to make sense of all this, because it's awfully confusing. Of course you're anxious, and I'll make decisions as soon as I can."

"Oh, that all right. I and Ezra been here a long time, since long before freedom cried out. We ain't playing the hog."

"I know that."

Ezra drank his coffee all at once and stood up, telling us he had work to do in the garden. Aunt Polly seemed in no hurry, however, and this was a chance to ask her about Amalia. So, despite her protest, I got up and poured more coffee for the two of us.

"My aunt, did she eat here often?" The room was not only friendlier than Avoca but in better condition. With the addition of electrical wiring, plumbing, perhaps a gas line, the quarters would make a very nice house. Aunt Polly had tacked up outdated calendars and magazine pictures, and an old-fashioned sampler, soiled from smoke and grease, was pinned to the wall next to me. Across its top was a crude alphabet embroidered in black, and beneath it were two dancing stick figures with black heads and the words *Wez Free*.

Aunt Polly saw me looking at the needlework and grinned. "Miss Emilie, she done the letters when she's a girl and throw it out for a rag. But I keep it and finish it off when freedom come. Miss Amalia help me with the words."

"It's extraordinary." The little piece of needlework was filled with life, so different from the samplers with which I was familiar, ones with formal patterns and dirgelike verses.

"I help Miss Amalia with her quilts all her life. We make a plenty of them. Miss Amalia, she love her needle. She say maybe so someday you finish her quilt tops."

"Ezra asked me about quilting. I don't know how. It was never anything that interested me."

"You learn by me. There's nothing brings peace like quilting. Maybe you need it." As if her remark had been presumptuous, Aunt Polly added quickly, "You ask if she eat in this kitchen, and I tell you she done it from the time she was a little thing and had the world in a jug."

"What about in her later years?"

Aunt Polly looked at me a moment, wondering about the question. "Sometimes."

"It's cozier here in your kitchen than over there in the house."

"Miss Amalia like the big house. Never did she ever live no place else."

That was as much of an entrée as Aunt Polly was going to give me. "I thought she and Miss Emilie lived in New Orleans, where my father was born."

Aunt Polly regarded me suspiciously. "I mean for a real home. She *visit* New Orleans, just like she visit New York and over there on the other side of the ocean. She meet the queen of England. You know that?"

Everyone in Natchez seemed to. "Avoca's such a lovely place. She must have missed it when she was away. After she lost her mother, she would have been glad to get back here."

"It home. She never left no more after that." The conversation put Aunt Polly on guard, so perhaps I had moved too quickly. After all, why would she tell me secrets she had kept for more than fifty years?

"What was she like when she was young?" I sipped the coffee, which was bitter with the taste of chicory.

Aunt Polly relaxed a little and pushed her tin plate aside so that she could lean on the table. "Like any other young'un. White chil'en play with the coloreds. Wasn't no difference. Less you see the fur, the mink skin the same thing as the coon hide. Course she still Young Miss. When she get ageable, she don't come around so much. She's off then"—she waved her hand—"places. She wild." Aunt Polly sucked her teeth, remembering. "The captain, he don't know what to do with her. She was his favorite and best. Anything Miss Amalia want, why, he wouldn't say no. He give her the keys to the kingdom."

"It's odd she didn't marry."

Aunt Polly picked at the wooden table with her fingernail. "I wouldn't know about that."

"There must have been plenty of young men in Natchez."

"Oh, not so many. There ain't been enough mens for white young ladies in Natchez since before the freedom. We got a shortness of white mens after that." She gave me a wry look. "That's what the white womens say. Me, I think we got a plenty of white mens. *I* don't need no more of 'em."

I laughed, and Aunt Polly chuckled, pleased with herself. I said, "Miss Amalia was engaged to the man who killed her, to Bayard Lott."

"Who say that?"

"Mr. Satterfield. Mrs. Long. It was even in the newspaper in Denver. Was she?"

Aunt Polly rose slowly. "I'm wearing out my sittin' chair. There's work to be doing."

I put my hand on her arm. "The two of you are to

keep the goat money. You're welcome to the goats, too. There isn't room in my suitcase to take them back to Colorado."

Aunt Polly didn't laugh or thank me, just watched me, waiting. It sounded as if I were bartering with her for information. Perhaps I was.

"There's no reason for me to cause trouble. I only want to find out about Amalia Bondurant."

"Why you trying to know into somebody else's business?"

"Because she's my business. She's my relative, and I want to know why she died." There was no reason to tell Aunt Polly that Amalia's death was becoming an obsession with me, that I felt compelled to understand why this relative had lived and died as she had.

"Ain't no more to it than you already know." She stared at me so hard with her good eye that I looked away.

"Besides, she left Avoca to me, and I don't know why."

"You her only kin."

"No, her brother Frederick had a child."

Aunt Polly sat back down and threw up both hands into the air. "Most likely dead. Besides, she don't like Frederick."

"I know that Amalia was engaged to Bayard Lott. Surely you know that, too."

She said, grudgingly, "He was her heartstring long time ago."

"Why didn't they marry?"

Aunt Polly stood and picked up the dishes, then placed them in a bucket of water that sat on an iron stove. "The captain buy this old stove. It smoke enough to strangle me. I ain't used it in fifty year. In this fireplace was fixed up all the meals."

"You were the cook?"

She smiled. "Still am. I cooks right good." She poured salt into a little dish, added a dash of water from a heavy iron teakettle, and stirred it with her finger. Then she set it on the table, along with a copper Turk's cap mold. She dipped a rag into the salt mixture and began polishing the tarnished metal. "I ever did like to see the shine come through. Ezra say I rather shine the copper than eat when I'm hungry, but that ain't so. I can't sit without I do something, and that's the truth."

"You cooked during the captain's time?"

She straightened a little and gave me a proud look. "I cook everything. You see that spit over there?" Aunt Polly pointed with the rag to the hearth. "That fit a young calf. I roast turkey, ham, venison, lamb on it. I fix burgoo, scalloped oysters, chicken shortcake—that be Miss Amalia's favorite. But my specialty my desserts"—she pronounced the word "*de*sserts"— "trifle, floating island, sweet-potato pie. My angel cake the best in Natchez, light as duck down. You can't mention nothing good to eat that I can't make.

"See that clock up there?" She pointed to an old timepiece with a pendulum that still swung back and forth. "The captain give it me to keep time on my cakes so's they don't get burnt. I don't have need of it, but I don't tell Captain that." She chuckled. "It weren't nothing to cook for twenty people, sometime thirty, maybe more. We cook it here and run it to the dining room. The captain call it the 'batter-cake express.'" Aunt Polly smiled at the memory of it. "That's why the captain buy me. He know I's a first-rate cook and nursemaid. I's Miss Amalia's nursemaid when she's hardly born."

Aunt Polly didn't seem to notice my consternation. "He bought you?" Of course he'd bought her. Slaves were a commodity. Still, the thought that my family had dealt in such commerce disgusted me.

"Oh, I be glad. My old marster, he mean enough to hatch monkeys." She pushed up the sleeve of her dress and showed me ancient scars like hash marks. "They worse on my back. He beat me scandalous. He done it 'cause I carry on when he sell my child, say that baby belong to him, not me. I been hurt to my heart ever since." Aunt Polly's face went rigid. "I guess I been in hell's kitchen and licked the spoon."

"Your master sold your baby?"

"Five year old. It his baby, too. He force me."

The idea of a father selling his own child away from its mother filled me with such loathing that I could not speak. Aunt Polly picked up the mold and began to polish it again. "Welcome. That what I call the baby, 'cause I welcome it. I never see Welcome again."

"How cruel." The words sounded patronizing and inadequate.

"Then I get Ezra. After that, no more children do I have. But everything be fine."

155

"You've been married a very long time, then," I said.

Aunt Polly cocked her head to one side and frowned. Then she laughed and rocked back and forth. "Why, God for Glory, Miss Nora, Ezra not my husband. Ezra my boy. His daddy the marster."

She gave a long, low chuckle as she looked at my astonished face, then found a clean place on the rag and dipped it into the salt again. As she polished, she hummed a tune, a spiritual. I was glad she was looking at the copper mold and not at my red face. It was embarrassing to mistake Aunt Polly for Ezra's wife, but I was stunned and revolted to learn that Captain Bondurant had fathered him. Watching Aunt Polly rub the metal in rhythmic circles, I suddenly realized that if the captain was Ezra's father, the blood that flowed in his veins also flowed in mine. Ezra was Amalia's half brother, and, if my suspicions were correct, my father's uncle. If Aunt Polly were aware of my shock, she didn't show it. She hummed, and after a minute, she began singing, "Sometimes I feel like a motherless child."

Ezra came back into the kitchen then. If he was surprised to see me sitting there still, he didn't let on, just set a handful of herbs on the table and rubbed Aunt Polly's shoulder. He washed the dishes that Aunt Polly had put into the bucket, dried them, then took the bucket of water with him and went back outside.

"Did Ezra ever marry?" I asked.

Aunt Polly nodded. "To his everlasting misery. Ezra so handsome that all the girls come 'round. He have his pick, but Sukey Pea the only one he want. She too

156

good-looking to be endurable. God ask her if she want good sense, but she say no, she take it out in hips, and hips was what she got. She gone crazy through the hips. Sukey Pea sure could tote herself. That must be what mens want, 'cause Ezra not the only one make a fool of hisself by her. Sukey Pea married to Ezra, but she like the other mens too much, and she cut loose. One day she just gone like a turkey through corn. I glad, 'cause she make Ezra crazy in his head. He can't bear to leave her, and he hate to kill her. We never hear about her again. I believe the Lord took her in His bosom by now, 'cause He welcome sinners as much as saints."

"Did they have children?"

Aunt Polly shook her head. "You don't have chil'en, neither," she said. She stated this flatly, and I stiffened to think that Amalia had shared my life with her servants. It was none of their business. But then, Ezra was none of my business.

"No." I got up then. "I don't."

Aunt Polly had finished polishing the mold and set it down on the table, tilting her head to admire the gleaming copper, which was the color of her hair. She must have been a beautiful young woman, I thought. Had Emilie known what was going on between her and the captain? Suddenly, the knowledge of my family's immorality, combined with the heat, the heavy air, and now the stench of a pair of goats in the doorway, made me want to be away from that place. I stood and thanked Aunt Polly for lunch.

She got up, too, and shuffled behind me toward the door. Aunt Polly's homespun dress was worn and patched and shapeless. Would it offend her if I made her a gift of a new one? I wondered. She felt almost like family, and in a way, she was. Then for no particular reason, I told her that I was unlikely to have children. "I'm divorced."

Aunt Polly studied me for a long time. She had to turn her head to one side to look up at me with her good eye. "You a widow," she said, correcting me.

My face went rigid, although it should have been no surprise that Amalia had read about David's death in the newspaper and shared the fact with Aunt Polly. "No." My voice was controlled. "We were divorced before my husband died. I am not a widow."

Then I turned and made my way back to the big house and the darkness of Amalia's bedroom.

David and I had met not long after I graduated from college. I worked as a secretary back then, a position that Henry had arranged for me at his bank. Except for Caroline, none of my friends held jobs. In fact, most of my contemporaries were married, and they filled their days with teas, luncheons at the Denver Country Club and the D&F tearoom, mah-jongg parties, and charity events. Such things didn't interest me then, and I preferred being a part of the business world, even if that meant taking dictation and typewriting letters.

David had moved to Denver from Fort Madison, Iowa, just a few months earlier to take a job at the law firm where he worked until his death, and he had come to the bank to straighten out the account of a client, a widow, who'd told him the bank was siphoning off her funds.

Since it was early on a Monday morning and none of the bank officers had arrived, David asked me to go over the woman's records with him. After a few minutes, I pointed out that the amount the woman claimed was missing was the same as the checks written to her son. Her signature on those checks differed from the signature of record.

Because the woman's family and mine were acquainted, I confided to David that the son was something of a rounder and frequented the back rooms of the gin mills on Lookout Mountain, west of Denver. The gambling games there were known to be crooked, and an ossified young man was an easy mark. Moreover, the boy was fond of women of questionable character, and he had a reputation for lavish spending. Although I did not tell David so, I actually knew the boy quite well, having gone out with him to a party a few weeks earlier. But he'd gotten drunk and treated me like a pushover, so I had taken a taxi home and refused to see him after that.

The fraud had been easy to detect, but David was impressed that I had done so. I was impressed with his pleasant manner and the fact that he treated me more like a colleague than as a member of the steno pool.

That night, David was waiting for me at the employee entrance with a box of Mrs. Stover's Bungalow Candies. He had noticed I was not wearing a ring and took the chance that I was unattached, he said. Then he invited me to dinner, and since it was Mother's and Henry's bridge night, I agreed. He suggested the Brown Palace Hotel dining room, but it was stuffy and expensive, and I believed David was a law clerk, since attorneys did not spend their time looking into bank records, but sent their underlings instead. So I told him that as he was new in town, he should visit the Manhattan Restaurant, which had steaks so tender that you didn't need a knife to cut them. The restaurant was much cheaper, too, although David didn't need to know that. When the owner, Richard Pinhorn, greeted me by name, I was pleased to think David might be impressed. Later, he told me he'd thought I might have worked there, probably in the kitchen.

"Let's have the porterhouse steak for two," David said.

"Oh, I'm not that hungry." The steak cost $1.90.

"I am, and I'll eat part of yours if you don't want it." He placed the order. "And we'll both take the green-apple pie with cheese for dessert." I thought he'd probably have to live on soup for a week to pay for the three-dollar dinner. I did not know that David's salary was sizable, and that even if it wasn't, he could have tapped his trust fund.

We said only a little about ourselves that night. David did not correct my impression that he was a clerk, and I did not apprise him of the fact that Henry was president of the bank. Instead, we talked about

160

moving pictures and books.

"Have you read *The Beautiful and Damned*? It's F. Scott Fitzgerald's best work, you know," David said.

"It's good enough, but *This Side of Paradise* is much better."

"Are you always so opinionated?"

"I try to be."

"Good. A girl who knows her own mind is interesting."

David talked about an exhibit of contemporary art he had seen in New York, and I told him about the Colorado Rockies. David once said the nicest thing I ever did for him was to introduce him to the mountains. By the end of the evening, I was stuck on him and thought he was fond of me.

"Well shucks. I've left my car at my apartment," David said when we left the restaurant.

It sounded to me as if he'd made that up, self-conscious that his car was a jalopy, or because he didn't have an auto at all. "Oh, I always take the streetcar," I told him.

David was too much the gentleman for that, so he called a taxi. He started to get into the cab with me, but I didn't want him to see the Marion Street house, because he might think me a wealthy dilettante whose family connections had gotten her a job—which was exactly what I was. So I insisted on going home alone. David paid the driver and then held the door long enough to ask, "Won't you meet me for a Saturday movie matinee?" Of course I said yes.

On Saturday, David apologized. "I'd been hoping we could make a day of it, but I've accepted a dinner engagement with a business associate tonight. It won't be nearly as much fun as being with you."

As I hadn't expected to make a day of it and had planned on dinner with Mother and Henry, I told him that was perfectly all right. We saw *The Custard Cup* at the Isis, and afterward, we walked over to the Loop Café, where we had hot tea and baked apples. We let the time get away from us, and when we finally realized it was quite late, David agreed to let me take the streetcar home this time. He walked me to the stop and when the trolley came along, he held my hand and said, "So long."

Mother had planned a dinner party that evening for several of my friends, including some boys who were considered quite eligible. She was concerned that, at twenty-two, I had not found anyone special. But though the boys were nice enough, they now seemed limited when I compared them to David. And that was exactly what I was doing when David walked into the living room with Henry. I was thrilled and rushed over to Henry, who said, "David, you've already met my daughter, of course." Henry winked at me. David turned and recognized me, and his jaw dropped.

"Am I the business associate you are dining with, or is Henry?" I asked him.

David grinned and replied, "Is this what you westerners call being buffaloed?"

"Nora had nothing to do with it," Henry told him.

Then he explained it all to me. "David wrote the bank a letter about the girl who had uncovered some improprieties in an account of ours. He thought I ought to know that she had averted an embarrassing situation for the bank. He even thought I should give her a raise. Your mother suggested we invite him to dinner."

"And what about the raise?" I asked.

"Would you really prefer it?"

Whether we were more embarrassed by Henry's cloak-and-dagger matchmaking or the banana oil we had fed each other, I didn't know. Both of us were glad that the little charade was over, although we couldn't have kept it up for long.

David was an immediate hit with Mother and Henry, as well as with my crowd. "He's as handsome as a man in an Arrow Collar advertisement," Caroline told me. David was not tall, but he was athletic and had an engaging smile. Two of my girlfriends made a play for him, but David confided to me that they were "dumb Doras." Besides, from the beginning, it was clear to both of us that we were a couple. We went to the parties and tea dances and dinners, but what we both liked best were the times we went for long drives by ourselves. David did have a car, as it turned out, a Cleveland Roadster, and he liked to drive fast. David was restless.

On the weekends, we headed west up the dirt road to Central City, an old mining town, where we peered into the windows of boarded-up houses. We drove over the mountain to Idaho Springs on the Oh My God Road, and when we got punctures, I helped David patch the tires. "Any other girl would sit on a rock, looking at her wristwatch," David said.

We explored the old mine workings and picked up curios. Once, I spotted a bent iron candlestick and showed it to David. "The loop at the top lets you carry it over your finger, and you shove it into the rock with the spike at the end. Or kill rats with it," I explained.

I threw it back onto the mine dump, but David claimed it, and after that, it became our mission to search the dumps and glory holes for candlesticks. "Want to know how you find a miner's trash heap?" I asked one day. "You stand in the doorway of a cabin and toss a rock, like this." I made an easy throw and watched the rock fall. "That's the dump."

"It makes sense. You can't blame a fellow for not taking out the trash in a blizzard," David said, squatting down near the rock. "This is a regular miner's midden." He held up a whiskey bottle that had turned purple.

"At this altitude, the sun turns them that color."

Over the months, we picked up candlesticks, picks, gold scales, buttons, once a solid gold locket with a woman's picture inside. David had it repaired and gave it to me for my birthday.

A few of the mines were still in operation, run by one or two men. We walked along the narrow-gauge rail-road tracks to the workings and stood in the shadow of the gallows frames, as the mine tipples were called, talking to the miners. They were always polite, courtly sometimes.

"How is the madam today?" one asked me, touching his leather cap.

We invited him to share the picnic lunch that Hattie, Mother's cook, had packed—a hamper of fried chicken, potato salad, pickles, cookies. We spread a quilt in an aspen grove, and the miner removed his cap and said a little prayer. "When you live in these mountains, you develop religious facilities," he told us.

"Have you found gold as well as God?" David asked.

"Here's your blossom rock," he said, tapping an outcropping of ore with a chicken bone. "I've done drudgery work on it, and it might amount to pay dirt, though the assay makes a hard decision against it."

"What would he do if he found it—pay dirt?" David asked me when we had given the miner the remains of the picnic and gone on our way.

"Spend it. In a few years, he'd be right back here."

"Isn't that what he wants? It's the search that matters. It's always the search," David said.

David liked to listen to the tales these old-timers told. One of his greatest assets was his ability to listen seriously to even the giddiest talk and to find gold among the dross. The prospectors found in David a kindred spirit, for David had dreams, too. At the time, they seemed to be for wealth and recognition, and perhaps a chance to make the world a little better place. Those were the things he talked about, at any rate. But as time went on, I realized he wanted something else, although I didn't know what it was.

Often we stopped to visit with my grandmother's

brother and his wife at their little house in Georgetown. They had no children, which might have been why they were especially kind to me. There were stories in the family that Uncle Billy had been an outlaw, which was difficult to believe, because he was gentle, and he and Aunt Emma seemed to be such an ordinary couple, honest as gold. Uncle Billy was even the treasurer of the First Presbyterian Church in Georgetown.

They captivated David with their tales of the old days in the West. "Why, a man couldn't walk down the streets of Leadville at night without he was attacked by footpads. There were more outlaws than honest men." He turned to Aunt Emma for confirmation. "There were women outlaws, you know." He winked at her.

She gave him a wry smile. "You'd not want to cross one of those."

"Oh no." Uncle Billy took her hand. "After all these years, she still makes my heart glad," Uncle Billy told us, and I thought I wanted a husband who would say that to me after such a long time.

Aunt Emma was embarrassed at his show of affection, but later she told me, "Your uncle was the handsomest-made man I ever saw. I thought he hung the moon." She paused. "I still do."

Driving home, I told David, "They ought to move out of the mountains. The coming of the leaves is hard on old people."

"They won't," David said.

And they didn't. They stayed on until they died. "Emma and I have lived side by side for forty years,"

Uncle Billy told Mother when she invited him to live in the Marion Street house after Aunt Emma passed on. "The good Lord didn't let me keep her, but her memory's here." So he stayed on in their little house, sleeping with a very tired heart, until he died less than a year later. Uncle Billy left the Georgetown house to David and me. When David and I divided up things in the divorce, he insisted the house was mine, although it had been a place of refuge for him.

Once, when David and I were dating, Uncle Billy showed him a pair of slats that a miner had left in the barn. "Snowshoes," Uncle Billy said. "That's how we used to get around in winter."

"Skis," David said. "I've seen pictures of them."

Uncle Billy helped David strap the long boards to his feet and showed him how to propel himself across the snow with a pole. David poled himself to the end of the street and back, then called, "Come along, Nora. You've got to try it." He strapped the skis onto my feet, and I attempted to push myself along, but the skis were heavy and my legs wouldn't move. "Try, try," David said, a little frustrated, for he expected me to be as good as he was.

I finally pushed myself a yard or so and fell down, laughing.

"You're a game girl, but this will never do," David said. After we returned to Denver, he ordered skis for both of us, and we taught ourselves to use them. We pushed along the old mining roads, then turned around and followed our trails back to the starting point. Or we skied through the aspen trees, making our own trail. Once, we got caught in a blizzard and spent the night in a deserted cabin. There was a sign on the door that read NO TRESPASSING AND WHEN YOU DO FOR CHRIST'S SAKE SHUT THE DOOR.

We had a lunch and a thermos of hot chocolate in my knapsack, and a pair of lap robes in his, so we were in no danger of either cold or hunger. "But what about your reputation? What will your friends think about your spending the night in a cabin with me?" David said.

"Or a week. With any luck, the storm will last that long."

"I mean it."

"Do you think I would preserve my reputation if I stayed outside and froze to death?"

"I could hang the blankets across the middle of the room. You could stay on one side and I on the other."

"Are you serious?"

At last, he saw the humor in the situation. We spent the night huddled together in the blankets, and by morning, the storm was over. We skied out through the fresh snow, which was such a dazzling white that it hurt our eyes. I told David, "I would risk my reputation just to see this."

There was a Kodak of David taken on that adventure. I had been snapping pictures of the snowdrifts, and I turned and saw David kneeling beside the cabin, putting on his skis. There was one picture left on the roll, and I called to David to smile. He looked up at me with sheer joy on his face. The snapshot, which was on my dressing table throughout our marriage, was one of the few pictures of David that didn't go into the dustbin when he moved out, because I knew the happiness on his face that day was real and that I had been a part of it. It seemed proof that our marriage was not always a sham.

The blizzard wasn't the only danger. Once, we skied up an old road almost to the timberline, the farthest trek we had ever made, when I spotted a mountain lion ahead and a little above us. It was large and muscular, and its fur was the bleached yellow of mine tailings. "Oh God, David, hurry. Let's go!"

David looked up and saw the lion, then gripped my arm. "Don't move. Stay where you are."

"And be eaten alive? Not on your life."

"Stay!" David ordered me. "If you race off, he'll chase you. He'll think you're dinner."

"I am dinner."

"Hold on. He may just go away." David slowly slid toward me on his skis, stopping a foot away. "Don't look him in the eye. You don't want to challenge him."

"Maybe we should curl up, so he'll think we're too small a supper to fuss with."

"That won't work. We'll wait him out."

The lion moved his head a little, watching us with eyes that were yellow and mean. He took a few steps toward us, hissing through yellow teeth.

"He's not leaving," I said as the lion began pacing back and forth. He did that for a minute or two, and then he stopped and crouched.

"We'll have to scare him off. Hold out your poles, so we look big."

"But he already knows there are just two of us."

"Animals can't count." David moved a little so that our ski poles, held out at arm's length, barely touched. "Now, make as much noise as you can, so he'll think we're going to attack him." Suddenly, David began shaking his ski poles. "Get! Get for home! Go on!"

I jumped up and down, as much as I could on the skis, made faces, and cussed. "You ugly cat. I'll rip your damn head off if you don't get out of here."

The lion stood his ground for a minute, while David yelled and I shrieked and carried on. Then David thrust his ski poles toward the animal, which turned and trotted up the mountain. When he reached the top of the trail, he stopped and looked at us again. David picked up two rocks and threw them at the big cat, and he disappeared.

"We did it, David."

"Not yet. Getting back to the car is the hard part. You go first, but not too fast. I'll follow." I started off, looking back to see that David was directly behind me, protecting me. The lion would have to go through David to get to me. But we saw no further sign of the animal. We were exhausted when we reached the car and ripped off our skis. David pushed me into the seat, then secured the skis and poles before he climbed in. He turned to me with a look of exhilaration on his face. "That's the most exciting thing I've ever done."

"You're nuts. We could have been eaten alive."

"You were magnificent. Any other girl would have fainted. But you mugged that cat like a regular Lon Chaney."

"Mugged?" I was embarrassed but had to admit that I was a little proud of myself. "Oh, applesauce!"

"Applesauce, my eye. You mugged him."

Over the years, those adventures spurred David on to greater challenges, and I could not always keep up with him. So I did not mind when David's college roommate, Arthur Ransom, moved to Colorado and the two of them climbed with the Colorado Mountain Club or hunted and skied with the other men in our set. David even joined a bird-hunting club, whose members sat all day in freezing duck blinds. That was not something I wanted to do, so I was glad women were not welcome.

I took to Arthur and his wife, Betsey, at once. Arthur, like David, was friendly, interesting, and fearless. And although Betsey was timid and got frightfully upset when Arthur went adventuring, she made fun of her fears and encouraged the boys, something I admired in her, since she had young children.

David was fond of Betsey, almost as attentive to her as he was to me, although I did not think anything of it at the time. The Ransoms did not move to Denver until some years after David and I married, about 1930, and by then, David's daredevil streak was obvious. He used to laugh and say that if he had not been a lawyer, he might have had a career as an auto racer or a stunt flier or even a flagpole sitter. That was not entirely a joke.

．．．

We had dated for more than a year when David and I became engaged. From the beginning, we had assumed we would marry, but we were having such a swell time that we were not in a hurry. David was thoughtful and romantic. Still, he did not propose with roses and candlelight, as I'd expected, but in an offhand manner, which came as a surprise. We had gone to the mountains to see the aspen, which had turned a glorious color, the leaves spilling onto the ground like golden coins, and decided to prowl through the Georgetown cemetery, where we read the tombstones.

"Listen to this," David said. " 'Little Freddie, age two years nine months ten days, 1880–1883. Oh, you must be a lover of the Lord or you won't go to heaven when you dies.' "

I smiled at the epitaph, then pointed to the gravestone of a couple, both born in 1841. She died in 1868. He lived until 1920. "Do you suppose when he got to heaven, she said, 'I'm not married to that old man'?" I asked.

"Think of all the things he had to tell her about— automobiles and airplanes."

"She'd more likely be interested in vacuum cleaners and window screens." I rubbed my hand over the faded letters carved into the stone. " 'Forever rest together.' "

"Do you think you could stand to lie beside me for all of eternity?" David asked.

"I shouldn't like to do anything for all eternity."

"I am serious, Muggs. You're a first-rate girl and the

best pal a fellow could have. You know I love you dearly. It would be grand being married. I think I'd better snatch you up before some other chap does it." He had been sucking on a stem of dried grass, which he took out of his mouth, then kissed me. "You will marry me, won't you?"

I did not realize how much I loved David until that moment, when a great sense of happiness came over me. And, of course, I said yes.

After such a wonderful courtship, we had a dreadful engagement. David was uncomfortable at the parties that Mother and Henry's friends gave in our honor. He'd never been crazy about social gatherings, and these were especially difficult for him because he was the center of attention. Mother had given her share of engagement parties for her friends' children, so it would have been rude of me to turn down the reciprocal invitations. David sulked when he got each week's social schedule, and he flat out refused to attend one party.

"I'll feel like I'm on display, like a lamb chop at the meat market," he said when he received an invitation for the tea that our neighbor Elvira Doud was hosting for us.

"With or without the skirt?" I asked, for we had always laughed at the paper frills the butcher put on the lamb chops.

David did not find that amusing and didn't reply.

"Oh, David, we have to go. Mother had a party for Mrs. Doud's daughter, Mamie Eisenhower, when she married. I can't turn down her mother."

"You'll just have to think of something, because I've had it. I'm not going," he said. So I went alone, explaining that David had just been called to the bedside of a client who was at death's door. Mrs. Doud probably scanned the obituaries over the next few days, searching for the woman's name.

David hated planning the details of the wedding. He took no interest in the color and style of my bridesmaids' dresses, had no opinions on the flowers for the ceremony. He didn't even care about the menu for the reception, and when Mother asked him whether one of his groomsmen should be seated beside a married or unmarried bridesmaid, he snapped, "For all I care, he can eat in the kitchen."

Of course, he apologized to Mother and sent her flowers, and she told me that Henry had been just as jittery before their wedding. But I was not so sure it was nerves. Just that week, David had walked out of a picture show, claiming he had a violent headache, and when I put my hand on his forehead, he'd brushed it away, saying, "For God's sake, Nora, it hurts enough. Don't touch me."

Another time, he had stopped his car in the park and said he wanted to go for a walk. He set a fast pace, and when I couldn't keep up, he snapped, "Why must you be so poky?"

"It's my slippers. They're not made for walking."

"You should have worn something else."

"I didn't know we were going for a hike."

"Well, damn it to hell."

"David!"

"Oh, don't be so shocked. You've said worse yourself."

By the time we got back to the car, he had begged me to forgive him, and I had, but I worried nonetheless that he might have changed his mind about marrying me.

Then one afternoon, as we sat in the living room opening wedding presents, David held up a crystal vase and said, "What idiot would think we would want something this ugly in our home?" He set down the vase so hard that the bottom chipped.

"David, you've found fault with every gift we've opened. You're acting like a jackass."

David turned to me with a look of rage on his face. "If you think I'm a jackass, why would you want to marry me?" Before I could respond, he added, "We ought to call it a day. I'm sorry, Nora, but this is not going to work. Forgive me, but I can't go through with it."

I was too stunned to speak.

"I'm sorry," he repeated, and rushed out of the house.

Mother heard the door slam and hurried into the room. "What is it?" she asked, sitting down on the sofa beside me and putting her hand on my arm.

"We've called off the wedding. I mean, David called off the wedding. He doesn't want to marry me." I sat with my hands between my knees, too dejected to cry.

"Oh, I doubt that. It's just a spat."

"It's true. I'll never show my face in public again."

"You've never cared about the public." Mother put

her arms around me and said it was far better to admit now that we had made a mistake than to do so after the wedding. "Let's just not say anything for a day or two. He'll come around. And if he doesn't, Henry and I will take care of everything."

But I knew David wouldn't come around, because he had been unhappy ever since we'd announced our engagement. "No. It's over. It's my mistake, and I'll handle the mess."

The next day, I began writing notes of explanation and packing up the wedding gifts. Mother helped me, while Henry sat in an armchair with a disheartened look on his face, for he thought of David as a son. From time to time, Henry said encouraging things, such as "He likes her. He'll be begging back." And later: "Why, of course he'll be back. He's just mulish. David thinks Nora's the Second Coming of Christ."

"Oh, Henry, don't blaspheme," Mother said as the doorbell rang. In a minute, Hattie ushered David into the room, and Henry shot Mother a triumphant look.

I had not expected David, of course, and looked a mess. My eyes were red, and my face could have used a powder puff. I'd put on a pair of britches and a shirt of Henry's, because I was going to have my arms in boxes of tissue and barrels of straw. David didn't look much better. He had not shaved, and his hair was mussed. His face was blotchy from driving about in the wind, or maybe from drinking. He wore a pair of old knickers and a sweater that was unraveled at the cuffs.

When he asked if I would go for a ride with him,

Mother said, "David, I think we all ought to sit down and—" But Henry touched her arm, and she was still. They thought David had come to make amends, but I knew he wanted to bring things to a tidy conclusion, and perhaps that was best for both of us.

"All right." My voice was unsteady. "I'll just change into—"

"No, don't. I've some things to say. My machine's outside. We'll go for just a short spin."

So I grabbed my old polo coat, and without even a comb or a compact in my pocket, went off with him.

We drove west on the concrete road to Golden, then into the mountains, the route we usually took on our outings. The roadster's top was down, and the wind was cold. I wrapped my coat tightly about me, wishing for a scarf to keep my ears from stinging. We did not speak for more than two hours, until we reached Idaho Springs, where David stopped the car in front of a coffee shop. Instead of waiting for him to come around, I opened my door myself and stepped out onto the street. The air was electric, and thunder was ringing in the mountains. I put my hands over my ears to keep out the noise and the cold.

We sat down in a wooden booth in the restaurant, and I would not look at David, just watched drops of water run down the steamy windows, leaving tracks like ski trails. I felt such sadness, not just at the broken engagement but in knowing we would never tramp the hills together again. Our trips to the mountains had been the happiest times in both of our lives.

David ordered coffee for us and asked if I wanted something to eat. "You're frightfully cold, I know. I should have turned on the heater."

"Just coffee." Those were the first words I had said since we'd left the house, and they came out rusty. We were silent again, David so lost in thought that he jumped when the waitress returned with our mugs. I put my hands around my cup and lifted it, letting the steam warm my face. I still could not look at David, just watched two old men in overalls and heavy boots sit down across from us. One of them ordered two slices of bread fried in grease and covered with Karo syrup, which he pronounced "Kay-row." Had I been alone, I would have remembered the word to tell David, because I always saved up things to tell him.

"Look at me," David said then, and I turned away from the men. David's eyes were red. I had never seen him cry, and I wanted to reach out and comfort him, but I would not do so, and I held on to the cup instead. "Dearest Muggs, do you think you could forgive a jackass?" He looked at me mournfully.

"Not just any jackass." I had used both hands to lift the heavy white cup to my mouth. But they were shaking so much that I had to put the cup down.

"A foolish, thickheaded, stubborn-as-a-mule jack-ass?"

"Maybe that one." And I hoped that in time I could.

He reached across the table and pried my hands off the cup. "I've been such a heel. I don't know what's wrong with me, because I want us to be married more than anything in the world."

I jerked up my head, too surprised to say anything.

"I know it's screwy, but I want you to be my wife right this minute. Can't we find a preacher and forget about this fancy show of a wedding? Do you love me enough to do that?"

I felt the blood rushing through my body, warming me. "Of course I do."

David leaned across the table and kissed me—to the delight of the two old-timers in the booth. One gave a low whistle, and the other stamped his feet and said, "I guess you got something in your coffee we didn't, young fellow."

"Must be she's his lucky piece," the other said.

"There ain't but one thing that's a lucky piece, and that's money," the first man said. Nonetheless, he held up his coffee cup in a salute to us.

David and I drove to Georgetown and asked Uncle Billy and Aunt Emma to stand up with us. While Uncle Billy went to find old Reverend Darnell, who had married them so many years before, Aunt Emma cut the last of the daisies and brown-eyed Susans in her garden for a bridal bouquet. "Did Mother tell you that David had called off the wedding? I thought everything was over," I told her, pinching off a wilted daisy.

Aunt Emma cut off another dead blossom with her scissors, then looked at me a long time, as if debating whether to say something. Then she told me, "The Lord and I were not always on the best of terms. There were things that happened. . . ." She shook her head as if to remove the memory of whatever those things were. "A friend long days ago, a colored man, told me about God's unending mercies. I didn't believe him at the time, but then I met Billy. I've learned that the Lord never abandons us. Like the Bible says, His mercies are new every morning." She laughed and searched among the daisies again. "That's too much gloom for a bride on her wedding day. Billy has always been my greatest mercy. I hope David will be yours."

So David and I stood up in that little mountain church to become husband and wife. We spent the night in a $2.50 room at the Alpine Lodge, a house that had once belonged to a silver king, and to explain our lack of luggage, we told the proprietor that we had had motor trouble and couldn't make it back to Denver, because we were embarrassed to say we were newlyweds.

Instead of a stylish wedding gown from Daniels & Fisher, I was married in the polo coat, which I'd buttoned up to hide my motoring clothes. I preserved the coat in blue tissue, taking it out to wear on our anniversary each year. After I returned from Reno, staying there only long enough to qualify for a Nevada divorce, I threw out most of the things associated with David. I forgot about the polo coat until several months later, when it went into the Community Chest clothing drive. By then, David was dead.

Chapter Six

RETURNING TO AMALIA'S BEDROOM, I sat for a long time in a worn leather chair, staring at the lines of light that came through the slats in the shutters at the side of the house. The shutters had been nailed almost shut, possibly to keep the Shadowland neighbors from looking in. But Amalia might have sat in the chair and spied through the thin openings at the Lotts. I leaned forward and peered out, catching sight of a house that was even more dilapidated than Avoca. Two rickety staircases led up to a second-floor gallery, whose railings had rotted away. As I watched, a tiny woman climbed out of one of the second-story windows and scrambled down the steps. Her footing seemed sure, but her head jerked as she moved. Magdalene, I thought—Lott's wife.

When she disappeared, I settled into the chair, whose back was to the open doors. Tufts of horsehair pushed through cracks in the leather, but the chair was large and roomy, with a high back and wings that curled around me. It was surprisingly comfortable, and I dozed off.

I awoke, checking my wristwatch, but the room was too dark for me to see the time. I did not know what had disturbed my nap until there was a rustle—possibly a goat. But the sound was so slight that it could have been made by rats, and I shivered and drew my legs tight against my body. Rats did not open drawers, however, and the sound was that of a drawer slowly being pulled out. Gripping the arm of the chair, I peeked around the wing.

The odd little creature who had descended the staircase at Shadowland was peering into an open drawer of Amalia's desk. She was perched on the chair where I had sat earlier, and her feet did not reach the floor.

The woman was so intent on rifling through the desk that she did not see me. From time to time, she glanced out the door, perhaps fearing that Ezra would discover her. She opened the drawers on the right side of the desk and searched through their contents, lifting out the account book, opening it, and running her finger down the page. But that was not what she was looking for, and she returned it.

When she came to the drawer that held Amalia's jewelry, Magdalene picked up the boxes, turning them over in her hand, looking at them curiously. She opened each one and inspected the contents, then lined up the boxes on the desk. After running her finger over the jewelry, she removed a large gold bow set with precious stones. She rubbed her knuckles over the gems and held the brooch to the outside light, then placed it against her dress, which was a pitifully worn piece of apparel, its tears held together with safety pins. Aunt Polly was better dressed than Magdalene Lott. I was ready to spring on her if she put the bow into her pocket. But she placed it back in its box and returned the jewelry to the drawer, pushing it shut.

She went through the rest of the drawers but did not

find what she was looking for, because she slipped off the chair and crawled under the desk. She touched something that released a hidden drawer on the right side, then sat on the floor and went through the contents. All at once, her hands fluttered up in a gesture of surprise and pleasure, and she lifted out a fat envelope and held it to the light coming in from the French doors. She muttered as she read what was written on the envelope, but I could not hear what she said.

The envelope appeared to contain money, so I stood up and asked, "What have you taken?"

Magdalene stuffed the envelope into the bosom of her dress, then got to her feet as she looked over her shoulder at the open doors, expecting to see Ezra or Aunt Polly. Saying nothing more, I stood beside the chair, waiting, while her eyes scanned the room and eventually came to rest upon me. She was even smaller than she had first appeared, less than five feet tall and as thin as a broom straw. The skin was drawn tightly across her face, and her nose stood out like a beak. Her head made the same uncontrollable jerking motions that I had noticed earlier, although the rest of her body was still. She looked as if she would blow away like a dried leaf, but she was less fragile than she appeared.

If she were frightened, she did not show it. Magdalene's face had a coy look, and she turned her head slightly, looking at me out of one eye, like a bird. She took her time before replying. "Why, you nice thing," she said in a voice that was raw and cracked from disuse. "I am purely looking for my receipt for lady cake. I loaned it to dear Amalia, who adored to eat it, you know, just adored to. Everybody did. I very plainly said she must return the receipt, but Amalia did not do so. I was afraid Ezra or Aunt Polly would toss it to the wind. They are that mean to me." She touched her breast. "So many grievous sorrows I have had."

I was not in the least taken in by her. This creaky old woman was out to rob Amalia—which was to say, me. Still, her audacity and quick wit amused me. "Is the recipe in the envelope you put inside your dress?"

"Why, I'm not even about to know what you mean." She gave me a smile that might have warmed the hearts of men half a century ago but did nothing for me now. Although she was an old crone, Magdalene Lott flirted like a young girl, as if she were unaware of how pathetic she appeared. Perhaps there were no mirrors at Shadowland and she did not know that her yellow face was as pitted and flaky as a corncob. Pickett had mentioned that during the war, mirrors were hidden in hay to keep the Union troops from breaking them. For Magdalene's sake, I hoped that Shadowland's mirrors were still tied up in ancient bales.

"Oh course, poor Amalia could never bake a proper cake. Mr. Lott, my husband who was"—she looked down dramatically and patted her breast—"he told me as much. He said my cake was blazing good and that it was surely his privilege to enjoy it, and Amalia's . . . well, if you must know, he said it tasted like old rags and sulfuric acid. I'm sure he didn't mean it." She dipped her head and looked up at me under pale eyebrows to let me to know that Bayard Lott had indeed meant it. I was surprised that with Aunt Polly in the cookhouse, Amalia had ever baked a cake.

I moved closer to Magdalene and saw that her face was covered with a white powder, which had sifted over her dress. It might have been flour. Whatever it was made her look even more like an apparition. She took a step backward, her hands clasped protectively over her bosom. "Let me see the recipe," I said. "I'm partial to cake, too, but I've never heard of lady cake."

"It's a secret—a secret receipt. I can't show you." Magdalene's voice was conspiratorial.

"But you said you shared it with Amalia."

"It's a family secret."

"I'm Amalia's family. I'm Nora Bondurant, Amalia's niece." I did not hold out my hand, for fear the white powder would attach itself to me.

"You!"

Not knowing how to respond, I simply looked at her until Magdalene dropped her gaze. She took a step backward and turned, but before she could scurry away, I grabbed her arm, throwing her off balance. She started to fall, but I caught her shoulder with one hand. She felt like a chicken whose tiny bones could be crushed if I squeezed her. With my other hand, I pulled the envelope from her dress. Magdalene grabbed for it, dragging her broken fingernails across my hand, leaving trails of white. But I held it high above my head so that she could not reach it. "Sit." I pushed her into the chair.

Magdalene crumpled and began to whimper as I looked inside the envelope and removed a wad of money—fifty dollars in one- and five-dollar bills. "There's no recipe here for lady cake." I felt just a little ashamed at my nastiness. Still, she had tried to steal money.

"The money's mine. It's owed me."

"Is that why you sneak in here like a thief in the night? If it was owed you, wouldn't you have asked for it?" This time, I smiled to offset the harsh words.

Magdalene cocked her head to one side and smiled as she batted lashless eyes at me and sighed. "How best to answer you? You're purely and simply not under-standing." She straightened up, resting her chin on a crooked forefinger. Then she smiled. "I do adore your blue glass buttons." She pointed to the buttons on my blouse. "I have not seen blue glass buttons that shade since a ball at D'Evereux away off." She paused. "Of course, the quality was better back then." Magdalene pursed her thin lips, as if she had said something she shouldn't have. "Your buttons are the color of morning glories. But then, I never took to morning glories. They're purely weeds, you know."

She must have passed for a wit in her time, and she still was adroit enough to have changed the subject. If it weren't for the money in my hand, I might have for-gotten what I'd asked her. "Why did you steal my aunt's money?" I asked again.

"Your aunt . . ." she mused, but I did not respond, so she changed tactics. "I did not steal it," Magdalene said hotly. "As you can see, you are holding it in your hand."

"But you would have stolen it if I had not caught you."

"You put too fine a point on it." As if talking to a child, she added, "Besides, one cannot steal what belongs to one."

I was impatient now. "Are you telling me you used my aunt's desk as a safety-deposit box? You must have spied on Amalia, for how else would you have known about the hidden drawer?"

Magdalene sniffed. "Every piece of furniture in Natchez has a hidden drawer. How do you think we kept the Yankees from stealing us blind? Besides, Mr. Lott had a desk just like this one. He had two made and gave one to Amalia as a betrothal gift."

"How romantic," I blurted out, and Magdalene laughed. Odalie was wrong when she said Magdalene was feeble; nonetheless, she did not appear to be capable of carrying out a double murder. Magdalene wasn't as frail as she seemed, but she certainly wasn't strong, either. And flirting, not firearms, seemed to be her weapon of choice.

She was shrewd enough to steal, however. I put the money into the pocket of my skirt and dropped the envelope onto the desk. "You can go along. Ezra will be here any minute."

"I shall not leave without my money."

"*Your* money."

"Look at the envelope." She was indignant now.

187

A name was on the envelope: Bayard Lott. It was written in indelible pencil, and I had seen enough of Amalia's writing to know it was in her hand.

Magdalene shot me a look of triumph. "You see! Now please kindly give me my money."

I was confused, but not confused enough to hand over the bills. "That is Mr. Lott's name, not yours. The envelope is torn and stained. My aunt may have reused it. Besides, why would she give anything to your husband? You have said yourself that they hated each other. It was in the newspapers."

"Oh, Mr. Lott loved her just like a dog loves a good whipping." Magdalene giggled, then grew serious. "She gave my husband fifty dollars every month, and now that he is gone, the money is mine."

I laughed at such a preposterous statement. "That's unlikely, but I'll talk to Mr. Satterfield about it."

Magdalene bounded out of the chair, startling me so that I put my hand over my pocket, but she did not grab for the money. Instead, she stood next to me and looked up into my face. She smelled a little.

"It's mine. You ask Ezra," she hissed. Suddenly, she spit on the floor. "You give it to me before that dries, or there'll be trouble." Perhaps she realized she had been unladylike and was unlikely to get anywhere with threats, because suddenly her mood lightened and she pouted and wrung her thin hands together. "You are as tight as Dick's hatband," she whined. "I am two and seventy years of age, too old for any good. If you don't give the money to me, I shall die starved. You can see

188

for yourself I am poorly thin and do not get a sufficient to eat."

She did look undernourished, and I wavered. "Why would my aunt support you? If she and your husband hated each other, why would she give him charity?"

"Not charity!" Magdalene stamped her foot. Then she changed her mood again and smiled sweetly at me. Magdalene Lott was as nuts as Odalie. Mr. Satterfield was right: I did not understand Natchez women.

"Then what else would it be? It's clearly charity." I hoped to annoy her enough that she would stop the posturing and blurt out something of interest.

And she did just that. "Amalia gave Mr. Lott a competence to keep what he knew to himself."

"She paid him money to keep a secret?"

"Money will do till God makes something better."

"He was blackmailing her."

Instead of denying it, Magdalene shrugged. "Call it what you like. It makes no difference to me. Just give me the money."

"What did he know about my aunt?"

"She wouldn't want you to know." Magdalene postured like a child with a secret. She seated herself in the chair again and gripped the arms with her hands.

I did not care to play her games any longer and told her so, asking her again to leave. But having decided she was in no danger and being unwilling to leave without the money, Magdalene showed no indication of going home. Cooped up in that moldering mansion with Bayard Lott, she must have missed the society of others. I was considering picking her up and carrying her out of the room, when Ezra entered from the great hall. He did not say a word, but when Magdalene saw him, she pulled back into the chair and her face took on a cagey look. Her eyes darted from Ezra to me. Ezra said nothing, just stood there with his arms at his sides.

"Mrs. Lott has taken an envelope with fifty dollars in it from Miss Amalia's desk." My words were unnecessary, since Ezra probably had been lurking outside the door during the entire conversation. "Mr. Lott's name is on it, and Mrs. Lott says the money is hers."

Ezra said nothing, just waited for me to continue.

"She claims Miss Amalia gave him the money every month." I rolled my eyes to show Ezra that I had not been taken in.

Ezra turned to Magdalene, his dark eyes boring into her, but Magdalene held her own.

"Why would she give your husband money?" I asked her again.

Magdalene had turned tenacious. "I said once, and I'll say again: He knew something that she didn't want spoken."

Ezra took a step forward and said, "Get!"

Magdalene stood up and stamped her foot. "Don't you warn me home. I will not be talked to in such a manner by a servant."

I dismissed her with a wave of my hand and turned my back on her. Ezra stepped forward and took her arm, edging her to the door. "Aunt Polly got a Coke-Cola bottle for you. Green, like you like. I hang it from

190

your tree for you." I realized the tree with the bottles that I'd seen on my way to the quarters must belong to Magdalene.

"Ooh," she cooed, and started for the French doors. But she was not done. She jerked her arm from Ezra's grasp, then held out her hand, palm up, for the money.

But I folded my arms to show that she would not get it.

"That her money," Ezra said suddenly.

I was too surprised to speak.

Ezra nodded. "She right. Miss Amalia give it to Mr. Bayard every and each month. She have me to take it to him."

I removed the bills from my pocket and handed them to Magdalene.

She counted them, then smiled up at me. "I kindly thank you." She started for the door, and when she reached it, she put her hand on the door frame. Long years ago, that might have been a dramatic exit, but now the gesture was pitiful. "Amalia led a corruptible life," she said. "What Mr. Lott knew was that Amalia was your daddy's mother. And who would know that better than Bayard Lott?" She laughed like a naughty child as she clutched at the doorjamb with a hand as veined and translucent as a dried leaf. "Please to have Ezra bring me the money next month."

After Magdalene disappeared through the French doors, I turned to Ezra. His face was stripped of emotion. Slaves would have had to develop that countenance to hide their feelings from their owners. And present employers.

"Should you see her home, Ezra? After all, she's seventy-two years old." It had begun to drizzle outside—no more than a fine mist, but the path through the underbrush would be slippery.

"Don't be telling me. I got nothing to do with her age." Ezra paused to get control of himself as he watched Magdalene disappear in the underbrush. "She ain't sugar. She won't melt."

"No." I waited silently until Ezra turned and looked me in the eye before asking, "What she said about my father, it's a preposterous statement, isn't it?"

"Yes, ma'am."

"Of course it is." I nodded for emphasis. "Still, Mrs. Lott isn't the first to say it. The same story was told to me last night."

Ezra's face remained placid, and he didn't reply.

"You yourself must have heard it before now."

"It get told over and again, but I don't pay mind to white folks' gossip. It just narrow-hearted littleness." Ezra shifted a little, as if the conversation made him uncomfortable. "If you ain't staying here the night, you want me to take you to the hotel in the automobile? I operate it. I drive Miss Amalia to town every day to sell milk. That a good car. I keep it first-rate. You be proud to have it."

I hardly intended to drive the REO back to Colorado and had decided to give it to Ezra, but this was not the time to discuss it. "Please sit down." I seated myself on the top of the steps that Amalia had once used to climb into her bed.

Ezra remained standing until I pointed to the chair by the desk that Magdalene had perched on; then he sat down.

"What do you know about Miss Amalia?"

"Everything and nothing."

This would not be easy. "What do you know about my father's parentage?"

"I a servant. It not my business."

"It is my business, of course. Don't you think if Amalia Bondurant were my grandmother and not my aunt that I have a right to know it?"

Ezra leaned forward in the chair, elbows on his knees, hands clasped together, looking at the floor. "I guess I see Miss Magdalene get home. Some of these days, she fall in the woods. Her feet ain't mates no more." He didn't get up, however.

"She must be home by now." We were silent a moment. "Did you hang all those bottles in the tree for her?"

He nodded. "Mr. Bayard a hard man."

"What was he like?"

"I got no use for him. If there a living devil, Shadowland be his home. Mr. Bayard lay them two open to trouble and sorrow. Miss Amalia say Miss Magdalene born to take other people's leavings, so Miss Amalia give Mr. Bayard the money to take care of her, 'cause Miss Amalia was sorry to her heart about Miss Magdalene's tribulation. You think Miss Magdalene treat her good for that, but she don't."

"You don't believe Mr. Bayard was blackmailing Miss Amalia?"

Ezra thought that over and shook his head. "She give him the money free of gratis. Miss Amalia have a heart like fine gold. She see Mr. Bayard smack Miss Magdalene after she say her mind one time. He tell her women and chickens ought to let somebody think for 'em."

"And Amalia believed otherwise?"

"Oh, yes, ma'am. Don't nobody think for Miss Amalia. She plucky all right."

"So Miss Amalia and Mr. Lott did talk from time to time."

"I never said not."

"No, but others told me they hadn't exchanged a word in years."

"Not a word they didn't have to."

"There's a path between here and Shadowland. I saw it from the window. Someone's been going back and forth."

"Goats," Ezra said. "Goats tromps where they wants to."

"But you go over there sometimes."

"I never had any tarry with him, 'cept for the money. Sometimes, I helps Miss Magdalene." He got up from the desk, slowly, stiffly. Ezra was older than I had thought, probably in his seventies. "Now, if you got nothing more—"

He had warmed to me a little, possibly because I had stood up for Amalia with Magdalene, and I wanted to take advantage of that. "I do have something more," I said quickly.

But it seemed that he had not warmed up much, because he looked at me warily as he sat back down.

"I asked you about my father's mother. Was she Miss Emilie or Miss Amalia?"

Ezra shifted, and I thought a look of sorrow passed over his face, but the light outside had grown even dimmer since the rain had started, and I could not be sure. "Your daddy born in New Orleans. How you expect me to know?" he replied.

"What I'm talking about took place nine months before that. Besides, people talk."

"Ain't nobody in this house talk."

"My father *could* have been Miss Amalia's baby."

"Child," he said, "he could have been the devil's doll baby, for all I knows. I'm hard of understanding why you want to stir up troubles."

Perhaps, I thought, it's because others are so determined that I not do so.

The wooden steps I was seated upon were hard on my backside, and I pushed myself up so as to sit on the quilt, my feet on the steps. The bed was very high, like a little island. There was a rustle as I settled into the quilt, the crackle of paper.

"Miss Amalia, she put newspaper on the bed to cover her sheet and pillow in the day," Ezra explained.

"Oh." I didn't like the idea that Amalia had been as eccentric as Magadelene, but of course she had. I leaned forward and looked at Ezra intently. "If Amalia was my father's mother, who was his father?"

Ezra nodded his head back and forth, a somber look on his face. He rubbed his eyes with his thumb and forefinger, then picked up the envelope on the desk and stared at the name Bayard Lott. He put the envelope back on the desk and looked up at me. "Aunt Polly say don't fault you for wanting to know, but some things don't bear a closer look."

"And some things do. My father was all but disowned by his family. And if the reason was that he was Miss Amalia's bastard"—the word hung in the air, but it had no effect on Ezra, perhaps because he was a Bondurant bastard himself—"I think I have the right to know who his father was. After all, that man was my grandfather."

Ezra tapped his finger against the envelope. "I could read her writing, but I sure couldn't read her mind."

I frowned, trying to figure out what he meant, shifting a little on the bed and making the newspapers crackle. I wondered if they were the Denver papers that Amalia had read to keep up on me. I looked at Ezra's finger pointing to the name in purple pencil on the envelope, then thought of Magdalene's oblique remark, asking who would know better about Amelia having a child than Bayard Lott? And why was there a picture of him among Father's things? Bayard Lott had gotten Amalia pregnant, then blackmailed her. That was obvious now. That meant something else was obvious: My grandfather had murdered my grandmother.

"You need a ride, do you?" Ezra asked. His eyes

moved toward the secret compartment in the desk, and I realized he had not known it was there. Ezra undoubtedly had gone through Amalia's things before I arrived, destroying what he did not want anyone to see. He could burn whatever Amalia had hidden in this secret place, too, if he had a chance. I didn't intend to give him one. "No, there's work for me to do yet. I'm in need of fresh air, and the walk back into town will do me good."

"It get dark before long. You not want to be on this road these moonshining nights."

The road did not strike me as sinister now. "It won't take long. There's Miss Amalia's receipt book and her quilt journal to pack, and some photographs I found. No need for you to wait. I'll close up."

"Best I stay."

"No." I sat down at the desk, using my foot to close the secret door, which Magdalene had left open.

Ezra bowed his head a little, then went out onto the gallery and passed by the side of the house. When he was gone, I crawled under the desk and pressed my hand at three or four spots along the molding until a drawer was released. Inside were scraps of paper, all with dates and the notation, "Paid to B.L., $50." Except for them, the drawer was empty. Disappointed, I closed the drawer and backed out awkwardly, bumping against the opposite side of the desk, where a panel opened, revealing a doll's trunk. When I lifted the lid, I found it filled with letters. Amalia must have hidden them from Ezra, but I would not take the time now to discover why. The little trunk in hand, I closed the panel and backed out from under the desk, then placed the trunk in a carpetbag of Amalia's, along with the two handwritten books and the pictures. Afraid that Ezra would return and somehow wrest the satchel from me, I quickly left the house and started for town.

Except for a man in overalls, who was on a white mule, and who tipped his hat to me as he passed, no one was on the road. The thick underbrush and the trees with their long, gnarled branches that formed a canopy over me seemed friendly. The foliage was damp and lush, and after the thin rain, the evening was cool. Mist rose like smoke from a campfire. Kicking up dirt with my new canvas shoes, I found the walk relaxing, the late-day shadows soft and enveloping. Fireflies darted in the dark recesses of the woods, their pinpoints of light like sparks from a cigarette lighter. The sounds were pleasant ones—the breeze rustling the leaves, the scurrying of animals in the woods, birds fluttering among the ferns, even the barking of a dog. An ugly mongrel followed me from the other side of a split-rail fence, growling softly. Then a voice called, "Let 'er pass, you mule-headed thing."

In a field of goldenrod, tall brick columns, the ruins of an antebellum home, stretched into the sky. Nothing else was left of the house, only the columns, like blackened pine trees after a fire. As the dirt turned to pavement, I came upon small houses with oversize pillars and tall windows and verandas with straight chairs and rockers. The houses grew larger, more imposing, and there were commercial buildings. As I reached the center of town, I saw a sign that read SHERIFF. To my surprise, for the sky was dusky now and it was long after business hours, the door to the building was open, and a light shone from a far office. When I knocked, a man leaned back in a swivel chair until he could see me and said, "Ma'am?"

"Are you the sheriff?"

"Yes, ma'am. Sheriff Cheet Beecham. Can I help you?" He pronounced the word *help* as "hep." The sheriff got up and stood in his office doorway.

"I'm Nora Bondurant, Amalia Bondurant's niece."

He nodded as if he were not surprised to see me. "I heard you was in Natchez. You come on in. I'm real sorry about Miss Amalia. She was choice."

I thanked him and said I hadn't known her, and he nodded again. He probably wasn't surprised by much.

"Do you have a few minutes? I could come back tomorrow."

"I got all the time you need right now. You come on in and take you a chair." He pushed aside a grilled cheese sandwich that rested on an ink blotter. "The wife died last year, God bless her soul. I nearly grieved myself to death, and even now I can't hardly stand to be alone in the house anymore. If I don't stay here, I got nothing to do but sit on the front porch and watch the cars go by."

"I'm awfully sorry."

"Cancer. The good Lord didn't give me hardly no

199

time at all to say good-bye. Before you could say Jack Robinson, Pie had passed. Pie, that's what I called her, for sweetie pie, you know. You married, are you?"

"I was." I sat down on a hard wooden chair in front of the desk and set the carpetbag on the floor.

He folded his hands on the desk and leaned forward, all business. "Now, what was it you wanted to ask about?"

"My aunt's death. First, is there any doubt that Bayard Lott shot her?"

"None that I could see. You'd not hardly think a man would shoot a person, then reload the gun and shoot hisself, especially being old and shaky like he was. They was shot with the same gun, of course, one of those old Odells that was made right here in Natchez 'bout the time of the War. They don't hold but one bullet. It had to take him a minute to reload, and you might think he'd've reconsidered. Old Bayard never struck me as a man wanting to die."

"Could she have shot him, then killed herself?"

"I thought about that, but it makes no sense. She was found in the bed, you know, in her nightdress. Looked like she'd been sleeping."

"The newspapers didn't print that."

"No, ma'am. It don't signify nothing. Never did I think he did anything to her in an unnatural way. But she was a lady." He paused. "Here's another thing: The gun was in Bayard's hand."

"Ezra or Aunt Polly could have put it there. Or even Mrs. Lott."

200

"Nope. We tested for fingerprints. They was Bayard's. There's no two ways about it. He done the deed, as the feller says."

He glanced at the sandwich, and I said, "I'm keeping you from your supper. Please, go ahead."

"You don't mind?" He picked up an open bottle of Nu-Grape and drank.

"Not if you don't mind my asking questions." Looking down at my dirty hands and skirt, I explained, "I was just out at Avoca."

"That would have been some surprise for you. What you going to do with the goats?"

"Give them to Ezra."

"That'd be my suggestion."

We were silent while he bit into a pickle and I moved around on the uncomfortable seat. "The biggest question is why Bayard Lott did it?"

"Don't none of us knows the answer to that."

"Yes, those were your words in the newspaper."

"Oh, I don't tell everything to the newspapers."

Intrigued, I leaned forward. "What, for instance?"

He lifted a corner of the bread and looked at the sticky cheese, then pushed the two slices of bread back together. He held the sandwich to his mouth, but before he bit into it, he replied, "I didn't tell them why I thought Bayard did it."

"And that is . . ."

The sheriff nodded as he ate from the middle of the sandwich. After he swallowed, he said, "I think he done it because she riled him some, and he couldn't take it

201

no more. She done something that day that made him snap, and it wasn't about no goats, although he complained about them often and on. Still, he put up with them every day of his life as long as I can remember. Besides, I have an idea that he and Miss Maggie drunk a plenty of Miss Amalia's goat's milk without her knowing it. Or maybe she did know it. She was a kindly hearted woman."

I didn't speak, just waited for him to continue.

He had eaten the center of the sandwich, leaving the crust like a frame, and he looked through it at me. "It pesters me that I don't have no least idea what it was."

I sighed with disappointment. "He must have hated her."

Sheriff Beecham shrugged. "Them two almost married, and as I hear it, Bayard didn't have no good time after they broke it off. It's my belief she ended things twixt them. For all I know, he was sweet on her till the end."

"Then why did he marry Miss Maggie?"

"You ever hear of a man marrying a woman he don't love?"

The chair made my back hurt, and my arms were tired from carrying the heavy bag, but those were not the reasons that I squirmed. "Did you know he was blackmailing Miss Amalia? She paid him fifty dollars a month."

He set down the remains of the crust. "Naw. What'd he go and do that for? What did he have on that nice old lady?"

"Sheriff Beecham, I don't know much about my father's family, didn't know anything at all about them until a few days ago."

He looked around for a napkin and then, not finding one, rubbed his greasy hands on his arms.

"I have been told twice that my father was not Miss Amalia's brother, as he was raised to believe, but her son."

"I wouldn't put much store—"

"And if Father were Miss Amalia's son, I'd put my money on Bayard Lott as his father."

"Well . . ." He looked at his hands as he rubbed them together. "God knows, you can't get that way when you don't have no man. Lordy."

"If all this speculation is true, why didn't the two of them get married?"

The sheriff leaned back in his chair, his hand over his mouth, thinking. "Could be it was somebody else got her that way. Or might be, if it was Bayard, she didn't have no use for him after. . . ." He cleared his throat. "Course, with that prop'ty, she could have kept busy running Shadowland and Avoca and the plantations she had. Back then, gentlemen spent most of their time hunting and drinking bourbon whiskey, so she wouldn't have had to see much of him."

"And as you say, people don't always marry for love."

"Exactly. The way I hear it, the Lotts was real glad when them two got engaged, 'cause the Bondurants had money, and the Lotts didn't. Bayard had almost about hit the jackpot with Miss Amalia. She was a fine-looking woman, too, icing on the cake, as the feller says. Bayard hisself was no yellow dog. Even at the end, he was a nice-appearing man, with black eyes that could see right through you." The sheriff peered at me, as if looking for any resemblance to Bayard Lott. "He wasn't the likely one to call off the wedding."

"If she refused to marry Bayard, why did Miss Amalia come back to Natchez after the baby was born? Why didn't she go someplace where people didn't know her, get a fresh start?"

"Now, how could she do that? Her daddy had need of her after Miss Emilie died. Besides, Miss Amalia wasn't one of your suffragettes, going off to the big city to get a job. And what kind of work would she've done? We train our women to be charming. Miss Amalia couldn't hardly teach or operate the typewriter. Best she could have done was wash clothes, and my guess is she never even done that before. We treasure our womenfolk in the South, but there ain't no market for 'em." He picked up a bottle of Nu-Grape, which had left a pattern of wet rings on the blotter, and took a swig.

The sky outside was very dark, and streetlamps had come on. So I picked up the carpetbag and told him he could find me at the Eola if he thought of anything else.

"I don't know what difference it'll make. All those folks are gone, and me and you will be, too, one day. Maybe we best let the dead rest easy in the heart."

"That's an odd remark for a sheriff to make."

"Maybe so, Miss Nora, but not for a Natchez gentleman."

On Main Street, I turned toward the hotel, walking under wooden awnings that covered the sidewalk. Moviegoers came out of the Star Theater, which was showing *The Kid from Spain* with Eddie Cantor, and a few bought food from a hot-tamale man who waited on the sidewalk with his cart. I passed a creamery and a barbershop, where back beyond the wire shoe-shine chair and the white porcelain sinks with their white bottles and black razor straps, a woman sat in a chair, getting a permanent wave.

Stopping in front of a drugstore, I peered at the window display of plaster reproductions of a banana split, a chocolate sundae, a pink ice-cream soda. Since I'd had nothing to drink since the coffee at lunchtime, I was thirsty. The store looked inviting, with its gleaming floor of hexagonal white tiles and a soda fountain of pink marble the color of melted strawberry ice cream. So I went inside, sat down on a swivel chair at the counter, and ordered a glass of soda water from a fountain man who greeted me with "*Hel*lo."

After I drank the water, the young man said, "You most likely got the indigestion. Nobody drinks soda water 'less they got the indigestion. I got it myself last night due to fish and green peppers." He rubbed his stomach.

"Just thirsty."

"I'm a real good soda jerk. I might could make you a

New Orleans eggnog, if you want me to." He was very eager. "You should try it."

"I should?"

"Course you should," he said. "Course you should."

"What's a New Orleans eggnog?"

"Vanilla ice cream, milk, egg."

"Does it really come from New Orleans?"

"Ma'am?"

It sounded tame enough, and I ordered one, watching with a certain amount of apprehension as the soda jerk added cream, molasses, and nutmeg to the shaker. He snapped on a lid and placed the container in a green stand, turning it on. The eggnog jerked back and forth. When it stopped, the soda jerk poured the concoction into a glass, setting it down in front of me with a flourish. He placed a napkin and a straw beside it and grinned as I sipped it and pronounced it good.

"You thought you wasn't going to like it," he said. "It's mighty damn fine."

"Mighty damn fine indeed."

"I can make a swell brown cow, too."

I held up my hand.

"And there's sandwiches. Most ladies like the cottage cheese, honey, and nut, but we got Roquefort cheese and Worcestershire ones, and westerns. That's with chicken and egg and cream cheese."

The combinations sounded ghastly, but his talk of food made me hungry, so I asked if he had peanut butter.

"You bet. You want sardines or bananas with that peanut butter?"

He was a good salesman, because the extras undoubtedly added a nickel or more to the cost of the sandwich. "Jelly. Grape jelly."

"I ain't seen you in here before." He took two slices from a waxed sack of Fresh Maid bread and opened a jar of peanut butter, stirring it with a knife to mix in the oil on top.

"No, I ain't been in here before." I almost corrected my grammar but then decided he might think I was making fun of him. "I haven't been in town long."

"You one of them reporters." He stopped long enough to take two sticks of chewing gum from his pocket. He unwrapped them, put one on top of the other, and fed them into his mouth, bending them in the middle as if they were ribbons.

"Reporters?"

The soda jerk went back to the sandwich. "They come here 'cause of the goat lady. You know about her?" Not waiting for me to answer, he continued. "She's an old lady that lived out yonder about a mile. She could cast spells, I guarantee you. You ought not ever to go there after dark. She's got an old colored man that'll get after you. He could whip the devil round the stump."

For an instant, I thought I should stand up for Ezra, but curious to see what the young man might say about Amalia, I asked instead, "What happened to her?"

He finished spreading the jelly on the bread and

placed a second slice on top. Then with a butcher knife, he sliced off the crusts and cut the sandwich in half diagonally. He placed the halves on a plate and added pickle chips and half a deviled egg. "She got herself kilt is what she did. You ask me, she cast a spell on the man what done it, cast it early and late. He lived over next door to her, and he raised cane about them goats eating his yard. I never did unduly care for goats myself. One of those blessed nights, he went over and shot her dead."

"And then killed himself."

"Aw, you heard the story." He put away the sandwich makings and washed the knife in a little sink across from the counter. Then he turned back to me with a sly look. "You sure you ain't a reporter? You look like you might could be a reporter."

I was using my tongue to get peanut butter off the roof of my mouth, so instead of replying, I shook my head.

"Well, darn it." He worked the gum hard.

"Avoca was a swell place once. I'd like to pick me out something from there. It's most generally known she had money hid all over."

I should have taken Amalia's jewelry with me, I realized. But if it had been safe at Avoca all these years, it would keep for one more night.

"I'm afraid of that colored man," the soda jerk continued. He leaned forward and, using his tongue, slid the gum in front of his buckteeth. "He killed a man once, maybe more than one."

"You know that for a fact?"

He shrugged. "Seems like he would of. There's haunts out there. The goose bumps jump up all over me just to think about it. The goat lady herself told it about that the place had spooks."

Amalia had been shrewd to give out such a story. It might have kept thieves and vandals away from Avoca.

"It's a shame about you not being a reporter. I sure would like to get my name in the newspaper. I'd glory in it." He watched me with a dopey grin on his face. "You'd tell me if you was, wouldn't you?"

Although I had eaten only half of the sandwich, I pushed the plate forward on the counter to show that I was finished. Doing so, I noticed Amalia's ring still on my finger. Ezra and Aunt Polly would have seen it, but what did that matter? "Yes, I would tell you. But I am not a newspaperwoman." I paused a little, thinking my dramatics were not unlike Magdalene's. "I'm the goat woman's"—I almost said "granddaughter"—"niece. And I most definitely can tell you there are haunts out there."

The fountain man's jaw dropped as he stared at me. "Is that a fact? You really kin to that old lady?"

"I inherited her ability to cast spells. I guarantee you." I laid a quarter and three dimes on the counter.

"Well, kiss the damn dog's foot!"

The bell on the screen door jangled as I went outside, then turned and waved at the fountain man, who was watching me through the window. Telling him who I was tickled me, made me feel more lighthearted than I had in ages. The soda jerk would embroider on my appearance and tell it around town, which amused me.

At the hotel, the desk clerk, friendlier than on the night of my arrival, asked, "The world treating you all right?"

"Just fine." He handed me my key, along with three messages, an airmail letter in my mother's handwriting, and a telegram. I slid open the telegram. SORRY FOR LOSS MISS YOU KIDDO BEST LOVE. It was signed CAROLINE.

"Bad news?" the desk clerk asked, and I wondered why people never asked what was in a telegram but only said, "Bad news?"

"Condolences from a friend." And I thought again what a good friend she had been. She'd refused to be put off when I turned inward after the divorce. She alone understood my grief when David died. I wondered if Pickett might be that kind of friend.

The messages were from Mr. Satterfield, each one more pointed, asking when I wanted to go to Avoca.

"That Mr. Satterfield—he called three or four more times, saying you're not to go to the goat lady's house without you take him."

"I've already gone. In fact, I was there all day."

"Oh. You shouldn't have done that. That Mr. Satterfield evermore will be put out."

I eyed the clerk for a moment before I shrugged. "That's just too bad. If he calls again, you tell Mr. Satterfield that he can just kiss the dog's foot."

Chapter Seven

WALKING TO MY ROOM FROM the elevator, I whistled—something I thought of as common, like chewing gum and smoking on the street. Had I always been as proper as an oyster fork, or had my sense of humor died with my marriage? I used to be fun, a wit, had even been considered a cutup. Perhaps my friends—all but Caroline, at any rate—shunned me not because I was divorced but because I'd become a bore.

I intended to enjoy myself tonight, since the bellhop was bringing me a bucket of ice and a bottle. "In Colorado, the best whiskey is sugar moon from a town called Leadville," I told him. David and I had gone there every summer to stock up. "Do you think you can do as well?"

"We got white mule. Tastes like pure silk. That 'shine suits me."

"Then your moonshine's bound to suit me, too."

While waiting for the man to return, I took out Amalia's quilt diary. An unfinished block for a crazy quilt fell out, and I ran my fingers over the rich scraps of fabric, outlining with my fingernail a horse that Amalia had appliquéd onto one patch with tiny gold stitches. I rubbed the silk velvet against my cheek. My hands itched to work with fabric again. It had been months since I had made anything, and I missed the peace and sense of accomplishment that sewing gave me.

Perhaps I would take out my scraps of fabric and lace and create a picture of Avoca in all its faded grandeur and aloofness. The technique was one I had thought up myself. Peering through a magnifying glass, I used tweezers to pick up threads and scraps of fabric, some less than an eighth of an inch in size, and glue them to cardboard to create landscapes and portraits. The materials were so minute that people mistook the collages for watercolors. "You've created a new art form," David had told me once, putting a brush into the paste pot, then spreading glue on the back of a fabric scrap for me. I realized there must be scraps of old fabric at Avoca that I could use.

After the bellman brought the bottle, I dropped ice cubes into my tooth glass and poured in bootleg until it was halfway up the glass, then sipped. The whiskey was strong, and I filled the glass with water, then took it to the desk and set it beside my mail and the carpetbag.

I ignored the messages from Mr. Satterfield, since it was too late to call him, and picked up Mother's letter, which was just like her—optimistic, chatty, and a little bit gossipy. She had tucked in a clipping about an event next month to raise money for caps and mittens for children of impoverished miners. The headline read CITY'S SOCIAL HEADS PLAN LUNCHEON and under it in smaller print, it said, "Fete to be presided over by Mrs. Frederic Atherton Adams and Mrs. Arthur Ransom." Mother wrote that she'd run into Betsey Ransom, who had asked to be remembered to me. "Betsey said to be sure and call her when you get back. She's such a lovely girl," Mother wrote.

I finished the drink, which did not taste like liquid silk, but more like ground burlap, and filled the glass with more whiskey and water.

Betsey Ransom. No, I would not call her, not for all the tea in China, for fear of what I might say to her.

Staring at the brown liquid in my glass, I remembered when Betsey and Arthur were new in town and David had asked me to attend to her. I liked her, of course. She was a pretty little thing, with skin as white as aspen bark and pale yellow hair that frizzed out over her head like a dandelion gone to fluff. She had a mischievous smile, but in fact, life bewildered her, and her interests did not go beyond Arthur and her children. Arthur appeared devoted to her. He was a buyer at Neusteter's, a women's specialty store, and when he brought her presents—jewelry, perfume, clothes—she'd clap her hands like a little girl and squeal, "Oh, Artie!" as she squeezed her eyes shut and held out her hands for the boxes. Arthur dressed her in the slinky gowns that were popular, although David had remarked to me that they made Betsey look like an usher at a movie theater. David had had a nasty streak, but in this case, he'd been right.

She was easily frightened. On summer outings, Betsey stumbled over rocks and scraped her arms against branches. Once, as we stood on a rocky escarpment on a mountain top, she became so dizzy that her legs buckled. David, who was standing next to her, swept her up and carried her away from the cliff, then set her down, propping her back against a lodgepole pine. While Arthur stood helplessly, David wrapped his coat around Betsey and rubbed her hands.

"Get some water," David told Arthur, who looked around for a stream. "In my knapsack," David added sharply.

Arthur simply stood there, looking stupid, so I grabbed the canteen and handed it to David.

"That's the stuff," David said as Betsey took tiny sips.

She ran her hands through her pretty hair and looked up at David with the trust of a child. "That was swell of you to catch me like that. I was awfully scared. You're a peach of a fellow. I suppose now I've spoiled our day."

"Oh, cut it out!" David told her.

"You hold on there," added Arthur, who had turned manly again. "It's a scary spot to be in. Why, any girl in the world would have passed out with fright."

As I was a girl and had not grown weak in the knees, I was annoyed and perhaps a little jealous at the way the two men fussed over Betsey. "Now that every-thing's back to normal, why don't we have lunch," I said brightly.

"Oh, I couldn't," Betsey said, and David seemed to glare at me.

After that, I saw less of Betsey, but David became closer to her. "Arthur's no good in a crisis, and Betsey does need looking after," he explained, then added,

"She's about as entertaining as a piece of chalk. How have you stood her all this time?"

When Betsey got pregnant with her third child, David was as solicitous of her as Arthur was. When the baby was born, a boy named James David, we were the godparents, and it was David who picked out the silver cup and had the baby's name and birth date engraved on it. Once, I heard David say, "Oh, I could just eat you up." At first, I thought he was talking to Betsey, but of course he'd directed the remark to the baby.

I began to think about children again, although we had put the hope of babies behind us years before, when the doctor said I wasn't likely to have them. David had always said children didn't matter because we had each other, but maybe he had changed his mind. One evening as we sat over cocktails, I brought up the subject of adoption. "It's the perfect solution. We would have a child of our own, and we would save some poor foundling from growing up in an orphanage. When you look at it, it's a selfless thing."

David stood up and looked out at the park, where a fresh snowfall outlined forgotten graves, for the park had once been a cemetery. With his back to me, he said, "No, it wouldn't work. If we had our own kiddie, well, we would do our best. But I'm really not cut out to be a father."

"You'd be a wonderful father."

"No," David said, and we did not discuss it again.

I wondered even then about David's preoccupation with Betsey, since she never read a newspaper or a book, never had an original thought. It was no surprise that Arthur spent so much time outdoors, mountain climbing, skiing, and motorcycling with David and the other men in our set. So it should have been no surprise when Arthur suggested that he and David take flying lessons. For some perverse reason, Arthur seemed to enjoy frightening Betsey. David once observed, "Arthur treats her like china under his hooves."

Much as I wanted to be a better sport, I agreed with Betsey that flying was out of the question. "You simply mustn't go up in an aeroplane," I told David. "I would fret so."

"How can you be such a ninny?" We were eating breakfast, and David put down his fork so hard that it fell off the edge of the plate and hit the table. "I spend my days holding hands with doddering old ladies. Aren't I entitled to a little excitement?"

Remembering that conversation now, I poured more whiskey into the glass, adding neither ice nor water. He was so seldom cross with me back then that his virulence had shocked me.

"It's just that you read about so many crashes. What would I do if something happened to you?" I picked up David's dirty fork, which had left a spot of yellow from his boiled egg on the tablecloth, and put it onto my own plate.

"You're as tiresome as Betsey."

"I thought you admired her."

David did not reply, just gave me a withering look. He stood and picked up his coffee cup by the bowl and drank, then set down the cup on the edge of the saucer, and it tipped over, spilling coffee across the tablecloth and onto my dressing gown. David did not apologize, just folded the newspaper under his arm and, without a word, left for work. We did not mention the squabble, and the following Saturday morning, he took his first flying lesson.

Looking back at it now, I realized it should have been obvious that David was unhappy, but that did not occur to me then. I thought only that we were having disagreements, like other married people who'd been together for a decade. We still had wonderful times together. In fact, those last months—that was the Christmas I gave David the silver tea set—were among our happiest. I had not known such contentment could exist.

The glass of whiskey was still in my hand, and I carried it to the window and looked out. The Mississippi was not visible, but I felt its presence, the way I felt the presence of the mountains at home, and suddenly I had a great longing to see the river, so I set down my glass and left the hotel.

I walked the few blocks to the Mississippi and stared into the silent blackness, then turned back to the hotel, walking past the dark bank building where Odalie had hailed me that morning. Just then, a very old man came out of the shadows, a rummy, from the smell of him. He put one hand on a stone column to support himself and said unsteadily, "Nobody's going to bother you when you're with me." He nodded solemnly to reinforce his statement and then asked, "You got any spare change?"

Ignoring him, I started off.

He took a step after me, stumbled, and put both arms around the pillar to keep from falling. "Hey, snooty lady," he called after me. "Jesus loves you."

I laughed, and not for the first time thought this would be a good story to tell David, then remembered I could never tell him anything again. But I could tell Caroline, and maybe Pickett. That made me feel better, and I returned to the hotel.

As I prepared for bed, I saw the miniature trunk of envelopes. Too curious to let them sit in the carpetbag all night, I spread them across the desk. To my disappointment, they did not contain real letters, only scraps of paper. Scattered among them were rose petals as faded and brittle as parchment. The notes, some thirty or forty of them, were written in pencil, and many were illegible where the lead had smeared or been rubbed faint. Most were only a sentence or two, sometimes just a word: "Tonight." One read, "Thank you, dear thing," and another said, ". . . when darkness covers daylight." They were written in the same hand. On a scrap of foolscap was "I glory in your love." One note said simply, "I love you." The signature was always an elaborate *B*.

B for Bayard. But when had they been written? There were no dates, no reference to current events. They could have been written half a century ago, for all I knew. The notes did not answer any of my questions, only added to them. Returning the scraps of paper to their envelopes, I picked up the quilt diary again and examined it more thoroughly. It was a record of the quilts Amalia had made. She'd sketched patterns and scribbled notations about materials she'd used. She'd even attached scraps of fabric with straight pins, which were now rusty. Paging through the book, I stopped to examine a swatch of white cotton with black horse-shoes printed on it. In places, the horseshoe shapes had been eaten away by the harsh chemicals in the black dye. Next to the swatch was the notation "B's shirt." On the next page was a drawing of two entwined initials, AB, the monogram embroidered on the quilt on Amalia's bed. The *B* was the same stylized letter Bayard had used to sign his notes. The initials didn't stand for Amalia Bondurant at all, I thought. They were for Amalia and Bayard.

Mr. Sam was breakfasting with his table of pals, whose ages appeared to range from thirty to ninety, when I entered the dining room the next morning. Before they could rise, I slid into a chair next to Mr. Sam, startling the men, and it occurred to me that I had joined a table reserved for males. I returned the surprised looks with a smile, knowing these gentlemen were too polite to ask me to leave. Besides, they knew Amalia, so they shouldn't be surprised that I did as I pleased.

"Good morning, Miss Nora. You're looking like fine china today," Mr. Satterfield said.

The waiter came, glancing around the table to see if

any of the men objected to my being there, then took my order for coffee and a boiled egg. "Oh, and may I have a basket of beaten biscuits, too, please?" I smiled at Mr. Satterfield.

"It appears you have taken to our ways."

"Only in matters culinary, Mr. Satter—Mr. Sam. I haven't acquired your good manners, or I would not have gone to Avoca by myself yesterday. But you see, I didn't know it myself until I did it."

Mr. Sam was much too polite to chastise me. Nor did he remark about Natchez women. "I forgive you for that," he said. "You must have wanted to get a feel for the place without an old man telling you what was what."

When I protested, Mr. Sam put up his hand. "You're safe enough out there with old Ezra."

"You find any haunts out there, did you?" asked a man dressed in a limp seersucker suit. He had a napkin tucked into his shirtfront; in fact, I was the only one at the table who didn't. The man sliced his ham into neat pieces and cut the pieces in half. "There was a story down to the drugstore this morning that somebody'd been out to Avoca and told Son Boy, the fountain man, that there was a plenty of ghosts there."

"That Son Boy, Wash!" Mr. Sam said. "It's just his foolishments."

"Not likely," Wash told him. "Son Boy says it was a woman, and she wasn't a ghost; she was real. Yes sir, he spoke the truth. No ghost ever left him a two-bit tip."

"No human being ever left that much to Son Boy, either," Mr. Sam said, and they all chuckled.

I ventured that rumors of ghosts at Avoca might keep the curious away from it.

"No, ma'am, not so's you'd notice," the young man told me. "Besides, there's not a one of these old places that isn't haunted by ghosts—or memories. You take your choice."

"And one or two by goats," I said.

They laughed, and Wash said, "Boys, she'll do!"

"Didn't I tell you she was a card?" said Mr. Sam. "Didn't I?"

"I didn't personally encounter any ghosts at Avoca, unless you count Magdalene Lott, but my impression is that she is still very much alive. Of course, I could be mistaken."

"Oh no, ma'am, no mistake there. She is with the living, God bless her," Mr. Sam said, rolling his eyes.

"Magdalene Lott," Wash said, looking pensive. "I recall her back when I first remember about things. She was a finely-looking woman with a morning-glory air, a real lady."

"No such a thing. That's what they call her, a lady, but she isn't. Never was. I'd call her everything but a lady," scoffed a very old man who had been eating scrambled eggs with a spoon. His head was as smooth as a darning egg, but his gray beard, which had gone to seed, was long as his arm. He was tiny, probably not much more than five feet tall, although since he was seated, I really could not tell. He sat up straight, making every inch count, and lifted his chin. "Back in them good old times gone by, she was pretty, but she was always a spitfire. We all thought it was passing strange that Bayard married her. He pro'bly reared and pitched and did it only 'cause Miss Amalia wouldn't have him." The man shook his head, which was criss-crossed with veins.

"Now sir," Wash protested.

"You are too young a man to have known her in her day." He turned to me. "I myself am eighty-eight." He pronounced his age "ada-ate."

The waiter interrupted, setting down my coffee and filling the other cups. The men busied themselves by pouring cream and sugar into their coffee, stirring and tasting, until the waiter finished and was out of earshot.

"Now, Uncle Doctor, Miss Magdalene was a badly used woman. You know that," said a man about my age, who sported a gold tooth. He turned to me. "Dr. Aldrich is a physician to nervous ladies, and as you might imagine, such are as common in Natchez as old clothes."

"What's that?" The doctor said in a loud voice to me, "Never nobody tells me a thing because I don't hear so good. If I get something wrong, it's no fault of mine. My left ear don't hardly track at all."

The nephew repeated himself.

"My knowledge don't come from treatment of Miss Maggie, for I never took her in charge in a professional way, never would. She is the most unpleasing woman I know." Looking at me, he added, "Begging your pardon for speaking so of any female woman."

We all waited for the old doctor to continue.

"It is generally known that Bayard married Miss Maggie to spite Miss Amalia, but he only spited hisself. And it served him right, the worthless pup!" The man laughed—a scratchy, choking sound. "Bayard was thought to fall on his sword, as was the saying then, when Miss Amalia cast him aside. He'd already bought the silver service and ordered up new draperies for Shadowland—and those Lotts couldn't hardly afford the expense. They been high-and-mighty at one time, with corn land so rich, it growed roasted ears, but no more."

"It's not the heights you come from that count; it's the depths you reach," Wash said.

The doctor frowned, whether from Wash's comment or from the interruption wasn't clear. He continued: "Their money was gone with the wind, as we say, and Bayard was too proud to work. But it was Miss Amalia herself that Bayard wanted. Seemingly, she was thought so precious that Bayard would have lived in the quarters on poke salad just to be with her."

"He didn't live much better with Miss Magdalene," Mr. Sam observed.

"No sir, he did not." Dr. Aldrich stirred the remaining eggs on his plate. "He purely and simply did not."

The waiter set down my boiled egg and the biscuits. With their fork pricks in the center, they looked like the giant oyster-shell buttons. The basket made the rounds of the table. "That's in the past and is all over and done

223

with," I said as the biscuits came back to me. Reluctantly, I took one and buttered it, setting it on my plate without biting into it.

Mr. Sam watched me, an amused look on his face. He had known all along that I did not care for the biscuits "Oh no, Miss Nora, it is not over and done with. In Natchez, the past is the present," he said.

"And anybody who don't like it, get out of here," added the nephew. Instead of laughing, the men all nodded.

Thinking of the scraps of paper I'd found hidden in Amalia's desk, I asked, "Did Miss Amalia and Mr. Lott ever make up?"

"If he done that, Miss Maggie would have killed him for sure," the doctor said, then gave a kind of impish grin. "Now, why did I say that?"

"Miss Maggie'd not have it in her to do so," the nephew remarked, glancing at the doctor, but the old man had returned to his eggs. "If Miss Maggie was to have got mad at Bayard, she'd have been a constant misery to him. They fairly hated each other."

Wash laughed. "It must have got to Bayard, him being smothered down by Miss Maggie, and Miss Amalia living next door, free as frogs."

"He was killing mad all right," Mr. Sam said. "Bayard suffered from the sin of pridefulness."

"Is there anything good to say about Bayard Lott?" I asked.

Mr. Sam reached for the biscuits and said, "Have you another" as he passed them again, and the others busied themselves with the butter and jam.

"He was good to his old people," Wash said.

"And he was right smart-looking. Age never seemed to come on him, and he always dressed rich as cream. Course, Miss Maggie dressed like a field hand," said the nephew.

"Gentlemen, I ask you not to talk again of Maggie Lott. I have my digestion to think about," the doctor said.

The big man I had seen in the lobby the day before sat down on the other side of Mr. Sam. He picked up his napkin and placed it on his lap instead of in his shirtfront, then said to Mr. Sam, "Good morning, young man. I see we have a new member at our table."

"Thank you for that 'young man' thing," Mr. Sam said. "Miss Nora, may I present to you Holland Thomas Brown. He semi-occasionally works at the law, and if you are not particular, you may engage his services if you find mine to be unsatisfactory to you."

"Or too expensive," Holland put in.

"Oh, this rapscallion would climb a tree to make a dishonest dollar, even if there was a twenty-dollar gold piece lying right on the ground," the nephew said.

Holland grinned and reached across the table for my hand. Surprised at the gesture, I brushed the crumbs off my fingers and shook his hand and told him I was pleased to meet him—and unlikely to require his services, as I had perfect confidence in Mr. Sam's.

"You may change your mind if you want an attorney familiar with any laws passed since the War of the

Rebellion—you know, the war that was won by the Yankees." He winked at me, then said, "I must watch myself, or these jaspers will lynch me late some evening."

"Why sir, we do not do such things in the dark of night," said Wash, looking offended. "But we may do it in the daylight."

Mr. Sam told Holland that we had been talking about Magdalene Lott.

"The goat lady," Holland said.

"No, Magdalene Lott lived next door to the goat lady," I said, correcting him. "Amalia Bondurant was the goat lady. My aunt."

Holland reddened. "I beg your pardon. I am only recently arrived from Chicago and not used to the country ways in Natchez." I noticed then that he was wearing a lightweight wool suit instead of a seersucker or linen one.

"Country," scoffed Mr. Sam. "As you can see, Miss Nora, my colleague lacks the breeding of a real Natchezian. But then we do not expect much of carpet-baggers."

Holland explained to me that his people had been one of the first families of Natchez but had lost their fortune after the war. "So my grandparents took my father to Illinois when he was a good-size child."

"And we had hopes this son"—Mr. Sam nodded at Holland—"would be as fine a man as the father was a boy. But in that, we were sadly disappointed."

Wash leaned across the table to me and said that Holland had come back to claim the family estate.

"And we didn't even have goats," said Holland. "Seven chimney spires and a cistern were all that was left of Holland Hall. I have had to sink so low as to practice the law." This appeared to be oft-repeated bantering. He waved to the waiter and asked for a dish of oatmeal and toast. "None of your beaten biscuits. Up north, we confuse them with sawdust. Both burn." He turned to me. "God Himself wouldn't eat them."

Holland spotted the biscuits in front of my plate then and glanced up at me with an apologetic look. Mr. Sam picked up the basket and said, "Why, Holland, here's you your order of crow."

The biscuits made the rounds again, and the old doctor took one, covered it with jam, and popped it into his mouth. He chewed and swallowed, and then as if he had not been interrupted at all, he continued the conversation of a few minutes earlier. "Bayard very plainly told me after Miss Amalia rejected him that he would get even with her, and I expect in the end he did."

"More than fifty years later?" I asked.

"Oh, here time means nothing," Holland said.

"At the rates you charge for your services, I would say that's not worth denying," Mr. Sam told him.

I ventured that Bayard Lott sounded like an awful person.

"Oh, when Bayard was in bad temper, he was as mean as Miss Amalia was good, some say the meanest man the sun ever shone on. He cuffed Miss Maggie

227

around, whipped her bloody as a pig," the doctor said, forgetting he had asked us not to speak of her. The table was very still, and he added quickly, "As a figure of speaking, that is."

"Miss Amalia told me that Miss Magdalene was not born for luck," Mr. Sam said.

"We weren't none of us born for luck," the nephew said, standing up and bowing to me. "The rest of you can talk forevermore, but those of us who have had to make our own luck must put in our day's work."

"In their daddy's bank," Mr. Sam said in a loud whisper.

The nephew pulled his elbows to his sides and looked hurt. He said petulantly, "Listen at him. You'd think *he'd* made his own way in the world."

As the conversation deteriorated, the men pushed back their chairs and stood up, taking the napkins from their shirts and wiping their mouths. One by one, they bowed to me and excused themselves.

"Come along, Doctor. Let's not drag out our leaving," Wash said.

The doctor wobbled a little as he took his first step. "They're expecting me in the barbershop for a shave and a shoe shine. I still keep my schedule, although I'm no better than a cracked plate." He took Wash's arm, and the two left the room, the doctor's cane tapping on the hard floor as he went along.

"He's as slow as a terrapin crawling in the shade, but he gets there," Mr. Sam said when only he, Holland, and I were left.

"Your aunt Amalia, was she born for luck?" Holland asked. The waiter had brought Holland's breakfast. He sprinkled brown sugar over his oatmeal and covered it with cream, but he left the toast unbuttered.

"She was richer than I'd thought." I caught Mr. Sam's stern look and added, "That is, if she counted her riches in something besides money. It appears she was a contented woman. She took what was offered her, which was not much in these last years, and she made do."

"Take tarts when tarts are passing," Mr. Sam said.

"What's that?" asked Holland.

"Miss Amalia's mother used to say that. You take you your happiness where it's found, and you got to recognize it when it's passing by. Now, that's not worth denying."

"'Take tarts when tarts are passing,'" Holland repeated. "I should not have had them pan up the oatmeal."

"My boy, my boy," Mr. Sam said. "You won't find tarts at the Eola."

Promising not to go poking about Avoca again without him, I made an appointment with Mr. Sam for midafternoon. Then both men rose as I walked out of the room.

Pickett, dressed in a summer frock the color of dark blue plums, was standing just outside the door to the dining room, and I found myself glad to see her. I would repeat the breakfast table conversation to her.

"What's news?" she asked.

229

"Men are worse gossips than women, and they don't know it."

"That's not news, but I love you for saying it." Picket glanced into the dining room and added, "You must be a suffragette or something. They'd never allow me to sit at their table."

"They wouldn't allow me, either, if I hadn't just done it. They were too polite to turn me away."

"That's the ticket. Any fine day now the people of Natchez will march into the twentieth century—behind you and Holland Brown. I see you did not need me— or Odalie—to introduce you." Pickett raised an eyebrow, which I ignored, but that did not stop her. "If you are interested, Holland is an uptown man, and he is eligible, of course. Mr. Sam says he's divorced and came to Natchez for a fresh start. It has to be the first time since Between the States that anybody's done that."

I told her I wasn't interested in meeting anyone.

"We've already put you on the spot about men," she said, then changed the subject. "I'll be just frank. I apologize for Odalie. She has the nerve of a brass monkey and the ignorance of an egg. If I had known she'd be so odious to you, I'd not have invited her. She ought to be in the booby hatch, although there's no law against being nasty."

"Odalie didn't mean to be rude," I said.

"Oh, she meant it entirely. I purely blame myself for inflicting her on you."

"Well, don't." I changed the subject again and told Pickett I'd spent the day before at Avoca.

"So I have heard."

"Nothing goes unobserved here. You probably know I had dinner at a drugstore last night, too—a peanut butter sandwich and something called 'a New Orleans eggnog.' It's not bad."

Pickett frowned. "Why would you eat there?"

"You'll probably hear about that, too."

She shrugged and told me she had come to give me a tour of Natchez. Pickett gestured at a smart Essex Terraplane convertible parked in front of the hotel, then asked if I had sandals and a hat.

I went to my room to change shoes and grab the braided hat from Natchez Under-the-Hill, then returned to the lobby, where Pickett was waiting with Mr. Sam. "We were talking about you," Pickett admitted. "Mr. Sam says you met Magdalene Lott at Avoca. I hope you were careful, because you'd not hardly be safe alone with her."

I replied that Magdalene seemed harmless.

"The most lethal women in the South seem harmless enough." She winked at me. "I do not include myself— or you." She made it sound as if we were coconspirators.

Ezra was there, I told her.

"Poor Ezra. Lord, I wonder what will become of him and Aunt Polly."

There was an edge to Pickett's voice, as if she were asking a question, not just wondering out loud. So I said, "They won't be put off the place."

"Of course not. But we do worry about our people.

Northerners don't always understand our ways." Pickett thought for a moment and then asked, "Does that mean you're staying on in Natchez?"

"No. It just means I won't kick two old people off the place."

"You see, I told you she is becoming a Natchez girl," Mr. Sam said.

Pickett kissed him on the cheek and told him, "I intend to show Nora about Natchez, or what's left of it, at any rate."

"It would be my joy to accompany you. I must needs be at my work, of course, but perhaps . . . ," Mr. Sam said by way of inviting himself along.

Pickett ignored the hint. "What a pity. Another time." She took my elbow. "So long, darling Mr. Sam." She steered me outside, and when we reached the curb, she said, "He very plainly wants to go. I hope you won't mind if we don't include him. Men can be so tiresome, you know—almost as tiresome as women."

I laughed, thinking how pleasant it was going about with a girlfriend. "To tell you the truth, I've had enough of men for one morning, although Mr. Sam is awfully nice. There's no Mrs. Sam, is there?"

After we got into the car, Pickett leaned over and confided, "Oh my word, no! He lives alone by himself. Mr. Sam is—how shall I say this?—our Oscar Wilde. Or to put it a vulgar way, he's a sissy. He prefers men. That's not worth denying, as he himself would say. Do you know what I mean?"

I did and felt a need to change the subject. "The

houses I've seen here are grand. Can we go inside any of them?"

"Only in the spring, during Pilgrimage, when we open our doors to the public. The Buzzard's Nest is one of them. There's a fee, of course." Pickett started the car and pulled into the street. She yoo-hooed at someone and waved as she braked for a touring car that had run a stop sign and pulled into the street in front of us.

"Where does the money go?"

"What money?" She concentrated on the big car as the elderly driver ground his gears and straddled the center line. When he reached the end of Main Street, he crooked his left arm to indicate he was turning right, but instead he made a sharp left turn. "Is it any wonder we lost the War?" Pickett asked as she shook her head at the man's maneuver. "You were saying?"

"The money you raise from your Pilgrimage. What worthy cause does it support?"

"Oh, us, of course." She stopped in the middle of the street. "Now, this house is Rosalee. The Yankees took it over for their headquarters during the War. Two old sisters live here now."

"On what?" The brick mansion with its four columns and long porches needed paint, and the gardens were in ruins.

"These old ladies discretely dispose of a few antiques, I suppose. If you want to sell Miss Amalia's furniture, I know someone who would buy."

"Who?"

"Me."

"I haven't decided what to do with it."

"Oh, I intend to pay you a good price. I'm not asking for a bargain."

"I didn't mean—"

Pickett waved her hand. "There's no need for you to give it away. There is a market for it. Besides, I would love to see inside Avoca." She glanced at me. "That's not a hint. It's a request."

I told her she was welcome to tour it with Mr. Sam and me.

Pickett pointed out Longwood, a curious eight-sided brick house with a balloonlike cupola, then drove me past great southern mansions named Magnolia Hall, Dunleith, D'Evereux, Auburn, Gloucester. She recited so many dates and occupants that by the time we were finished, the information had all run together in my mind. I would never remember which house was once a tavern or left to a nephew of the owner on the condition he take the uncle's name.

"I wanted you to see what Avoca would have been like in its day. It was every bit as grand as any of these houses," Pickett said. "What a pity it is gone."

"Not completely."

"Oh, but you couldn't restore it."

"No, it's out of the question. If I sold everything in the house, there wouldn't be enough to put on a new roof, and a roof is only the start. There's nothing to do but let it crumble."

"You wouldn't be the first heir to do that," she said.

"Would you like to see Miss Amalia's grave?"

I was embarrassed that I hadn't even thought about visiting the cemetery.

Pickett drove north out of town on a dirt road lacy with shadows from live oaks. We passed two boys with fishing poles and a black man who was barely visible in the deep shadows of the woods, then turned into a large cemetery. In contrast to Natchez and its mansions, the cemetery was plain, with simple tombstones and only a few monuments.

Pickett turned down a narrow lane and stopped beside a plot enclosed by a low cast-iron fence. Inside were small white marble stones and an enormous rose-bush. "That's a Souvenir de la Malmaison," Pickett said as we got out of the car. "The roses are as big as coffee cups. The bush came from Avoca in Miss Emilie's time."

Miss Emilie's and Captain Bondurant's names were engraved on stones at the heads of graves, and there were markers with the names of other Bondurants, the dates going back to the eighteenth century. I would have to ask Mr. Sam about these relatives of mine. No tombstone identified the newest grave; I would order one before I left Natchez.

"No matter what we do in life, it all comes down to your name on a rock," Pickett said.

"Dust to dust."

"I should like to think I would make pretty dust." Pickett shaded her eyes and looked out across the cemetery, then waved to a black man who was standing near an open grave. "You come and get you your Nu-Grape, Jake," she called, then told me, "He is a favorite of mine."

Pickett went to the car and reached into the backseat, taking out three bottles of soda pop that were stored in a champagne bucket of ice. She removed the tops and handed one to me. When the black man, cap in hand, reached us, Pickett gave him a bottle and said, "It's plenty hot to work this morning, Jake."

"I ain't going to lie. It's as hot as a cotton field. I'm just stumbling round 'mongst the toes of God out here, trying to keep from the heatstroke. I sure would like to get shed of this sun." He gulped down the Nu-Grape and handed the bottle back to Pickett.

"You rest now," she told him.

Jake shook his head. "I weren't born to be lazy. My mama learned me to work, and I ain't sorry." He went back across the cemetery, and when he reached the open grave, he spit into his hands and rubbed them together before picking up a shovel.

"Where are they buried, the Negroes?" I asked.

"Not here. There's a colored cemetery."

"Separate in life and separate in death." I stared at Amalia's grave and noticed for the first time the bouquet of flowers set in a jar of water. They were fresh, perhaps put there this very morning, probably by Ezra.

"Not necessarily," Pickett said, sipping from her bottle.

"What's that?"

"I said black and white may be separate in death, but

not always in life, if you know what I mean."

I didn't and had to think for a minute. "Are you talking about miscegenation?"

"Does that surprise you?" A breeze came up, catching Pickett's full skirt, which went billowing up. She caught it and clutched it around her.

"Of course not. There are plenty of light-skinned Negroes in Natchez."

"It didn't happen just back in slavery times."

"You're saying there are white men today who keep black mistresses hidden away."

"Not all of them are hidden. I could name you a dozen mixed couples in Natchez. One of them was a prominent Natchezian who lived openly with a black woman and their children, just as if they were man and wife. When he died, he left her better fixed than most white widows."

"But he didn't marry her." My voice was edged with scorn.

"He couldn't. It's illegal." Pickett waited until I looked up at her. "Is it legal where you come from?"

"You've put me in my place," I said, admitting to her that I did not know. I sipped the Nu-Grape, found it too sweet, and wondered if I could pour it out when Pickett wasn't looking.

"Rightly or wrongly, it happened then and happens now and evermore will be. In the old days, dallying with a servant girl was a rite of passage for a planter's son. It kept the white girls safe. The slave owner himself had his pick of the women in the slave quarters. I expect half the slave women in the South gave birth to a light-skinned baby or two."

"What happened to the children?"

"They were sold down the river by the father or sometimes his wife. Or if the father cared about them, they went to work in the big house instead of in the fields. Look at your own Ezra. I do not believe he is a pure-blooded African." She raised an eyebrow.

Not wanting to give Pickett time to wonder if Ezra and I shared the same white blood, I said quickly, "How could southerners do that? How could they let their own children be slaves?"

"We pretended it didn't happen." Pickett stared across the cemetery at Jake. "Pretending is one of the things we in the Old South do best." She put the bottle to her lips, sipped, and poured the contents onto the ground. "Just as I'm pretending to like this dreadful Nu-Grape, dearie. And so are you."

Chapter Eight

PARTHENA HAD LEFT A MESSAGE at the hotel, telling me that Mr. Stroud, the editor of the *Natchez Democrat*, would be delighted to have me to call anytime that day. She apologized for not being able to introduce us personally, but she was being called away to attend to a relative who was ill.

"That is the lot of southern women. Nothing comes before sick relatives, and Parthena's relatives are sicker than most," Pickett said, reading the message over my shoulder. "It's what keeps Dr. Aldrich in business. He's made sacks and sacks of money off sympathy and sugar pills."

"He's an odd little person."

"Yes. He was considered quite the gay creature until Miss Magdalene turned him down when she was young. It's pretty generally known she broke his heart."

After all the nasty things the doctor had said about Magdalene, I said, I was surprised he had proposed to her.

"She was the only woman in Natchez who was shorter than he, and she went and married a man who was a foot taller. Poor Dr. Aldrich is still pouting."

"He had not a single good word to say about her at breakfast."

"He hasn't since the end of Reconstruction. A man scorned . . ." Pickett put out her hands, palms up.

"I've never heard of such a thing."

"Oh course you have, my dear—Bayard Lott. He'd been seething since Miss Amalia broke off the engagement."

"Men are more troublesome than women."

"Tell me something I don't know. Come along. I'll drop you."

Pickett left me at the newspaper office, where I asked for Mr. Stroud, telling the receptionist that Nora Bondurant was calling.

"A lady, who I already lost her name said you'd be stopping any next minute," the woman replied. She turned to a man who wore a hat made of folded news-paper, which perched on his head like a saucepan, and said, "You take your foot in your hand and go out to the press and get him."

A few minutes later, Wash, the man from the break-fast table, walked in and bowed. "Good day again, Miss Nora."

"You run the newspaper?"

"In Natchez, we set store by who we are, not what we do. Besides, I warrant you people like me better when they don't know I own the paper." He ushered me into an office that was cluttered with photographs, a type-writer, and carbon copies of stories, all spread across a desk. He removed a stack of newspapers from a chair and offered me a seat. "You are a newspaperwoman yourself, I understand."

"If you have that impression, then I sail under false colors. I'm just a scribbler who writes stories for ladies who like to fancy up their flower beds. But I accepted Parthena's offer of an introduction in hopes you'd let me into your newspaper morgue."

He did not look surprised. "Thought so. That's why I had Gladys, out front, to put together a file of our sto-ries about the goat-lady murders."

"There is something more. I'd be awfully glad if you'd let me go through your old newspapers."

He looked at me curiously. "How old?"

"Eighteen seventy-seven."

He mulled that over. "I'm guessing your father was born in eighteen and seventy-eight."

I looked away.

"Oh, don't be embarrassed about that. You know yourself that it's a reporter's job to figure out all those things." He cleared his throat. "Besides, once you're murdered, you can't hide out your secrets anymore. Miss Amalia is ever our favorite topic of conversation at the Eola's eating table these days. Mr. Sam told us about Miss Odalie's speculation. That woman wears herself out with minding other people's business. She's the meanest kind of woman. Still, a big number of folks would not be surprised if what she said is true. You won't find it in the newspaper, however."

"Perhaps there's something else from back then—an engagement announcement or a notice of the engagement being called off."

"Oh, we didn't believe in such in those days. We respected our womenfolk. If Miss Amalia's name had been in our columns in such connection, the old captain would have come boiling in here with a horse whip."

"I'd like to see the papers just the same."

"No harm to it. We've got a library, although it's mostly put to use as a lunchroom. I'll have Gladys to clear off the bologna and bread crumbs."

He called to the receptionist, who took me into a room lined with bound volumes of newspapers. She warned me about the ink coming off on my clothes and handed me an apron. As she searched the shelves, looking for 1877, she pointed to a thin volume. "That's 1865. We had plenty of news then, but we couldn't hardly get the paper to print it on. Some publishers used wallpaper." She set a thick folio on the table. "Here's you your 1877." She opened it to the first January issue and left me alone.

Wash was right, of course. There was no society page, although the paper printed mentions of balls, parties, and outings. In a July newspaper, there was a brief article on Captain Bondurant, "who will be traveling to New York City and abroad. He is to be accompanied by his daughter, Miss Amalia Bondurant." There were no details about Amalia, no adjectives such as *lovely* or *popular,* nothing to indicate what she hoped to see or do.

No further mention was made of the Bondurants until the end of the year. Under the headline NATCHEZIANS AT HOME was an article about Amalia and her father returning to Natchez after an extensive trip to New York and London.

After finishing the 1877 newspapers, I took down the 1878 volume and found in June a mention of the Bondurants. Inside a black box was the headline NATCHEZ LADY IN ARMS OF MORPHEUS and an article telling of the passing of Emilie Bondurant in New Orleans. The piece did not reveal the cause of death but hinted that it might have been yellow fever, which had been bad that year. Captain Bondurant, the article said, had undertaken the "grievous journey to New Orleans to claim the body of his beloved wife, one of the kindest ladies who ever drew breath." Neither Amalia nor Frederick was included in the article. In further editions of the paper, there was no record of the captain returning home or of Miss Emilie's funeral. And no mention anywhere of my father.

But there was something about Bayard Lott in a September issue. The piece was only a few sentences: "Bayard Lott is returning to New York on business. Mr. Lott hopes to enjoy the social season there, just as he did last year. Then he will proceed to London, where he was in great demand a year ago."

After returning the newspapers to the shelves, I took off the apron and found a washroom where I could scrub the ink off my hands. Once presentable, I went in search of Wash.

"Find anything?" he asked.

"Miss Amalia went to New York in 1877, along with Bayard Lott. They both were in London, too."

"So he followed her first to one place and then to another."

"It looks that way. Of course, we'll never know if they actually saw each other."

"She certainly saw somebody." He looked uncomfortable. "I ought not to have said such a thing."

"Perhaps they ought not to have done such a thing." We both chuckled. "It appears that Miss Amalia and her mother went to New Orleans for the summer of 1878. Miss Emilie died there."

"Who ever heard of anybody going to New Orleans for the summer? And that year, the yellow fever was bad."

"So the paper said. The article suggested that Miss Emilie might have died of the fever, not childbirth."

"Oh, we wouldn't have put anything in the paper about a lady dying that way. We never mentioned childbirth. Ours was a world handicapped by ignorance, and it was sure a wonder where little babies came from. My dear mother told me every chick and child was found in the cabbage patch." He thought a minute. "We didn't hide out the women when they were in the family way. We just ignored the condition. We still do."

"So do we." Then I asked the question I'd asked everyone else. "Why did Bayard Lott kill Miss Amalia?"

Wash ran his hand through his hair. The room was hot and close, and his shirt was damp with sweat under his arms. There was perspiration on his face—and on mine, too. "I couldn't hardly say, and I have tried to figure it out since that first doggone day she was found. Why did Bayard go over there that day? From what Mr. Sam says, Bayard and Miss Amalia didn't have truck with each other. Make a heck of a story, wouldn't it?"

"Oh, you won't print any of what I told you, will you?"

Wash grinned at me. "No, Miss Nora. The *Democrat* is not a yellow sheet, bless God, and Miss Amalia was as sweet as honey in the comb. We still respect our women in Natchez." He paused and added, "Course, if it'd been Miss Maggie . . ."

I asked if she were really as bad as Dr. Aldrich claimed.

Wash took out a handkerchief and wiped the back of his head with it. "Miss Maggie turned down our good doctor's advances because he was too old. It is a terrible thing to wound a southern man's pride, and the doctor is a good hater. When she went to housekeeping with Bayard Lott, Miss Maggie left the doctor in a misery so deep that he has had vexation about it ever since. That did not prevent him from trafficking with a plenty of women—he was a scalawag and an alley cat in his time, if you don't mind my saying so—but he never did find a woman to his liking. He likes 'em pert, and Miss Maggie is that."

"Perhaps with Bayard Lott dead, he can press his suit again. Don't you think Miss Magdalene would enjoy being courted?"

I intended the remark to be funny. After all, there was something outlandish about the aged old man pursuing such an odd little creature, but Wash looked up in surprise and said, "By golly, I hadn't thought of that, and I bet Dr. Aldrich hasn't, either. His old mind runs slower these days. I will make it my business to suggest it to him. Miss Nora, I warrant you have a true understanding of Natchez women."

Mr. Sam followed us in his auto as Pickett drove me to Avoca that afternoon. After she turned off the motor, she reached into the back of the car, taking out the three empty Nu-Grape bottles. "They're for Miss Magdalene's bottle tree. Ezra will hang them for her."

Ezra was not waiting for me, as he had been on my last visit. Instead, Aunt Polly stepped onto the porch from Amalia's room. When she saw us, she took a few steps forward and dropped a rock clutched in her hand. She wrapped her hands in her apron and stood motionless, leaning against a pillar for support, waiting for us to reach her.

Alarmed, I called, "Where's Ezra?" Ignoring the ladder, I climbed directly onto the porch.

"Ezra to the quarters. There five, maybe six mens here last night. They make out to crook you." She stopped and waited until Mr. Sam helped Pickett up the ladder. Mr. Sam removed his hat and said, "How do, Aunty."

"Middlin'," she replied. "I tell Miss Nora we got mens here last evening—varmints. Ezra see them passing and repassing in their autocars just as dark come on, and he hide by the house and stand watch." Aunt Polly took a breath and continued. "They stop and get out the car and was drinking and carrying on so, it sound like Judgment Day. That yard was overstocked with white mens. See you the carcass of their doings." She motioned to the front yard, where the weeds were trampled. The area was strewn with jars and bottles. An ax handle leaned against the porch, and big sticks, probably clubs, were scattered about.

Mr. Sam picked up a stone jar lying on the porch and smelled it. "Corn liquor." He tossed it into the weeds.

"Ezra, he stand by the house, looking out at 'em, not saying nothing, and he think they don't see him. After a time, the mens gets up whiskey courage and they starts for Miss Amalia's room. They meant to prank with it. He say stop, but they don't stop, and two of

246

them go after Ezra with a club. Ezra, he old, but he strong, and he break their heads with that old ax handle." She looked proud when she pointed to the handle. "But then the others come on him, and Ezra can't come nigh doin' all of 'em. They get Ezra down, and they wear him out with a cowhide. Then they cut on him. It ain't right what they done. It ain't right at all." Aunt Polly began to shake. "They meaner than bulldogs, just like the patterollers and the Ku Kluxers. Last night just like them terrible times come again. Lord have mercy, I never been so worse scared. I 'sturbed in my mind 'bout that."

"How badly is he hurt?" I asked, putting my arm around Aunt Polly to stop her from shaking. Under my hand, the fabric of her dress was thin, and her bones felt loose, as if they had come unhinged under her skin.

Aunt Polly wrung her hands. "He don't say. Ezra savin' on his words. You know that. They ain't kilt him, but they gave him good attention. He cut some and bruised some, and he got his licks and lumps. His eye shut, and he got misery in his arms. But he been hurt worst in his time, and I don't find no bones broke. I doctor him, and he all right now, to my knowing. He resting at the quarters."

"Aunt Polly's known for her doctoring," Mr. Sam said. "On occasion, I myself have preferred her services over those of Dr. Aldrich." He winked at me. "The good doctor treats nervous men as well as nervous ladies." When no one found his remarks amusing, he cleared his throat.

"It don't look like nothing's mortifying on Ezra," Aunt Polly added.

"Mortifying?" I asked.

"Infected," Pickett said.

"I blames myself," Aunt Polly continued. "I heard them old squinch owls all week, so I put salt on the fire. I put me a fork in the door, too, but it don't do no good." She looked at her hands while she talked, then glanced up at me, shamefaced. "I thought it was you bring us grief. But turn out it were them mens. They worse than the Bad Man."

"The devil," Pickett muttered by way of explanation.

Aunt Polly must have remembered our earlier discussion about her being a Presbyterian, because she added, "Salt in the fire ain't hoodoo. It's just common sense."

"Common sense indeed. I do it myself," Mr. Sam said without a trace of sarcasm. I tightened my arm around Aunt Polly to show that I agreed.

"You tell Ezra he did a fine job," Mr. Sam said. "Tell him Miss Nora is grateful to him."

I said I would tell him myself and would stop by before we left. "That was a courageous thing he did for me, standing up to those brutes."

"He didn't done it for you, Miss Nora. He done it for Miss Amalia," Aunt Polly said, drawing away from me a little. "He don't want such as that picking amongst her belongings, poking through her life like they got the right. Ezra always look out for Miss Amalia."

"Of course." I wanted to thank her but was afraid she

would think my gratitude presumptuous. The lives of those three—Amalia, Ezra, and Aunt Polly—had been intertwined for three-quarters of a century. "Did Sheriff Beecham catch the men?"

By way of answer, Aunt Polly, Mr. Sam, and Pickett stared at me as if I were an imbecile. Finally, Aunt Polly said, "I don't know about no sheriff."

"Oh." I felt foolish. "How did Ezra get away?"

Aunt Polly gave a little smile at that. "I and Ezra knowed they'd come, now that you're here."

Mr. Sam answered my questioning look. "Larcenous folk figure you'll be taking anything of value that belonged to Miss Amalia. So they know they best loot Avoca whilst they got the chance. This may be the first attempt to rob you, Miss Nora, but it will not be the last."

Aunt Polly nodded. "That how come Ezra been keeping watch. Last night, from down at the quarters, I hear them passing and passing and I knowed there's a plenty of 'em and Ezra can't take every and each one. So I wrap up in a old sheet of Miss Amalia's and paint on a scare face with flour, and I go through the garden calling 'Whoo whoo' and clattering two tin pie plates together, *a-wick, a-whack,* and those mens scatter off. Jesus Christ, peas and rice! They don't tell their heads from their foots. The big hat, he run like Old Scratch after him."

"The devil," Pickett whispered, "and 'the big hat' is the most conceited one."

Mr. Sam said, "Unfortunately, when they sober up,

they'll realize you were just cutting the monkey for the white folks."

Aunt Polly nodded. "They won't hardly lose no time coming back. So I stand out here waiting for 'em." The old woman must have loved Amalia a great deal to risk her life to defend Avoca.

"They're too cowardly to bother you in the daytime," Mr. Sam said. "But come nightfall, the infidels will be back."

"My cake, Aunt Polly, I pray to God to watch out for you," Pickett said.

"Oh, I taken care of myself. No need to wear God out," Aunt Polly replied. She straightened up a little and looked away, embarrassed by her pride.

"Of course you did, but we don't dare ask you to do it again," I said. "Can't you arrange for a guard, Mr. Sam?"

Mr. Sam said he would hire someone, then told Aunt Polly to go back to the quarters and jolly up Ezra. "Anything he needs, just let me know."

Aunt Polly thanked him, then took my hands in hers and made me promise to see Ezra before I left.

After Aunt Polly disappeared, Mr. Sam said, "Poor stove-up black devil. It's a wonder he wasn't stroked. That would certainly scare me into heart failure."

"There's something here that puzzles me," I said. "In Natchez, can drunken white men beat up a Negro with impunity?"

"I declare it to be wrong, but that's the way of it," Mr. Sam said.

"It's not so easy," Pickett interjected. "If Ezra didn't recognize them, what good would it do to report the fight? Who would the sheriff arrest? And if Ezra did know who attacked him, it would be the word of a Negro against the word of a white man—more than one, in fact. People in the South class off, and the word of a Negro isn't worth much against a white's. No white jury would convict those men on Ezra's say-so, and of course colored folks don't serve on juries. Just by bringing charges, Ezra would be asking for trouble. Negroes have been hanged for less in Mississippi."

"It's not right," I said.

"That's not worth denying," Mr. Sam agreed. "But that's the way of it."

Since I couldn't change anything and commenting further would antagonize my friends, I said, "I know about the Ku Klux Klan. What are patterollers?"

"The real pronouncement is patrollers," Mr. Sam said.

"They were low-born white trash mostly, mean old boys," Pickett explained. "Back before the War, they hunted slaves who were off the plantation without permission. They chased down runaways for the reward money. The Negroes were scared to death of them."

"With good cause," Mr. Sam added. "God bless anybody they caught. The patrollers gave them pecks of trouble, turned their dogs loose on them, beat them so bad that they died sometimes. Of course, we don't have patrollers anymore."

"Don't you?"

"Ma'am?" Mr. Sam said as he and Pickett exchanged glances.

I had gone too far, so I said quickly, "Why don't we go inside."

"Don't think hard of us," Pickett whispered as she set the soda-pop bottles on the porch, placing them beside the door, then followed me into Amalia's room. "We're getting better. Things were much worse in my coming-up years."

None of us cared to pursue the conversation. I went directly to the desk and opened the drawers, relieved to find that everything was as I'd left it the day before. "The jewelry goes with me. I won't be so lucky the next time somebody comes around."

"We can all commence," Pickett said, taking a large kerchief out of her pocketbook. She folded it on the diagonal, then wrapped it around her hair and tied it in a knot at the top of her head. "There are some Nu-Grape boxes in the car. You pack whatever's worth saving, and I'll carry it off to the Buzzard's Nest for safekeeping." When she returned with the cartons, she was wearing a man's shirt over her dress.

We placed Amalia's jewelry and other valuables on the desk and her papers on top of the bed. Mr. Sam would take the latter to his office. Pickett went around the room, picking up mementos and objects d'art and showing them to me. "How big is this place, Mr. Sam?"

"I'll measure it one day," Mr. Sam replied, then indicated the volumes he had taken from the bookcase. "These have always been a favorite of mine." He pro-

252

nounced the word "fave-or-right." "The captain was partial to first editions. I shall store them in my office, where you can go through them at your leisure," he said.

"You're welcome to keep them."

"I'll thank you till you're better paid." He bowed.

"It's not so much of a gift, since it would cost a fortune to ship them to Denver."

"You'll find no better home for them. Mr. Sam is the best-read man in Natchez," Pickett said. She laid the AB quilt on the desk. "It's a beaut, isn't it? I insist most emphatically that you keep it. Do you know that at one time Miss Amalia was considered the most accomplished needleworker in Natchez?"

"Miss Amalia joyed to quilt," Mr. Sam said. "She and Aunt Polly sat here of an afternoon making story quilts. Aunt Polly drew her stories from the Bible, but Miss Amalia . . . Lord, I don't know where she got hers. She gave me a big and fat quilt once, said the story was about a man who took care of his neighbors." Mr. Sam paused so that we would know without his having to tell us that the story was about him.

"Why, of course she did, you helpful old thang," Pickett said. "If they weren't all used up, those quilts must be stored somewhere around here."

While Mr. Sam concentrated on the books, leafing through them and reading passages out loud, Pickett and I packed the items we had collected, marking the cartons for Mr. Sam's office or the Buzzard's Nest. The things I wanted to take back to the hotel went into a separate box—Amalia's jewelry, a workbasket with bits of fabric inside, a silver candelabra, and the quilt that had caught Pickett's fancy and mine. Because I might find other things to add to my carton, I set it on the floor beside the desk, while Pickett and Mr. Sam carried the rest of the boxes to the cars.

When she returned to the house, Pickett ran her hand over the footboard of Amalia's bed. "This was made by Prudent Mallard. It's very rare."

I told her I'd already decided to keep it, and I asked Mr. Sam to arrange for shipment to Denver.

"I shall give it my full attention," he replied.

After Pickett examined the rest of the furniture in the bedroom, the three of us went through the great hall and then into the dining room. Pickett waved her hand at the water-stained furniture. "Ruined! Shame on you, Miss Amalia!" But she clapped her hands when she saw the china, exclaiming, "This is exquisite! Families like the Bondurants ate off this priceless Old Paris. There was no such thing for them as a second-best set of china or crystal. If I didn't already have a dining room full of dishes, I'd buy them from you. Have you a use for them?"

"My mother," I said, delighted with the idea. "She'd love them." Mr. Sam said he would arrange to have the china crated.

"Now this," I said, going into the hall and pointing at the marble statue of Amalia and her dog. "What in the world can be done with it? Even if the thing could be shipped home, there's no place for it."

"Pity to let it go to ruin," Mr. Sam said. "That statue was quite a conversation piece in its day, you know, what with the dog's tail lopped off. And this head." He pointed to the riding crop Amalia held in her hand. "You can see where there's a man's head engraved on it. We never knew the truth of who it was. Of course, we had our suspicions."

"Maybe it's a likeness of the sculptor," Pickett said.

"Maybe," Mr. Sam replied.

"Or Bayard Lott," Pickett suggested. "After all, he was the handsomest man in Natchez in his day. Quite a catch." She gave me a sly look. "And hips! Oh my. Even as an old man, he had those hips. Didn't he, Mr. Sam?"

"Oh, indeed not!" Mr. Sam blushed.

Pickett gave me a sideways glance and said no more. Instead, she volunteered to check with the library to see whether there might be a place for the statue there, but she was not hopeful. "Marble statues go begging here."

I asked if she wanted the gold chairs in the parlor.

"One can't have too many ballroom chairs." She looked at the staircase that curved around the statue of Amalia. "Are we going up?"

"Ezra says it's not safe."

"Why, what is safe in Natchez?" She eyed the steps expertly. "It doesn't look so bad. Shall we?" Without waiting for an answer, she started up the stairs, then turned and said, "Fraidy cats."

Mr. Sam followed, wheezing a little. "I have never been above the first floor," he told us as he tested each

255

step before putting his weight on it. When the three of us reached the top of the stairs, we looked around, disappointed at the shabbiness.

Floorboards were broken through, and the ceiling was soiled with water stains. Where the roof was torn away, we saw sky. Tattered wallpaper curled away from the walls, leaving bare plaster like onion skins. The remains of a chandelier lay in one corner, and the floor in the center of the hall was damaged from where the fixture had fallen. The only furniture in the hall was a large table with a mirror beneath it.

"The mirror doubles the amount of light in the room," Mr. Sam said. "Look you." He used his cigarette lighter to light a kerosene lamp that sat on the table, then set the lamp on the floor in front of the mirror. The hall glowed.

"No such thing. Who'd put a lamp on the floor? Why, it's like hiding your lamp under a bushel," Pickett scoffed. "Miss Emilie put the mirror there so she could see if her petticoats showed. You'll find petticoat mirrors all over Natchez."

We peered into the bedrooms, where sheets heavy with dust covered the massive beds and dressers. "It smells like a dead Dutchman in here," Pickett said, holding her nose as she walked into one of the bedrooms. With her free hand, she pulled back the dust cloth that protected a love seat. Mr. Sam held the lamp close to the intricately carved wood, and Pickett exclaimed, "It's a Belter!" I knew Belter and told her I did not care for the fussy style. In a second bedroom, she announced, "Another Prudent Mallard."

"Would anybody steal furniture?" I asked.

"No, but they'd burn it," Pickett replied. "There's a dealer in New Orleans who would dance a jig to have these things. The least I can do is to arrange to sell them for you."

As we inspected the rooms, I picked up a handful of items to take with me—a crystal powder box, a handful of tin soldiers, bits of ribbon and lace, a sampler dated 1824, which was beautifully executed but not as interesting as the one in Aunt Polly's kitchen—and set them at the top of the stairs. Pickett opened a wardrobe in one bedroom and discovered a cache of Amalia's quilts, which I said I wanted shipped home.

We made a full circle of the hall, until only one room remained; the door to it was closed. I opened it and found a bedroom flooded with sunshine. The rest of the second floor was dark, with only slats of light coming through the closed shutters, but in this room, the louvers were open. Old lace curtains at the windows fluttered like laundry on a line.

"What in the world?" I muttered. Filling almost the entire room was a tepeelike tent. Its peak was too high for the room and had been folded against the ceiling. Ropes attached to the sides were stretched to the corners of the bedroom to hold the canvas structure in place.

"A Sibley tent," Mr. Sam said. "Now where'd the Bondurants get hold of a Yankee tent?"

The flap was open, and I pointed to a bed inside.

257

"The tent keeps the rain off the bed—and the plaster from falling on it, too," Pickett said, pointing to the ceiling, where light came through the broken places. The tent was badly water-stained. "It's probably the bed Ezra slept on."

"Ezra sleeps in the quarters," I said.

"He *lives* in the quarters. He slept here in case Miss Amalia had need of him," replied Mr. Sam, correcting me.

"To protect her?"

"Oh that, and to administer to her wants. It's quite common really," Pickett said. "My nursemaid, Sugar, slept on the floor beside my bed until I was married. I think she'd still be sleeping there if Buckland hadn't put down his foot." She sighed. "I do miss her. If I tell Bucky I need a blanket or a glass of water, he gets crabbed and cross and says to get it myself. Sugar was much more accommodating."

"Sugar's been dead for some time," Mr. Sam reminded her.

"Yes, that's another reason she doesn't sleep beside me anymore."

I started to laugh, but Pickett had not made a joke, so catching myself, I said, "If this is Ezra's room, we shouldn't intrude."

"Nonsense. It's your house. You have a perfect right to go wherever you like. Ezra understands that," Pickett said. "You won't want this bed. It's just an old slave bed—wooden legs with canvas stretched over them. But Ezra does have another one of Amalia's quilts—or maybe it's Aunt Polly's." She handed a folded quilt to me. "Too bad it's so worn."

"Too bad." I returned the quilt to the bed.

Pickett walked across the room to a wardrobe and opened it. "Nothing much here, either. Just a few clothes." I looked beyond her and saw a pair of worn shoes and faded shirts and canvas pants, wash-worn and folded.

Pickett picked up a large unframed photograph that was mounted on cardboard. "Is this Miss Amalia? The workbasket looks like the one you found downstairs this selfsame day, Nora." She handed the picture to Mr. Sam.

"Oh, yes, that's Miss Amalia, maybe forty years ago." He gave the photograph to me.

The picture, printed in sepia, was faded, but Amalia's face was clear. She sat on the steps of a gazebo, a book in her lap, the workbasket beside her. Behind her, chickens pecked in the dirt near a stable, and a man—Ezra perhaps—held a horse by its bridle. Next to him stood a woman wearing a turban and a calico dress, but she had turned her head as the shutter opened, so her face was out of focus. The woman might have been Sukey Pea, and perhaps Ezra had kept the photograph because it was all he had left of her. The moving blur could be the way he remembered her, a kind of whirlwind in his life.

"Is this Ezra's wife?" I asked.

"Did he have one? I'd not heard of it," Pickett said.

"Oh, you wouldn't have. That was a long time ago,

about the time this picture was taken, most likely. But I remember her." Mr. Sam chuckled. "She was nice and soft-goin', with a backside that looked like she had melons stuck in her hip pockets. I guarantee you she was wild. She did not walk a chalk line."

"She did not what?"

"She wasn't faithful," Pickett explained.

"Miss Amalia told me Ezra was a punkin head to jump the broomstick with her." He laughed.

Without my having to ask, Pickett explained, "'Jumping the broomstick' means they got married. That was how they did it in slavery days."

"I thought Miss Amalia'd run the both of them off the place when they got married. Wasn't nothing happened on Avoca without her say-so, and she figured if Ezra, who was her especial favorite, did as he pleased, the others would, too, and it bothered her mind. Of course, that marriage didn't last long. Sukey Pea mistreated Ezra terrible, and Miss Amalia joyed when Sukey Pea ran off with some brutish fellow. It didn't surprise anybody. Sukey Pea was a prodigal. She flirted her skirt at every man who passed, and fornicated up salt crick."

"Why, Mr. Sam!" Pickett said.

"I beg pardon." He took the photograph and held it close to his face to hide his blush.

Pickett said, "How can you say such a thing even about a colored woman, Mr. Sam? You're just like a possum. The longer you live, the less sense you've got."

"The longer I live, the plainer I see things," Mr. Sam retorted, handing back the picture. "I can't be positive certain whether that's Sukey Pea, but it might could be. She never did stand still. Ezra didn't study anybody after she left, just stayed on with Aunt Polly to take care of Miss Amalia."

I put the photograph back into the wardrobe, knowing that Ezra would be aware that we had snooped. But he would not say anything to me. As Aunt Polly had told us, he was saving on his words, and as Pickett had said, he probably believed I had the right to snoop.

Ezra's chamber was the most interesting of the upstairs rooms, the only one that still contained life, and I wanted to spend more time there. But Pickett and Mr. Sam had started down the stairs. When I reached the hallway below, Pickett was holding her wristwatch to the light. "Nora, we'll meet here at nine tomorrow to commence our work. Mr. Sam, would you be a darling and take her to town? I must scoot."

I said I would walk back into town after visiting Ezra, and I waved to Mr. Sam as he drove away slowly, the car straddling the center of the road. Only after he disappeared did I remember that he had not taken my box of plunder with him. So I turned back to go to Amalia's room, and I noticed then that the three bottles Pickett had left on the porch were gone. Perhaps Magdalene Lott had snatched them. I glanced around the yard, then looked beyond it to the woods, but I saw no one.

Magdalene had been bold enough to enter Amalia's

room, and next time, she might steal something. So the box would have to go with me. I picked it up, adding the things from upstairs—the toys and fabric scraps and an opera program for *The Marriage of Figaro* at the New York Opera House in 1877. I was surprised that I wanted so little from this house.

Walking along the path of scattered shells, I wondered if Amalia had liked opera. I did not care much about opera, and David—I had discovered just last year—had actually disliked it. In our ten years of marriage, we attended only one opera, the opening-night performance of *Camille* at the Central City Opera House. That was only a year ago, and we went not so much to hear the opera as to support the restoration of the opera house.

Central City once had been a prosperous mining town, but when I knew it, the only activities were kids selling ore samples to tourists in the summer and old men sitting on benches, speculating about the price of gold. The Central City Opera House, which once drew famous performers from New York, had been turned into a movie theater, but then it closed, and the roof was caving in. The interior was filled with fallen plaster, broken chairs, and pack-rat droppings. A group of Denverites, including Mother, decided to restore it, bringing culture to Colorado and economic development to Central.

Opening night was the highlight of Denver's social season, and everybody dressed in Victorian costume.

David and I made the rounds of the secondhand shops on Larimer Street, Denver's skid row, where we purchased a fine beaver hat and a black cloak lined with white satin for David. Then we found an antique velvet dress the color of the blue time, which was what we called the late afternoon, when the distant mountains turned blue. As we were dressing that evening, David presented me with a necklace—a gold chain with a drop of two aquamarines a few shades lighter than the dress.

We rented a little Victorian house on the Casey, a promontory just below Central, for the weekend, and after the opera and the festivities were over, the two of us, me twirling a lace parasol, David carrying the beaver hat, which had begun to smell, walked the dark streets to the Casey. Neither of us was tired, and the rented house, long boarded up, had a peculiar odor of rot and rodents. So we sat in rocking chairs on the porch in the moonlight and talked. When I shivered, David put his opera cloak about my shoulders.

He lighted a cigarette; then, holding it between the fingers of his right hand, he pointed out the star formations. Far below us, smoke curled up from a chimney, and I told David the old joke about the houses in Central, which were built on such steep hillsides that when the housewife on top threw out her stove ashes, they flew into the chimney below and thus worked their way from house to house, all the way down to the bottom of the mountain.

Then David said, "I read about the man the Casey

263

was named for—Pat Casey. Do you know about him? He struck it rich here."

"Hmm," I muttered, my rocker creaking. I knew all about Pat Casey, but there was no need to spoil David's story.

"Pat was illiterate and dumb as a clothespin. He carried a big gold watch, which he'd pull out from time to time. It was strictly for show, because he couldn't tell time." David rocked back and forth while I chuckled.

David flicked his cigarette over the hillside, and we watched the sparks scatter in the dark as it bounced from rock to rock. "Pat showed up at one of his mines and called into the shaft, 'How many of youse are down there?' A miner yelled back, 'Five.' Pat scratched his head, then said, 'Well, half of youse come up for a drink.'"

David's rocker stopped, and without turning his head, he shifted his eyes to get my reaction—a gesture he often made when he said something funny—and I laughed. "You've probably heard that story before," he said.

"Never so well told. I didn't know about the watch."

David reached over and took my hand. "Could you have lived up here in those days, do you think?"

"Probably not. I'd have hated not being able to take a bath for weeks at a time and having to carry water and use an outhouse. And I couldn't have slaughtered an ox for food. It's much nicer to go to the butcher at the Piggly Wiggly and have him do it for me."

"You sell yourself short." David's seriousness surprised me. "You could deal with almost anything, if you had to."

"Well, so far I haven't. And with any luck, I'll never find out." It struck me then how easy my life had always been. The Depression, which had devastated so many people, had barely touched us. "What about you? Could you have been a pioneer?"

David lighted another cigarette as we sat in the dark and looked at the lumps of mountains across from us. I was glad for my husband's cape around me, because a wind blew down the Casey. There were occasional sounds from up the hill—drunken shouts mostly. A motorist switched on headlights, and a car started down Eureka Street in Central. I leaned out over the porch and watched as it made its way along the twisted street far below. It reached Black Hawk and stopped, then turned onto the Denver road.

David took a long time to answer the question. "There's something awfully appealing about being self-sufficient. Every male wishes he could be a caveman."

"Pioneers and cavemen aren't exactly the same thing."

"Perhaps they are. Living in a cave is a lot closer to settling the West than taking the trolley to the office and sitting in a chair reading legal documents."

David seemed to be working out something. He snubbed out the cigarette on the porch floor, then picked up the hat and stroked the beaver pelt. I put my hand to my throat and rubbed my fingers across the aquamarines.

"Sometimes it's all so pointless. Last week, I listened to two women with more money than God argue over which one got the diamond brooch and which the emerald ring. And I knew damn well that neither woman cared. One just didn't want the other to get her first choice."

"You're being unfair." I reached for his hand, but he was still holding the hat. "You know that's not what you do. You help people through difficult times, and you let lonely old women know that somebody cares. Whatever you say, you really do care."

David dismissed my remarks with a wave of the hat. "Maybe they'd be better off if I told them to go on home and stop feeling so sorry for themselves."

He had never talked like this before. "What's gotten into you, David? You've always loved your work."

David didn't answer. He put the hat on the porch and leaned forward in the rocker, resting his arms on his knees.

"Is that why you go off with the boys on those dangerous outings?"

David turned and looked at me, but in the dark, I could not make out his features.

"Those dangerous things you and Arthur do, is that the reason for them, because your work frustrates you? Tell me."

David looked down the mountain. Pinpoints of light were coming from the windows of two or three houses now. The occupants had returned home, or they had just gotten up. He sat silently for a few moments. "Nothing's wrong. Blame the damn opera. Don't ever ask me to go to one again, will you?"

"I never knew you didn't like opera."

"Neither did I." David relaxed a little and sat back in the rocker, moving to and fro. "Do *you* think I could have been a pioneer?"

"We're lucky we live in the twentieth century and won't have to find out." When David didn't respond, I said, "But I suppose you would have done all right. You're awfully good in an emergency. Look at how assured you were when we came across that mountain lion, and how you kept Betsey from falling off the cliff."

"Those weren't hardships. They were adventures."

"You don't lose your head in an emergency. And you're not afraid of hard work. I think you could have been a pioneer, don't you?"

David's rocker squeaked rhythmically, and he didn't reply.

Then I wondered if this might not be just an idle conversation. "Is something wrong?"

"Oh, no."

"Are you sure?"

"Everything's all right."

I put my feet under me and wrapped the cloak around me like a blanket.

"I could have been a pioneer if you'd been there." David turned his face to me in the dark.

"What?"

"With you beside me, I think I could do anything."

"Oh, David, that's one of the nicest things you've ever said to me."

"I mean it." His voice was so ferocious that I shivered. "I'd be lost if you ever left me."

I sat upright and tried to make out David's features. The intensity of his words troubled me a little, so I said lightheartedly, "I don't have any plans to leave, so you needn't worry."

"I hope not." David turned to look up at the stars, and at the same time, he reached over and took my hand, squeezing it so much that it hurt. "I love you, Nora. Don't you ever doubt that."

I didn't, not then.

Chapter Nine

AUNT POLLY SAT ON A white-painted bench in front of the quarters, a wooden bowl of green beans in her lap. She seemed in no hurry as she picked up the beans one at a time, broke off the ends, tossed them aside, and then snapped the beans in two. She dropped the broken halves into the bowl and picked out another bean, sliding over on the bench to make room for me. Placing the box of Amalia's things on the ground, I sat down beside her.

"Ezra sleeping now 'cause he feeling all punylike. I dress his wounds with spiderweb. Them that bleeds too much, I put on sweet apple-tree bark. Then I bind 'em up. Before you know it, he as good as he was, though Ezra never ain't goin' be good as new. He too old."

"How old is he?" I wanted to help with the beans, but Aunt Polly seemed to be enjoying the rhythm of snapping them. Besides, I knew my place.

"Lemme see." She paused with a string bean between her old fingers. "Ezra born eighteen and fifty-eight, so he seventy-five now, 'cause this nineteen and thirty-three. I ain't never studied about how old I is, but I expect I been ninety for one or three years. I got no desire for one hundred, so I stay ninety. I about sixteen when Ezra's born, maybe twelve when Welcome comes. Maybe less."

Aunt Polly stared off in the direction of Shadowland. "My mind rest easy if I knowed Welcome growed up. But I ain't ever goin' know 'bout some things, and there's no use wrecking my mind over it."

"Aren't there any records?"

Aunt Polly shook her head. "None I ever knowed about. Even if there was, who'd keep track of a darky after the War's done with. 'Sides, it's a long time gone. By now, Welcome's most likely passed." Aunt Polly had grieved for her child for almost eighty years.

We sat quietly for a few minutes. A goat came out of the bushes behind the quarters, and Aunt Polly stroked her affectionately, muttering, "Look at them goat legs. They got a wood-keg look to 'em, just like Miss Magdalene." Since Miss Magdalene had worn a long dress when I'd seen her, I wondered how Aunt Polly knew about her legs. The goat wandered off. "I milked the goats and paid a boy a nickel to haul that milk to town. I go a piece of the way to make sure he done it right."

I hadn't thought about the goats. "Ezra must have done a good job of defending himself last night."

"Oh, he good at that all right. Ezra ain't easy scared. He's a fighter when he's young. He was a good-looking man back then—still is, if you asks me—and had all the girls pursuing after him, and that make all the mens mad, so Ezra have to fight 'em. Then when he marries with Sukey Pea, he's got to defend her. I try to keep it out of his ears about what that fractious girl is up to, but he find out anyways. If it still been slavery days, the captain sell him just 'cause all the trouble he make round here. Once, the captain say he put Ezra off the place if he don't behave, but Miss Amalia beg for Ezra to stay."

She paused. "There's times when Ezra the only one can protect her. She need him. When she look at her brother, fear stares her down." Then Aunt Polly added quickly, "Miss Amalia not afraid of much else." She ran her hands through the beans to feel for any she'd missed, found one, and snapped it hard.

"Why was she afraid of her brother?"

"I don't get no full understanding about it. You like these beans? I cook 'em up for supper with a little piece of pork."

"That sounds tasty."

"I hoping Ezra don't have no backsats with his healing."

I pondered the word *backsats,* then decided Aunt Polly meant setbacks. "So the captain didn't force Ezra to leave Avoca after all."

"There ain't nothing the captain won't do for Miss Amalia. He cherish Young Miss, love her better than anybody, even Miss Emilie. Miss Emilie sick all the time."

"He took Miss Amalia to New York."

"Oh my, yes, after slavery done gone. He take Miss Amalia and three, maybe four servants to look after her. I don't go 'long, but Ezra done. He think maybe so he stay in New York. Up there, he a pass-for-white man. But he come on home instead, and after a while, he marry up with Sukey Pea."

"Did Miss Amalia's brother go to New York?"

Aunt Polly nodded. "Miss Amalia don't want him to, but he did."

"And Miss Emilie?"

"No, Miss Emilie too poorly. She tell the captain take Miss Amalia, get her out of dis bad house."

"Bad house?"

"Sick house, I guess. Miss Emilie say Miss Amalia deserve her fun. She tell the captain make sure she have the time of all times."

"And did she?"

"I ain't the one to ask." Aunt Polly stared hard at me, then returned to Ezra's marriage. "None of us didn't care if Sukey Pea run off, most especially me and Miss Amalia, and maybe Ezra, too, after he get used to it. The leaving was the best thing she done for him. He put

271

all his badness behind him after she gone. Folkses say he met up with a gospel bird and that the reason he give up the fightin' and the drinkin', but I know better. Ezra wasn't never much for religion, not like some that wears out their knees crawling to the cross, then wears out the seat of their britches sliding back. It was Sukey Pea what made him crazier than a betsey bug, and he never have peace in his mind till she gone."

I changed the subject back to Amalia. "There was an opera program among her things. It's dated 1877. That was the year the captain took her to New York."

"I don't study too hard on years, 'less they has to do with me and mine, 'cause I ain't got no learnin'. Now Ezra, he read and write. Miss Amalia teach him when he's a chap, before the War's over. The captain beat Ezra if he know about it back then, but Ezra do trick him. One day, marster see Ezra with a book, and he reach for the whip, but quick as a mouse in the flour bin, Ezra turn that book over, so when old marster come up close, he see Ezra look at it upside down. Marster laugh so hard, Ezra don't get no whipping." Aunt Polly chuckled and leaned her head back against the brick wall of the quarters, closing her eyes. "He never say he read till freedom come. Then marster glad, 'cause Ezra help him with the lumber company. He better than Miss Amalia's brother at figurin'. If the captain give Ezra the lumber company, instead of Mr. Frederick, it still be hummin'."

"Did Miss Amalia like New York?"

A shadow crossed Aunt Polly's face. "She come

home full of misery for a long time. Then Miss Emilie get sick and they boat the river to New Orleans, and I never see Miss Emilie again. I ain't never talked to Miss Amalia about New York." She paused, then sat up straight and looked at me. "How come you wanting to know so much into Miss Amalia's business?"

"Because she was my aunt," I replied, then added slowly, "Or my grandmother."

A muscle twitched in Aunt Polly's face, but she leaned her head against the bricks and closed her eyes again. "That's something I ain't never paid no attention to."

The old black woman was silent then, and her face was so serene that I thought she might have fallen asleep. Perhaps she had been through so much in her life that my prying questions meant nothing to her. I felt drowsy myself, sitting there in the afternoon sun with the sounds of birds and insects flitting about. There was a noise from the direction of Shadowland, but I had no way of telling if it were Magdalene or a goat in the underbrush. I put my head against the wall and lifted my face to the sun, closing my eyes, and I might have gone to sleep had Aunt Polly not asked suddenly, "What gatherin's you got from Miss Amalia in that box?"

"The things I want to keep. I was afraid someone would come back and steal them. They'll be safer with me at the hotel."

Aunt Polly leaned over me and peered into the carton with her good eye, the eye closest to me.

"There's her workbasket and some silver, a quilt and a sampler, this and that," I said. "And her jewelry."

"Her jewelry the best there is. It never need no polishin' up nothin'. I proud to see her wear it."

I took out the jewelry boxes, opened them, and lined them up on the bench.

Aunt Polly looked at the pieces and smiled as she recognized them. "That belong to Miss Emilie." She touched the sapphire ring and added, "Just like that one you got on belong to Miss Emilie one time." She picked up the diamond earrings tucked inside the tortoiseshell box and held them to my ears and laughed, then put them back.

"Miss Amalia beg the captain to buy her this. She wear it lots of times." Aunt Polly pointed to the pearl necklace. Then she looked at the spray of diamonds and pearls and frowned. "Mr. Bayard give her that. She ain't never wear it."

"When did he give it to her?"

"She come home from New York with it. Mr. Bayard, he go up there to try to get her to marry with him, thinkin' life be a mess of cornmeal dumplings if she done it. He taken that fancy jewelry piece up with him and give it to her. Miss Amalia don't marry with him, but she don't give him back that pin, neither. I tell her sell it, but she say what people think? She rather let Avoca shamble down than sell her jewelry." Aunt Polly shook her head as she examined the contents of the boxes. "Miss Amalia love her pretties. She wear 'em even when she's old. Sometimes she get dressed up in her fancy dress and her ear bobs and that pearl neck-lace, and she dance around the house." Aunt Polly smiled at the memory. "She wear her jewelry some-times when she sell the goat milk. She always a lady."

"Which piece do you like best?"

"Oh, I can't rightly say."

"Choose something. Miss Amalia would want you to have a piece of her jewelry, don't you think?"

Aunt Polly stared at me, but whether it was with plea-sure, surprise, or suspicion, I couldn't tell.

When she didn't reply, I picked up the dragonfly, thinking the bright rubies might appeal to her. "What about this? It's one of the prettiest pieces." I held it against her dress, which had been red once but had faded to the double pink color of old quilts.

Aunt Polly looked at me skeptically. "What I do with it?"

"You could wear it."

"Folkses think I all biggity-acting if I wear some-thing like that, think I steal it from Miss Amalia. Can't no colored person wear that jewelry."

I hadn't considered that, and I hoped my offer did not emphasize the class distinctions she had suffered all her life. Still, she deserved something valuable of Amalia's, even if she kept it tucked away in a drawer.

Aunt Polly leaned close to the boxes. "Them sparkly stones sure is pretty with the sun all shining over 'em." She meant the diamonds.

I picked up a pendant, a large pink diamond sus-pended on a diamond-studded gold chain, and thought that if the stone were good—and Amalia wouldn't have had diamonds that weren't—it was the most valuable of the jewels. I tested the chain to make sure there were no weak links, then inspected the catch to see that it fastened properly. For a moment, I had second thoughts about giving it away, then chided myself for my selfishness. There were other pieces for me to keep. "You could wear this under your dress, where no one but you would know you have it on. It would remind you of Miss Amalia and how much she loved you."

Aunt Polly held her face tight for a moment, then slowly looked up at me as if expecting me to change my mind. She took the necklace and held it to her eyes. The catch was tricky, but she opened it easily. Of course she knew how to work it, because she had fastened it around Amalia's neck. Aunt Polly put on the necklace, straightened it, and ran her fingers over the diamond drop. "The captain give this to Miss Amalia when she sixteen. It richer than top milk. She pleasured herself with it often and on."

"I hope it will pleasure you."

Aunt Polly sat up rod-straight and ran her fingers through the green beans, searching again for any that hadn't been snapped. Her right hand went back to the diamond, and she fingered it, then moved to feel the diamonds on the chain. She buttoned the top of her dress so that the pendant was hidden. "I thank you most sincerely. You quality, like Miss Amalia and Miss Emilie. You a true Bondurant."

Her compliment went to my heart, and I couldn't

reply. Aunt Polly was emotional, too, because she didn't say a word after that. From time to time, she touched the diamond through the faded fabric, and I smiled to think that under that old dress, she wore a diamond worth more than a house—a stone far better than any of Odalie's little ole antebellum diamonds.

Bending over to put away the jewelry boxes, I noticed a black telescope lying on the ground and picked it up. It was scratched and rusted, but the lens was good, because looking through it, I saw the weathered and broken columns of Shadowland as if they were but a few feet away.

"Miss Magdalene give that to Ezra 'cause he put the bottles on her tree. It a spyglass. Mr. Bayard find it under a tree one time when he get wood to chop. He say it there a long time, maybe since the War."

"A spyglass would suit Miss Magdalene."

Aunt Polly laughed. "Yes'm, but she can't hardly tote it. Ezra say we use it to hunt up the goats."

"What did Mr. Lott use it for?"

"He sit on the porch of an evening and look at the stars."

"Or Miss Amalia?"

Aunt Polly's head jerked up. "You think that?"

I shrugged. "Did she say when Mr. Lott found it?"

Aunt Polly thought hard. "Maybe just before he die. My old mind won't remember." She added, "There ain't nothing worth seeing at Avoca, just old furniture. What you do with that furniture?"

She had changed the subject on purpose. So I replied

that the furniture would be moved the next day, then asked if she wanted any of it.

"Only Ezra's bed upstairs. I reckon you seen it," she said, perhaps as a way of telling me she knew that I had snooped in his room.

"What about the chairs?"

Aunt Polly chuckled. "What I need with a gold chair? Only gold chair I want's waiting up yonder. I almost went looking for it this past June gone by, when I felt death creeping up on me, but the Lord don't want me to go before my mist'ess. Maybe now Miss Amalia gone, He take me to look after her. 'Cept I got Ezra down here to care for."

"That chair will be waiting for you whenever you get there. So will Miss Amalia."

"Yes'm." She touched the diamond again with a hand that was the color and texture of a wrinkled brown paper sack. She looked down at the bowl and said, "I best put these on," but she made no move to get up. "What you do with the big house?"

"What do you want me to do with it?"

"It not for me to say."

"No one would buy it."

"Don't s'pose."

"There are better houses for sale in Natchez."

"There is."

I waited.

"You could move in. I and Ezra got nobody to take care of now. We look after you, just like we done Bondurants in bygone days."

278

I reached into the bowl of beans and squeezed her hand. "Thank you for that, Aunt Polly, but how could I leave Denver? My family's there, and I don't know anyone here."

"Your family here, too. You a Bondurant. Folkses be all over you like gravy on grits to be friendling with you."

"That's a tribute to Miss Amalia and Miss Emilie, not to me. I don't fit in here."

Aunt Polly gripped my hand. "This your place," she said. "You the last leaf on the tree."

I thought that over. "Where would I live? Avoca's ready to fall in, and I don't intend to put you out of the quarters."

"You doesn't have to live inside the big house. There's the hothouse and the poultry house and the captain's billiard house."

I looked at her curiously, for I had not seen a billiard house.

"The billiard house." Aunt Polly shook her head, remembering. "Miss Emilie don't like the captain's gentlemen friends in her house smoking cigars, so she has a special house put up for them. It got a billiard room and a room where they plays cards and two or three other rooms where the gentlemens sleeps when they drink too much—and whatnot." She glanced at me to see if I understood "whatnot." I did. "It built real nice, all brick, better than the big house now. I tells Miss Amalia to move in there, but she say ladies don't live in no billiard house. She say what folkses think?"

"Where is it?"

"Ezra take you there when he's up. Maybe you want to live there. You give it time, you might like it in Natchez. You never can tell in this life what's going to happen."

I nodded, and Aunt Polly seemed encouraged. "You and Ezra look after each other. When I's corpse-dead, there he will be."

"Ezra doesn't want me taking Miss Amalia's place."

"That's the truth, but he don't mind if you take *your* place. Without me and Miss Amalia, you got the care of him."

That already had been made plain to me.

"The Lord have His reasons for bringing you here. Might be it a good thing you get to know Ezra. The Bible say the Lord give us new mercies every morning."

My aunt Emma had quoted that bit of Scripture to me in Georgetown on the day I married David. "Am I Ezra's mercy, or is he mine?"

"Maybe so both. Miss Amalia want to home you here. That why she give you this house. Maybe your daddy want you here, too." Aunt Polly sighed and got up, and as she went through the door into the quarters, she said, "You ain't got no husband no more. You come here to Avoca, maybe you find yourself a new one. Now I go wrassle up these beans."

It seemed as if half the people I'd met in Natchez wanted to marry me off.

Inside the quarters, Aunt Polly put kindling onto a

banked fire and used a bellows to create a flame. She took down an iron pot and added water and the beans. Watching her through the doorway, I thought about living in Mississippi. The idea was absurd. A river never could take the place of mountains for me. And I never would fall in love with a man in a wrinkled suit.

Inside the quarters, it was cool despite the fire. Ezra stood in a corner, his head wrapped in a bandage made from a red kerchief, supporting himself with a walking stick made from a tree branch. Its knob was smooth, polished by the hands that had gripped it over the years.

"You did a fine job of looking out for Avoca. I think Miss Amalia would have been proud of the way you smashed those men to protect her home."

Ezra gave me the glimmer of a smile. "I crumple their feathers."

I smiled back and said, "Mr. Satterfield's bringing in men to guard the place tonight. We'll move furniture tomorrow. Miss Amalia's bed and her quilts are going to Denver."

"Miss Amalia like them quilts. You take care of 'em, not put 'em on mules."

"I won't."

"What you do with that statue of Miss Amalia?"

Perhaps I'd been hasty in agreeing to offer it to the library, but surely, I thought, Ezra wouldn't want it. The idea of a marble statue of their mistress inside the slave quarters was grotesque. "I thought it could go to some public place, like the library. Wouldn't that be nice?"

"Miss Amalia won't want that." Suddenly, he laughed, the first time he had really laughed in my presence, and the sound was warm and infectious. "She won't want it to go to no library, have peoples stare at her. She tell me throw it in the river when she gone. She never like that statue and ask her daddy after it's made to keep it in the barn. But the captain think it mighty pretty, and he set it up in the big house so everybody see it."

"Why didn't she move it after the captain died?"

"The captain too smart for her." Ezra laughed again. "He cut out a place in the floor for it; then he brace it down below with a big pole. He tell Miss Amalia the house fall down if she move it. Maybe it will."

That would solve my problem of what to do with Avoca. "Is there anything of Miss Amalia's that you want to keep?"

Ezra shook his head back and forth. If he had wanted to keep anything—a chair, a book, a picture—he'd already taken it, just as he had destroyed anything he didn't want me to see. The scraps of paper hidden from Ezra in the desk were all that I was likely to find that would give me a clue to Amalia's life. "That a kindly thing you done to give that neck bob to Aunt Polly."

I wasn't sure what to say in response and was glad that Aunt Polly interjected, "Ezra, you take young miss to see the billiard house. Maybe she live there."

"Why she want to live in there? Ladies don't smoke no cigars and play no billiards."

282

"'Cause she can't live in the big house without the roof fall down on her head."

"Bondurants always live in the big house. It good enough for Miss Amalia." He rubbed his right hand over his left arm, which was taut and corded. At his age, Ezra still was a powerful man. I would not have wanted to be one of the "varmints" he had attacked.

"No it ain't. You know we try to get our mist'ess to move out that place, and she don't do it. Now go on with you."

I suggested we wait until Ezra was steadier on his feet, but Ezra said defensively, "I ain't strattledy-legged." He did indeed appear to walk normally as I followed him from the quarters down a path overgrown with foliage. "This where Miss Amalia have her blue garden when she's a girl. Every flower blue. Miss Amalia like her flowers. When she walk to town, she stop in folkses' yards and plant what she think they need. She leave vegetables by the door of them that needs, too. Miss Amalia keep her own garden till she die. I pick the flowers for her every morning."

"And you still do." I remembered the rose he had left in Amalia's memory on her desk and the jar of blossoms at the cemetery.

Ezra kept on until we came to a Greek Revival–style cottage that looked like a small temple, situated at the edge of a long slope that ended in a meadow. The building was the size of a bungalow and was shaded by magnolia trees. Ezra opened the front door, and then, his walking stick tapping on the wide floorboards, he led me through a wood-paneled hallway and into a large room where a billiards table was set up. In the center of a wall was a fireplace so large that he could stand up in it. Corn-colored brick surrounded the opening, which was set off by a dark wood mantel. Four-foot-high firedogs were spaced far apart to let the captain burn enormous logs, and it appeared from the blackened bricks in the fireplace that he had done so often.

Ezra showed me the dining room and a pantry, the bedrooms and storerooms. One of the bedrooms could be made into a kitchen, I thought, and the linen press into a bathroom. It would not cost so much to make the building habitable.

Back in the billiards room, I asked about a place where boards had been ripped from the wall. "Rats?" I'd never live in a place that had rats.

"Maybe so." Ezra smiled to himself at the question. "One anyway—Mr. Frederick. When the captain build this place, Miss Amalia a snot of a baby. The captain order wine special from France and have them to plaster up the bottles in the wall. Captain say they stay there till Miss Amalia's wedding day. Frederick and his chaps steal them and drink the wine, and what they doesn't drink, they pours out. Only time I ever know of the captain cowhiding a white boy."

"You didn't like Frederick."

Ezra didn't reply. "Look you how nice this place is in the hot of the day." He raised the top half of the sash, then unlatched the paneling below, which swung to the side, turning the window into a large doorway. I nearly clapped my hands with delight.

"This called a jib window. Two of 'em here, two across, so the breeze just go right through."

"You can see all the world from here," I said.

"And maybe Texas." He paused. "You believe maybe you live here?"

The question surprised me, because it seemed as if Ezra was encouraging me to stay, too. "What would you think of that? Do you want another generation of Bondurants to look after?" I asked.

"I never done nothing else since my way back yonder time. You Young Miss now. Aunt Polly say maybe you find a husband here. She worry about that."

"She can't have worried very long, since I just met her." I heard the edge in my voice but wasn't sure Ezra had.

"She worry about you before, ever since you get you a divorce. Her and Miss Amalia worry."

"And you?" Ezra could not have missed the sharpness in my voice this time.

He looked at the place in the wall where the wine bottles had been hidden and touched the end of one of the laths, which was broken and ragged. "You all Miss Amalia has got."

"Had."

Ezra ignored me. "When we get that letter long time gone past saying your daddy die, Miss Amalia's heart drop below her knees. Folks say she turn queer when the boll weevil come and she lose her plantations, but it was your daddy passing. Onliest thing that keep her going on was you. Then your husband go to glory. Don't none of us know why, but Miss Amalia real smart about folks. She afraid you die of sadness, and she worry even more about you."

"I was divorced by then."

Ezra looked at me with dark eyes that I could not read. "Miss Amalia think what happen no accident. She say you hurting in those terrible times. Aunt Polly tell her write you a letter. She say if Miss Amalia don't do it, she will. But Miss Amalia know Aunt Polly can figure but she sure can't write."

Pushing aside one of the dust cloths, I sat down on an oversized leather chair, because my legs suddenly were wobbly. "If she cared so much, why didn't Miss Amalia contact me when I was a child? After all, Father died thirty years ago."

"She say wait till you old enough to come looking for her. She wait a long time."

It was not necessary for me to point out one more time that I did not know about Amalia. "Why did she care about me and not Frederick's child?"

Ezra looked outside, and I realized that the shutters in the billiard house had been opened before I got there. Perhaps Ezra and Aunt Polly had intended to show me the place all along. "I can't say," he replied.

He could, but he chose not to.

"She tell me onliest thing she want was to see you before she die. Maybe she do that if Mr. Bayard don't kill her."

"You found the body, didn't you?"

Ezra dipped his head.

"How long after Miss Amalia was dead?"

"Maybe a minute, maybe not so long."

Startled, I looked up at Ezra, who was leaning on the walking stick, his body hunched. He was tired but would not sit down unless I told him to. I threw off the dust cloth covering another chair and gestured to it, and Ezra lowered himself into it. "You were right there when Miss Amalia was killed?" I asked.

"Not there. If I there, I stop him." Ezra hit the floor hard with the walking stick.

"Of course you would have."

Ezra watched me a minute to make sure I believed that. "I upstairs. I hear them fight."

"You mean he struck her?"

"He never hit Miss Amalia. They were fighting with words."

"What did they say?"

Ezra looked away. "I can't make it out."

I didn't believe him. "Not any of it? How did you know they were quarreling?"

"I reckon I know when somebody speak hate." He placed the walking stick upright in front of him and put one hand over the other on its knob.

"Who was hateful, Miss Amalia or Mr. Bayard?"

"Mr. Bayard. She too good—good as gold."

"You know Miss Amalia was my father's mother." I leaned toward Ezra and waited, but he neither confirmed nor denied it. "Were they fighting because

Bayard Lott was his father?"

Ezra didn't move. He stared out the jib window, looking across the meadow to the woods beyond. Then his thumb stirred a little on the stick. He took so long to reply that I thought he would not answer. "Maybe he is; maybe he isn't." He dropped his head and looked at the floor. Ezra's answer came with a great effort and with sadness.

"But Miss Amalia was my grandmother."

"That the Lord's own truth." He stood and walked heavily to the window and closed it. Then he shuffled around the room, closing and latching the other windows. "Aunt Polly got supper ready." I followed him outside, where he closed the front door and secured it with a key the size of a hammer.

We walked back to the quarters in silence. Ezra had told me as much as he was going to, so I didn't annoy him with more questions. He walked quickly, silently, resentful that he had revealed so much about Amalia. Perhaps he wanted to get back at me for my prying and that was why, just before we reached the quarters, Ezra said cruelly, "It too bad you don't come see Miss Amalia after you get you a divorce. She help you. Might be if you done it, your husband don't die in the airplane crash."

Or perhaps Ezra meant nothing at all by the remarks. How could he understand my guilt? Ezra knew only what had been in the newspapers. Still, I felt hollow inside, and when we reached the quarters, I told Aunt Polly I was not feeling well. Before she could reply, I picked up the box of keepsakes and hurried off.

The first newspaper account of David's death had been a straightforward report of the facts about the aeroplane crash. David was killed when the craft he was flying hit the side of Lookout Mountain, west of Denver. His flight teacher told reporters that David had been a careful and methodical pilot but that he'd lacked experience. The instructor speculated that the plane had been caught in the vicious winds that sweep along the Front Range, and he said that even a seasoned pilot would have had difficulty controlling the little plane.

The subsequent newspaper articles were sympathetic. The reporters found no evidence that David had been careless or that he had been drinking. There were a few sentences speculating that someone might have sabotaged the plane. After all, David had handled messy divorce cases, and there had been occasional threats against him. David himself, it was pointed out, had been divorced just recently, but, fortunately for me, the idea that the end of our marriage might have had something to do with the crash was dismissed out of hand.

Mostly, the articles told about David and his career, describing him as a successful lawyer who was active in civic affairs. There was information about me, about the "socially prominent" family David had married into, and there were photos of the two of us at society events, "in happier times," as the papers put it. An anonymous friend of mine was quoted in the *Denver*

Post as saying that the divorce had been amicable, that David and I had grown apart but remained firm friends. That was untrue, of course, as the friend—most likely Caroline—knew.

Henry learned about the accident first, and he hastened to my apartment to tell me. His voice breaking, for he was very fond of David—and the two of them had continued their weekly luncheons even after the divorce—he said, "It was one of those terrible things that happen for no reason. Sometimes God makes mistakes."

But it wasn't God who'd made the mistake. I knew the instant Henry told me the circumstances of David's death that it had been no accident, that David had deliberately flown the plane into the mountain. He had committed suicide, and I was responsible.

I had walked perhaps a quarter of a mile from the quarters when my shoulders began to ache from carrying the heavy box, and I sat down on a log beside the road. A boy came along in a jalopy and slowed, offering me a lift into town. But I could not bear to talk to anyone just then, and so I turned him down. A few minutes later, a man in a wagon drawn by a pair of mules stopped, but I waved him off. Then it was quiet, and I stared into the tangle of woods, which were soft and friendly and mulberry-colored under the rich shadows. I let the memories come back then—the sordidness and the revulsion, my love for David and my hate, and, most of all, the fear that my love for him had been worthless, his love for me a fraud.

Mother and I had made plans to spend the weekend at the Broadmoor, and we were motoring down to the Colorado Springs resort in David's car when she suddenly took ill. We turned around and drove to the Marion Street house and summoned her doctor, who diagnosed a case of the flu. He assured me she would be fine in a few days and that I'd been wise to cancel the trip. When Henry came home, I promised to check in with Mother the next day, then left for the apartment. I thought David would be surprised and pleased that none of our friends knew I'd returned and that we would have the weekend to ourselves. He had been distracted lately. In the morning, he could sleep late and have breakfast in bed. I would set it on a silver tray with a flower, because David liked things done elegantly.

The apartment was dark. David must have gone out, I thought, perhaps with friends or to the movies by himself, as he'd begun to do lately. But there were voices from the bedroom. I decided that he'd gone to bed early and fallen asleep with the radio on. I tiptoed down the hallway so as not to awaken him, but at the bedroom door, I realized the voices were real and that they were coming from the bed. Without thinking about it, I pushed the button on the wall. As the bright light came on overhead, David half-rose from the bed, ashen-faced. Then slowly, a second head turned to me, eyes wild and confused, like those of an animal caught in the light of car lamps on a mountain road. The face and hands were tan, but the body was as white as a dishrag.

"Arthur!" I cried.

The three of us froze for a painfully long time, staring at one another in the harsh glare of the overhead light. As the scene sank into my consciousness, I felt disgust and rage and betrayal and finally a sadness so overwhelming that I could have drowned in it.

I was not naïve. I knew about such things, of course, but until that moment, it had never crossed my mind that David was a homosexual. Such men were supposed to be frail boys, like satyrs, with nervous darting eyes, or pudgy fellows with big soft lips. David was masculine and fit. So was Arthur. The great irony, of course, was that I had wondered if he were infatuated with Betsey.

"For God's sake, Nora, turn out the light," David said at last. His voice was high-pitched and filled with anguish.

My hand was still attached to the light button, but I could not push it. At that moment, my body would not function. My legs were limp, like empty Christmas stockings, and I had to clutch the doorjamb to keep from collapsing onto the floor. I gaped at the two of them, until finally Arthur pulled the sheet over his pale, firm body and buried himself under the spread—a spread that I had made from remnants of lace and silk and velvet.

"Nora," David said. "Nora, let me explain."

"No, David." My name coming from that horrible bed pulled me out of my transfixed state. "You can't. You can't ever explain." I turned and ran from the apartment then, not knowing if David called me or came after me. I hurried down the stairs and got into David's car, and without making the decision to do so, I found myself motoring west, rushing into the mountains and driving on and on. I tried to explain away that awful scene, but my mind was so filled with the picture of David and Arthur in the bed that I knew there was no explanation other than the obvious one. Something precious had become rotten. Or maybe there had never been anything precious about our marriage.

David was all the ugly words—*queer, pantywaist, fairy, sissy,* some even worse. I knew so little about homosexuality. Had I caused it? Could David be cured? Did he want to be cured? Had there been other men? Perhaps this was the first time, but thinking back over the friendship between David and Arthur, the excuses they had made to be together, I knew it had happened before. Later, in the one very long talk that David and I had, he told me a great deal. But that night, I had no answers, only the knowledge that David had never loved me, but only used me to cover up his horrid secret.

Late in the evening, I stopped at a filling station high in the mountains. An oxbow hung beside the door of the little shack. When I switched off the motor, a man in greasy coveralls emerged from behind the remains of a Conestoga wagon. "Fill 'er up," I said, rolling the window all the way down and shivering in the cold air, realizing there was snow on the road. I had been too lost in thought to see it.

"You got money, do you?" he asked suspiciously. "I don't give up nothing I've worked for without a pretty fair trade."

Not knowing whether the man was drunk or just surly, I fished a five-dollar bill out of my pocketbook and held it up. Then he stood silently with one foot on the running board, holding the long hose against the tank while the gasoline went up and down in the big glass pump.

"Where you headed?" The man had hung up the hose and was using a rag to wipe spilled gasoline from the side of the car.

"West," I replied vaguely, realizing I had no destination.

"Shouldn't drive it at night if I's you."

"Is the road bad farther on?"

"If I can't say nothing good about it, I don't talk. And I'm not talking."

"What do you think I should do?"

"I can't tell you. I got troubles of my own." He took the bill, breathing on me with his liquory breath, and went inside for change, while I pondered whether his information was good or just whiskey talk.

The man came back and counted out the dimes and nickels and dollar bills, then said, "I guess you're between the rock and a hard spot about going over Suicide Pass yonder."

I had never heard of Suicide Pass and did not know if it were a proper name or a local moniker. I wouldn't for anything let on that he had upset me. Mountain people depended on the flatlanders, as they called those of us who lived on the plains, but they resented us and enjoyed deriding us. Sometimes, they played practical jokes on us. Tomorrow, the man would sit with his chums on the bench in front of the filling station and embroider on the story of the foolish woman from the city who had tried to drive across the mountains at night. They would find me even more amusing if they knew why I'd fled, I thought bitterly.

Snow glinted in the moonlight on either side of the dark road ahead. I knew I would not like to be caught on a mountain pass in a blizzard, especially when my mind was so troubled. There was no choice but to turn back. I put the car in gear and drove across the road to a café.

A woman wiping a table with a rag looked up as I came through the door and said sourly, "You don't want supper, do you? I'm about to close. Got to wash my feet and go to bed."

"Just coffee." I could not swallow food.

A man at a table nodded at me and said to her, "I guess she must have heard about your cooking, Sis. The meat's so tough, you can't cut the gravy with a knife."

"Oh, go on with you, Folger. I notice it ain't stopped you from coming in." Sis had become more good-natured now that she didn't have to fix food for me.

"Well, I'm going to stop, 'cause I got laid off at the mine. Anymore, if you're not twenty-five or thirty years old, you can't get a job."

"You never worked that hard anyway." Sis poured so much coffee into a heavy china mug that it slopped over. She didn't wipe the cup, just shoved it across the counter.

"The Blind Tom owes me for two weeks, and it owes the whole town for letting it throw all them tailings down the mountain."

"Oh, that mine don't owe we a dime. It's kept us going for years."

I wiped the side of the cup with a paper napkin and paid the woman for the coffee as well as for the mug, so that I could take the hot liquid with me. It would keep me awake during the drive back to Denver. I did not know that I would not sleep that night—and, in fact, would not sleep much at all for a very long time.

As I left the café, Folger said, "They're so spiteful, they don't know what to do with theyselves. They's weighted down with grievements."

He might have been talking about me, because my life, which had seemed perfect only a few hours before, was indeed weighted down with grievements. Back in David's car, I looked for a place to set the coffee, but the auto's dashboard was sloped and the cup would not fit on it. So I propped it on the seat beside me and drove back to Denver, taking a perverse pleasure in the way the coffee sloshed onto the seat. David disliked seat covers and had refused to install them. He would be furious at the coffee spill. Then I realized that David would not care now about stains.

As I came down Lookout Mountain and saw the lights of Denver spread out below, I realized that I did not know where I was going. The apartment was out of the question. I would have to face David sometime, but not now. With neither suitcase nor kitbag, I couldn't check into a tourist court. If I asked to stay with Caroline, she would ask questions. The only place for me to go was home to Mother and Henry. I would let myself in with my key and think of something to tell them later.

But as I opened the door of the Marion Street house, Henry emerged from the living room, a cup of tea in his hand. "She's all right. You mustn't worry," he said.

"I couldn't sleep and thought she might need me," I said, grateful that Henry had provided me with an excuse. Our aborted trip to the Broadmoor seemed so long ago that I had forgotten Mother had the flu.

"That's not necessary."

"Oh, but it's what I want."

Henry turned on the hall light and took in my ghastly face and swollen eyes and the wrinkled motoring suit that I had put on in the morning for the drive with Mother to the Springs. The hem was out where the heel of my shoe had caught it at the mountain stop. "What's wrong?"

I started to tell him that nothing was wrong but knew he would not believe me. "David and I had a spat. He knows I'm here."

"He must have forgotten, because he's called three times." Henry caught my arm and said, "It can't be all

297

that bad. Don't you think you ought to make up?"

"Make up?" I shrieked. *"Make up?"*

Henry put his finger to his lips and pointed upstairs to where Mother slept.

"Oh, Henry, we'll never make up. I'm going to file for divorce." I made the decision at that instant, knowing that there was no other choice. My marriage had ended when I pushed that light button.

Perhaps Henry called David after I left the house in the morning, because David was waiting for me at the top of the stairs when I returned to the apartment. He was looking even more haggard than I did. He held out his hands, but I could not take them. "Not now. I need a bath."

"Let me draw one for you."

"No." I locked the bathroom door, turned on the hot water, and threw my clothes onto the floor. Then I got into the tub, sitting there until the water turned tepid. I brushed my hair and put on the soft wool robe that David had given me for an anniversary gift. Although the heat was on in the apartment and the sun shone through the windows, I was cold. In fact, I would be cold for weeks, cold to my bones, sitting in the hot sun with a coat on and sleeping in a flannel nightgown under heavy quilts. The warmth never seemed to reach beneath the skin.

David had set cups and saucers on the table in the sunroom, and when I joined him, he poured coffee into the pot that was part of the Christmas silver service.

"Do you want eggs—scrambled eggs or a soft-boiled egg?"

"Is that what we're going to talk about—eggs?" I asked shrilly.

"Nora . . ."

"What?"

He sighed, and his whole body shook. "What do you want me to say?"

"Oh, well, why don't we talk about the weather. Or Mother's flu—or in the excitement last night, did I forget to tell you about it? Or maybe the coffee I spilled on your car seat. So sorry." I drew in a deep breath, for I had intended to be civil. "Or maybe we should talk about the divorce."

David drew into himself. "That's pretty drastic, isn't it? We can work things out. I promise never to see Arthur again."

"That is a promise you cannot keep."

"I can try. We don't have to be hasty."

"Yes, David, we do. Our marriage is over. I can't stand to be married to you, can't stand to even look at you."

"But all the years . . ." David had tears in his eyes as he reached across the table for my hand, but I would not give it to him. "Dearest, I'm so sorry."

I felt a little sad for him then and said, not unkindly, "Tell me about it. I want to understand. You owe me that." Then, because I could not stop wondering, I asked, "Is it my fault?"

David's open hand turned into a fist, and he put it into

his lap. "It doesn't have anything to do with you. It started before I even met you, back in college. I thought by moving here, I'd end it. I've always had those feelings. You remember when I broke our engagement. It was because I was all balled up inside and wasn't sure it wouldn't happen again." He glanced up at me pleadingly. "Then I decided that you were such a dear girl and that marriage would cure me. And it did."

"Until Arthur moved here."

"Yes, that."

"Did you ever love me?" It was the question that had repeated itself over and over in my head as I drove through the mountains.

David started to answer, but I interrupted. "No. Don't say anything. I wouldn't believe you anyway."

We talked for a long time. The morning sunlight slipped away from the room and was replaced by afternoon shadows. David made a second pot of coffee, and a third. I fixed cinnamon toast, but neither of us ate it. We talked about David's homosexuality, our marriage, and finally the divorce. At times, I wanted to comfort David—as he did me. He said we could be friends, but we could not. Sometimes, I was so overtaken by rage and betrayal that I could not speak. By the time we got up from the table, my palms were bleeding from where my nails had dug into them, and my hands ached from being clenched.

I agreed that David could spend that night in the guest room, for he had nowhere else to go but Arthur's place. The irony of that did not escape either one of us.

In the morning, David would make other arrangements. We joked that he might rent an apartment from me, and I thought that because we found humor in the situation, we would be all right.

But I was not all right. We worked out the details of severing our marriage, dividing up the furniture and art, the sheets and the flatware. I did not ask for alimony; he insisted on my keeping the apartment building and the house in Georgetown. Less than a week later, I took the train to Reno for a quickie divorce, staying in a downtown hotel, where women told stories about unfaithful or drunken or useless husbands. But I was silent, confused.

After six weeks in Reno, I appeared before a judge, threw my gold wedding ring into the Truckee River, and returned to Denver, the divorce papers in my pocketbook, shame and bitterness in my heart. I telephoned David to say that the divorce was final. But we did not see each other. I kept to the apartment or spent time with Caroline and my family. Hostesses were careful not to invite David and me to the same events, but as solitary males were preferable to unescorted women, I did not receive such a quantity of invitations. After a while, some of the single men in our set invited me to attend the movies or have a quiet dinner. I turned them down.

One morning, David called and asked if he might pick up the drapes, which I had promised him but had not yet taken down. He still had a key, and we agreed he would let himself in that afternoon while I was out.

David was delayed, however, and when I returned, I found him and Arthur sitting in the living room, drinking tea. I was overcome with anger.

"Hello, Nora," Arthur said, as if he were making a social call.

"How dare you be here?" I spat the words.

"It's all right," David said. "Arthur is helping me with the drapes. You remember he helped us hang them."

"I never said you could bring him into my apartment again."

"I thought you wouldn't be here."

"Get out."

"Nora, dear, I'm sorry about all this," Arthur said smoothly. He wasn't sorry at all. He had exactly what he wanted—a wife and children at home and now a secret life with David in David's new apartment. Arthur reached for the box on the smoking stand beside his chair, took out a cigarette, and lighted it. After a puff or two, he placed the cigarette in the ashtray and leaned back in his seat, apparently enjoying our little scene.

I began to shake, so I sat down, for fear my legs would give out.

"There's no need to be uncivil," David said. "We're all adults."

"Aw, she'll get over it," Arthur told him. He saw that his stocking had slipped down, and he pushed up his pants leg while he refastened the sock to the garter.

The gesture repulsed me. "Get over it? Get over that my husband is a damned—"

"Don't," said David, interrupting me. "Don't let's talk about it."

"You mean it's okay for the two of you to do what you do, but it's not okay for me to talk about it? Isn't that a bit twisted?"

"Muggs," David pleaded.

"Don't you ever call me that."

"It's not really wrong, but simply the way it is. There's nothing any of us can do about it, so don't be sore," Arthur said. He had picked up the cigarette again and now blew smoke out of the side of his mouth. "Buck up, Nora."

My hands were so icy that I took out my gloves and put them on. Then I shoved my gloved hands deep into my pockets. "Does Betsey think there's nothing wrong with it?" From the wary expression on Arthur's face, I knew that Betsey was no more aware of their homosexuality than I had been a few weeks earlier. "I'll ask her myself. Yes, I'll call Betsey, and we'll have a little talk."

"Come on, Nora," David pleaded.

Arthur said nothing, but he gave me a smug look, as if he knew I wouldn't follow through. He muttered out of the side of his mouth, "No soap," and then he patted David's arm. The homey gesture, one I had made so many times myself, made me white-hot with anger. I stood up and removed the glove from one hand and went to the telephone and dialed a number. "Betsey? It's Nora. Can we get together next week? I've something to tell you."

Would I have told her? I want to think it was only a bluff, that my better sense and my compassion would have kept me from doing something so cruel. All my life, I had acted out of love, not hate, but I had never really hated anybody until I caught Arthur with my husband. Of course, I would never know what I might have done. The threat that afternoon just five months ago had been enough. Two days later, David crashed his plane into the mountain.

Chapter Ten

GUILT WEIGHED ON ME LIKE the box of Amalia's belongings that I carried. After resting for a few minutes, I walked on, shifting the burden in my arms to check my wristwatch, but I had forgotten to wind it, and the hands were stopped at 2:20. The sky had turned ink-colored, and the deserted road, black with shadows now, was less friendly. Wood smoke from burning brush filled the heavy air with an acrid smell. Crows cawed from deep in the woods. A snake crawled out of the green slime in the ditch beside me, forcing me to wait as it slithered across the road. A dead turtle lay in the dirt, crushed by some vehicle. The woods were alive with insects, and gnats attacked my eyes and nose. When I shook my head to get rid of them, something damp and clammy, like a lizard, scratched at my neck, and I dropped the box, grasping at myself, but the thing was gone. The touch remained on my skin, and I rubbed at it with my hands to rid myself of the sliminess.

The carton lay in the dirt, its contents spilled across the road. A jewelry box had opened, disgorging a diamond that glittered in the black dirt like the eye of a crow. The candelabra was bent, and the glass on the sampler had cracked. I swore a little, gathering up the things and shoving them into the box, while the wind blew leaves off the trees, swirling them around me until my hair and body were speckled with the remains of dead foliage.

As I started off, there was a noise in the underbrush, as if something were following me, and I realized I had heard it before. I stopped, and the noise stopped. I went on, and so did it. Only a human would track me that way. I hurried as fast as I could, my legs aching and my arms limp from the weight of the heavy carton. I looked over my shoulder but saw nothing in the gloom of the trees.

Behind me, I heard the motor of a large car and then two staccato beeps of a horn. I moved as far to the side of the road as possible without stepping up onto the embankment, hoping the driver was not stalking me, too. The car slowed, and there was a second quick honk. I turned angrily to glare at the headlamps, hoping to forestall some masher before he could give a wolf whistle or yell, "Hey, girlie." The car crawled alongside of me and stopped, and a man reached over and rolled down the passenger window. "Hello there."

The auto, a bulky Packard, was dark inside. I did not

recognize the voice. Then the driver, realizing that I did not know him, said, "It's Holland Brown. We met at breakfast."

"Oh." I was surprised at how relief washed over me. I was not used to being frightened.

Holland put the car into neutral and set the emergency brake, then got out and stood on the running board as he leaned across the Packard's roof toward me. "How about a lift back to the Eola?"

"It's not far."

"If you won't let me drive you to your hotel, I'll have to walk along beside you, for the gentleman in me won't allow you to carry that box one more step."

"Was that line bred in your bones, or have you learned it since you've been in Natchez?" I hoped my words did not sound as abrupt to him as they did to me.

"I'm trying to learn southern manners, and by the looks of things, I'm not doing such a hot job at it."

Embarrassed by my rudeness, I explained, "Walking along this road, I've been imagining all sorts of awful things. You could have been a fiend."

"No such luck." Holland Brown's amusement made me feel better. "That box you're carrying says 'Nu-Grape' on the side—horrid sugary drink, that—but my guess is you've got the family jewels in there. You can hold them on your lap, if you think I'll snatch them."

The remark made me laugh, because the box did indeed contain the Bondurant jewelry, although I had no intention of telling that to Holland Brown. "It does make more sense for both of us to ride." Then, to show

306

that I had learned manners, too, I added, "And yes, thank you, a ride would be nice."

Holland came around the car and took the box from me. "Ye gods! If these are your family's valuables, they're made of iron. It's a wonder you were able to carry them at all." He put the box into the backseat and opened the front passenger door for me, then got in on the driver's side. "I'll wager you have been out in the country, looking at your patrimony. I've been doing the same." He stuck out his elbow to indicate his rolled-up shirtsleeves as he put in the Packard's clutch and switched gears. "I've been tramping around it, at any rate. I hope your place is in better condition than mine. The land's sour and parched, and the house burned down years ago."

"In the war?" I asked.

"Heavens no. The Hollands would have been better off if it had. That might have forced the lot of them to move sooner. These old places just catch fire—lightning, tramps, naughty boys sneaking a smoke. Have you insurance?"

"You've not seen Avoca." I'd assumed that everybody in Natchez knew all about Avoca.

"I haven't had the pleasure. My condolences on your aunt's death, by the way. Mr. Sam said she passed under mysterious circumstances."

"Thank you. She didn't die under mysterious circumstances. She was murdered. After he shot her, the killer committed suicide. That's it."

"Oh, I *have* missed a plain-spoken Yankee woman

307

since coming down here." Holland grinned at me, showing teeth that were very white but a little uneven. He was a large man, not fat, but powerfully built, with big features. His hand on the steering wheel was large. Holland was not especially handsome, but there was a wholesome look to him. David had had delicate features, and he'd been trim—sleek almost—with fine hair that he'd had carefully trimmed each Friday morning. Holland Brown had curly hair that appeared to have a mind of its own, the kind of hair a woman might like to comb into place with her fingers. I was not that sort of woman, however. I would keep my hands to myself.

Holland seemed to be waiting for a reply, so I said, "They do have a way of talking, don't they, as if they sprinkle their words with sugar."

"They sprinkle everything else with sugar. I've never been offered so much treacle in my life."

"What doesn't have sugar has salt. Have you tasted the ham? And I don't believe I have to say anything to you about beaten biscuits."

"My sentiments exactly," Holland said. "And grits! What sane person could grind up a perfectly good cornstalk and turn it into sand?"

"Perhaps it's their punishment for losing the Civil War."

"You mean the Lost Cause."

I leaned back against the woolen seat of the Packard and relaxed. Holland Brown seemed like a boy from home, his words clipped, instead of melting into one another. But unlike the boys in Denver, he did not know me, did not know about David, so he was not looking for hidden meaning in what I said. I felt more comfortable with him than I had with a man in a long time.

He stopped in front of the Eola. "I'll carry that box to your room for you, unless you think people will talk. They do have a way of minding each other's business here."

"They have a way of doing that everywhere. We'll just tell them to get lost."

"Why, Miss Nora!" Holland said in mock shock.

"It's just plain Nora. Do you think they'll talk even more if I offer you a drink up there? The bellman sold me a bottle of something called 'white mule.'"

"I know it well—the devil's poison."

"It's not nearly as good as sugar moon from home. Colorado makes the best bootleg in the country."

"I'm partial to Chicago whiskey. It's as nice as you please."

"Either one's bound to be better than white mule."

"You've got my number."

My room was too stuffy for comfort. So after locking the jewelry boxes inside my suitcase—while Holland discretely stared out the window, pretending he was not interested in what I'd taken from Avoca—I stuck the bottle into my purse, and we walked to the river, where the water was the same lead color as the sky. We watched as the night came on, taking nips from the bottle like a couple of bums, and I told him about the drunk who had approached me the night before. Sharing the story with him made me feel good. Then we walked down to Natchez Under-the-Hill and had dinner in a little dive. People ignored us, and for the first time since arriving in Natchez, I felt invisible.

As we ate fried catfish and hush puppies, Holland told me that he had come to Mississippi after his divorce but was not yet sure he would stay for good. He did not talk about his marriage, but instead spoke about Natchez. "The people are fine, and despite what you'd think, there is plenty of legal work here, even though these are drowsing years and some folks don't hit on all six, but . . ." He shrugged. "It's still an alien place to me. I ain't a southerner, not yet, at any rate."

"Me, neither." I told him that I was divorced, too.

"Love dies, doesn't it?"

"If it ever existed at all." I added quickly, "I intend to be here only long enough to settle my aunt's estate."

"Well, that's a shame."

"There is a little building on Avoca that I could turn into a house, but the idea seems awfully far-fetched."

He raised an eyebrow but said nothing, and after that, like countrymen who have found each other in a foreign land, we amused ourselves with stories about what Holland called "the natives." "A client of mine came in wearing the oddest-looking pair of shoes, which he said were made during the war," Holland told me. "The family couldn't get leather, you see, so when their dog died, they skinned it and sent the skin to the tanner, and the shoes lasted into the third generation. They were so grateful, they damn near held a wake for that dog." He paused only a moment. "Have you heard about their wakes? They serve a drink made of bourbon, cooked oatmeal, and cream. Fortunately, with the heat, the laying out is brief."

"It's a good thing I arrived too late for my aunt's funeral," I said. Then I related Parthena's story about a Natchez woman who had been told by a Union officer during the war that if all the women in Mississippi were as pretty as she, he had no desire to conquer the South. "You know what she replied?" I asked, then told him. " 'If all the Union men are as ugly as you, we have no desire to conquer you, either.' "

After dinner, Holland walked me back to the hotel. For a moment, I thought he would kiss my cheek, and I wanted him to. But we were in the lobby, and so we shook hands. "I would like to see you again before you leave," Holland told me.

I said that would be nice, and I thought, That would be very nice indeed.

As if in punishment for the pleasant evening with Holland, I awoke with the shivers. I turned off the fan and covered myself with a blanket, although the air was still and hot. I lay in bed, my toes and fingertips cold, thinking about David, about his last minutes in the aeroplane as he maneuvered it toward Lookout Mountain, wondering if his final thoughts were not of me but of Arthur. I took a sleeping powder and did not awake until nine o'clock, the hour I'd agreed to meet Pickett and Mr. Sam at Avoca. Seeing the time on the clock ticking on the bedside table, I jumped up and threw on my work clothes, brushed my teeth, and dusted my face with a puff I took from my compact. It might be all right for me to be late in Natchez, but it would certainly be improper to arrive with a shiny nose.

By the time my cab reached Avoca, Amalia's bed was being disassembled in the driveway and Pickett was waving her arms at a workman carrying a small table. "Over here," she said, and he set it down. A tiny man dressed in a white shirt and pants and carrying a walking stick, examined the table, his fingers tapping his chest.

"It's sure a beaut," Pickett said, beckoning me.

He squatted and looked underneath the table. "It's fabulous." He pronounced the word "fabalas."

"I told you so." She indicated me. "Nora Bondurant, may I present Philip St. Vrain, the New Orleans antiquities dealer. Some people would say he knows more about American antiques than anyone else in the South."

"And they would be right." Philip stood and dusted off his palms, then took my hands between his. "Miss Nora, you pretty thing, it is such a pleasure. When I heard last night what was inside this house, I could not sleep. My driver and I left New Orleans before the sun was up."

"I hope you don't mind," Pickett said. "I didn't encourage him. I simply telephoned to ask about prices. Watch him. He'll try to honey up to you."

"She embroiders. You understand, of course, that with the economy in such a muddle, what I can afford to pay . . . But there it is." He held out his hands, palms up. Then he said he would make a more pleasing arrangement if I would consign the furniture to him.

"Philip, if you push her like that, you can just go on home." Pickett turned to me. "Mind you, you aren't obliged. I told Philip what was inside, and he insisted on seeing for himself. If you'd rather not make a decision about selling just now, we'll tote the lot over to the Buzzard's Nest. You can store it there till it rots."

"*Cher!* You are an unbalanced woman!" Philip protested. "Now run along and powder your nose like a good girl, and leave me with Miss Nora."

Pickett ignored him. "Your things are going in the driveway for now, Nora, and we'll haul them to the shipper's this afternoon. Tilly's taking apart Miss Amalia's bed for you." She looked at Philip. "Prudent Mallard, Philip, and she's keeping it."

Philip pouted until Pickett said there was a second Prudent Mallard bed upstairs.

"The things you've offered me"—she dipped her head in appreciation—"go onto the big truck. The rest will stay in the yard, where Philip can haggle over them." She waved to a man carrying a chair and indicated the lawn. "Philip can tell you what he wants, and the prices are up to you. Don't accept his first offer, of course. He adores to steal things."

Pickett smiled at Philip, who huffed and said, "I believe you'd skin a gnat for hide and tallow."

313

"Stuff and nonsense. The Mallard's not anything for you to sell it, and you know that's right." Pickett dismissed him with a flip of her hand, and when he had gone off to examine another piece of furniture, she whispered, "That little twelve-ounce man is a dear, but he's so touchy. Of course, those Oscar Wildes are. You can always tell, can't you?"

"Can you?"

Pickett was directing a workman with a chair in his arms. "What?"

"Ezra says Miss Amalia wanted the statue thrown into the Mississippi."

"I hope you're not sob-hearted woman enough to do it."

"He also said the thing is supported from the cellar and that the house will fall down if it's moved." Then I added, "But the house will fall down anyway."

"Tell me something I don't know. But perhaps we'd better leave it there for now." She called to a workman who was carrying out the petticoat mirror, "Oh, my cake, Mobile! Be taking care with that looking glass."

While she went to see if the mirror had been chipped, I wandered onto the driveway to look at the chair Tilly had set there, a Belter. I picked it up, but Philip took it from me. "I was hoping you'd sell that." A goat had wandered over to him and now began nibbling on his shoe. Philip pushed it away with both hands, then brushed his hands together.

"It's a Belter," I told him. "I *love* Belter. There are two more chairs, a sofa, and a table that match.

They're in awfully good condition."

"People these days prefer those horrible davenports."

"I know. That's why I think I'll keep the set."

Philip sized me up while I looked at him stupidly. "You stinker. You are every bit as cagey as Miss Pickett—and as tight. When she opens up her pocket-book, moths fly out." He sat down in the chair. "I'm sure we can work something out, *cher*."

After he left, Pickett said, "That poor fish doesn't stand a chance. You told me you don't like Belter. Why, you can fib as fast as a horse can run."

"Or at least as good as you can."

As I went into the house, Pickett yelled at Tilly that she'd step on his corns if he dropped the marble bust he was carrying. From the back of the house, a man's voice said, "She cackles so much, she'd give a hen the blues."

I went into the dining room, where a man with moles all over his face and rolls of fat under his chin, which gave him a screw-neck look, sat at a table. He was watching a woman use newspaper to wrap the Old Paris china. When I thanked her, she said, "You got a gracious plenty here—enough for you here, enough for you there. Your family wouldn't want nothing better." The table was covered with china, and as she finished filling a box, she looked for someplace to set it. "Gimme that chair you setting in, Pretty. I rather have your space than your company." She turned to me. "We call him Pretty 'cause he's so ugly."

"You ain't no Miss Bessie Smith yourself, sugar."

Impulsively, I asked the woman to set aside place settings for eight, for I'd begun to wonder about restoring the billiard house. It was an absurd idea, of course, but I could always ship the china later.

I wandered into the great hall and went upstairs, where the shutters were open and the rooms flooded with light. The tent and Ezra's bed were gone, along with his quilt. The other quilts were still in the cupboard of one of the bedrooms, so I shook out a dust cloth, set an armload of quilts on the clean side, and wrapped them up. I carried the bundle down the stairs and out to the driveway, where Pickett had set my things, then returned for a second load, and a third.

As I set down the last bundle, Philip took out a pair of round gold glasses and put them on, commenting, "I wear eyeglasses for show and for seeing close." He leaned over for a better look at the quilts.

"My aunt made them. I'm keeping them."

With his walking stick, Philip flipped through the quilts. "Oh yes, do. I thought they might be Baltimore Albums, but they're just primitives." I straightened the quilts before returning to the house, where I asked two workmen to haul Amalia's desk to the quarters. Ezra and Aunt Polly might want it.

At noon, Aunt Polly, wearing a starched apron, her hair tied up in a crimson bandanna, brought biscuits and vegetable stew, pickles and stewed apples, and sweet-potato pie for Pickett, Philip, and me. We three whites sat on the porch, eating off china, while the black workers gathered in the yard with tin plates.

I hadn't thought about lunch, and I asked Pickett if she had given Aunt Polly the makings. "And insult her? Why, she used to cook for dozens of people at a time."

"Today reminds me of such good times as that, Miss Pickett, and I happy as a dog in the smokehouse to wrassle up that somethin' good to eat," Aunt Polly said, coming up behind us. "This morning, we don't have enough to make a fly a snack, but I tell Ezra to go in the garden and fotch the takin's, be they small or big, and he come back with enough to fill the cook pot. I expect this the last party I make for Miss Amalia."

By midafternoon, everything worth saving, except for the statue, had been removed from the house. As I stood in the yard with Pickett, watching the workmen start off, Mr. Sam drove up. He pulled over to let the caravan of trucks pass, then got out of his car and observed that they looked like "Confederates fleeing the accursed Yankees."

"When will you stop fighting that war?" I asked.

"When you surrender." As he walked toward the big house, he called over his shoulder, "I believe you are in retreat—cornered up north, eating beans."

I followed him into the big house, where he peered into the empty rooms on the first floor. "Bondurants have lived here for near a hundred years," he said, mopping his eyes with a handkerchief, wiping away either sweat or tears. He passed the statue of Amalia, removed his hat, and bowed low. Then he gazed up at the marble face and said, "Miss Amalia, it has been a pleasure to serve you, a pleasure." He stood up but kept his hat in his hand. "I remember standing in this very spot when I was a boy, watching Miss Amalia come down these selfsame stairs in a yellow satin dress and yellow satin slippers with the toes covered in gold. The house was lit up by candles. Natchezians called Avoca 'the house of a thousand candles.' Miss Amalia glowed in that candlelight like a flame, and folks stopped talking to stare at her. The next season, every woman in Natchez ordered a yellow satin gown of her dressmaker. They looked like honeybees. Miss Amalia was the only woman who could ever wear that color." He glanced at me and added, "I believe yellow would be becoming to you."

Yellow made me look like a banana, but I smiled at the compliment and asked Mr. Sam if he wanted to go through the rooms on the second floor again. "The workmen have been going up and down all day, so we should be safe on the steps."

"I have not the slightest doubt." He led the way to the upper floor, pausing when he reached the hall to say, "You have taken hold here."

I did not understand, and he explained. "That is to say, you have come to belong to Avoca."

"Not belong," I said, taken aback, "but I like it. Of course I do."

"You should have seen it when Miss Amalia was in her time of blossoming. But she's gone now. Yes, she's gone." He raised his head and looked me in the eye. "Aunty said Ezra showed you the billiard house. Would you stay?"

318

"I don't know."

"If you don't, they would be left lonesome."

The sun beat down through the broken roof onto my face, and my shoulders ached from lifting boxes. I was tempted to hurry Mr. Sam, but I knew I might not find him in such a reflective mood again. "It makes me uncomfortable that others know my family's secrets when I don't."

"Do you have need of knowing them?"

"I do."

"What if you don't like what you find out? What if the weight of it puts a grief on you?" Mr. Satterfield looked troubled. "Had you thought you might be better off not knowing the Bondurant secrets?"

"I think you have opened a door."

"No, Miss Nora, not even a window."

"Perhaps a peephole."

Instead of sparring with me, Mr. Sam sat down on the top step and waited while I seated myself below him and wiped my damp face on my dirty skirt.

"You already know the half of it, that Miss Amalia was your father's mother. That's not worth denying."

"And it's not worth denying that Bayard Lott was my grandfather. You know that every bit as much as Ezra and Aunt Polly do."

"Oh, servants." He gave a dismissive wave of his hand. "No need to pry on that score. There are burdens no descendant should carry. You needn't ask me his name, because I'm not going to say it. That's a thing past telling."

"It doesn't matter. I already know it. But I still don't know why Bayard Lott killed Miss Amalia. I believe you could tell me something about it. I would like to know before I go home."

Mr. Sam stood up. "The light's fading, and I should like to see the rooms downstairs for the last time."

I did not stand, however, and good manners forced Mr. Sam to wait for me. "Bayard Lott was primed for more than fifty years," he said. "Ezra won't tell you the truth of what lit the fuse, but Aunt Polly might could do so. Nothing ever happened on Avoca that she didn't know about."

He reached his hand for me, and I got up, and together we descended to the first floor, where Mr. Sam stopped and bowed again to Amalia's statue. "Good-bye, my dear girl."

Aunt Polly hadn't confided in me before, of course, but armed with the knowledge that if anyone knew the reason for Amalia's death, it was she, I decided to try one more time. After Mr. Sam drove off, I went to the quarters.

Aunt Polly was sitting a little distance away, under the shade of a live oak. Bent over a quilting frame, she was sewing in the dappled light. The frame was propped on the backs of chairs turned outward, and I sat down on one. "Mr. Satterfield's shipping Miss Amalia's quilts to Denver for me."

"She like that." Aunt Polly took half a dozen stitches on her needle; then, with her free hand steadying the

320

quilt from underneath, she pushed the needle through the fabric. "This a string quilt, mostly tore-up clothes. Miss Amalia make the toppen part."

My grandmother Bullock had made string quilts, sewing together tiny strips of leftover fabric, but in Amalia's quilt top, the strips formed stars. The fabrics were yellow calicos, handwoven butternut, indigo-dyed homespun, and double pinks, but the predominant color was red.

"Thread you a needle," Aunt Polly said. "I show you to quilt. It bring me peace. It bring you peace, too."

I shook my head.

Nonetheless, Aunt Polly set down her needle on the quilt top and cut a length of thread. She took a second needle from a piece of folded cloth and, holding it to her good eye, threaded it, then laid it at the edge of the quilt in front of me and picked up her own needle. "Watch me. You starts when you want to." I made no move toward the needle, and she resumed her stitching. "Ezra take you to town in the car, so he don't have to follow you through the brush no more."

I jerked up my head. "That was Ezra following me yesterday?"

"He afraid some of those mens go after you when you got Miss Amalia's gatherin's. He think you don't want him to look after you, so he stay to the trees, not drive the car."

After telling her that Mr. Sam would transfer the title of the REO to Ezra, I stopped, embarrassed. "I don't know your last name."

"Oh, it Bondurant, like you."

"I suppose that makes sense. After all, the captain was Ezra's father."

Aunt Polly's head jerked up. "What you say?"

Had I offended her? But she had told me that herself. "Forgive me, Aunt Polly. I didn't know it was a secret."

"That ain't no secret. That ain't even no truth. Bless God, what Miss Amalia say to that!" Aunt Polly laughed, shaking her head back and forth. "Ezra's daddy the marster but one. The captain buys me when I pregnant for Ezra. My other marster in my way back yonder time a dog that mistreat me terrible, gave me bread and water and lashes for no reason. He just mean. Slavery do that to white men. He hurt me fearful, and I pray for a new marster. God is awful kind to me when I need Him, and He give me the captain. The captain never laid no hands on me."

She poked her needle in and out of the quilt with fingers as frail as curled leaves. "I sure do have sharp luck when the captain buys me. The more I see, the more I got to give thanks for. Miss Amalia passes, and we gets you."

"Then Ezra's not Miss Amalia's half brother."

Aunt Polly laughed again. "After freedom come and we gets to pick us a name, Miss Amalia herself say me and Ezra ought to be Bondurants. She never like the name Ezra 'cause Mr. Frederick pick it for Ezra when he born. Miss Amalia call Ezra 'Bon.'"

I stilled Aunt Polly's hand with my own, and she looked up, waiting. "Mr. Sam says you can tell me why

322

Bayard Lott killed Miss Amalia. Please."

Aunt Polly did not look away, just narrowed her eyes, focusing on my face. "Ezra say you don't want to know."

"And you say?"

"I say maybe you got the right of knowing it."

"Mr. Lott saw something through the telescope, didn't he?"

Aunt Polly looked down at her needle, but her hand remained still. "Maybe so he did."

A piece of Spanish moss hanging like smoke from the branch above us suddenly swung down over the quilt. I broke it off and threw it onto the ground. "He saw something that made him mad enough to kill Miss Amalia."

"She always keep that shutter on the window by Shadowland closed, but maybe he see through it with the spyglass."

"And saw what?"

Aunt Polly put down her needle and ran her hand over the quilt, her eyes cast down. "Maybe he seen Ezra in the bed with Miss Amalia." Her hand was still, and I sucked in my breath.

What had I expected? That he'd seen goats grazing on Shadowland's lawn? Amalia and Maggie plotting together? No, of course not. But I had not expected that. For a moment, I did not breathe as I let that revelation sink in. Then I let out my breath in a whoosh. "And so he killed her. And then he killed himself." It was not a question, but a statement.

"No." Aunt Polly waited, slowly raising her head until she looked at me. "He just kill Miss Amalia."

I narrowed my eyes at her, confused.

Aunt Polly's hand moved slowly on the quilt, making its way toward the needle. She touched it but did not pick it up. "Ezra kill Mr. Bayard."

I sat very still, waiting.

Aunt Polly put the point of the needle into the fabric and looked at me. "Ezra already gone upstairs, and that where he's at when he hear the shot. Ezra have the captain's gun up there to kill rats, 'cause Miss Amalia, she hate rats. Ezra grab it and runs to Miss Amalia, but she laying there dead in the bed. Mr. Bayard next to her. When he see Ezra, he cusses fire to Ezra's heart and raise his gun. So Ezra shoot him. Ezra don't think till it too late that Mr. Bayard's gun don't have but one bullet to it and he ain't got time to get him another. Those two get killed with two guns, but nobody didn't know it."

The sheriff had told me only that he'd checked Bayard's gun for fingerprints. He'd just assumed that both bullets had come from the same gun. "What did Ezra do with the captain's gun?"

"He throw it in the river."

"That's what I would have done." I nodded my approval. "Was Ezra the reason Miss Amalia didn't marry Bayard Lott?"

"Ezra or no, she never marry with him!" Aunt Polly spat the words. "Mr. Bayard go to New York and tell her she his, that he want her since their creepin' days.

When she say, 'See the door,' he have his way with her. You know what I talkin'?"

I did.

"Ezra, he comfort her, just like he always done. They love each other since they both little chips.

"Miss Amalia teach him to read, to sign his name with that fancy *B*. Miss Amalia embroider that *B* on her quilts. Ezra right proud of that letter." *B* for Bon, not Bayard, I thought.

"If he loved Miss Amalia, why did he marry Sukey Pea?"

"He a man. He got his needs." Aunt Polly grinned. "It make bloody footprints on Miss Amalia's heart, and she act grievous. But after Sukey Pea leave, Ezra and Miss Amalia stop talking with their tongues and start talking with their hearts." She nodded as she said, "You got to give heart-room to love, not hate."

Aunt Polly resumed her quilting. In a few minutes, she laughed, "There ain't no colors in heaven." She took a few more stitches. "The Lord give us love like a new mercy every and each morning. He got all kind of love to give us. Maybe it ain't what you want, but the Lord got His reasons. God don't want us to be left lonesome on this green earth. Any love's a gift of God." She set down her needle and put her hand on my arm. "Honey baby, maybe the Lord give you this place as your new mercy, to stop the hurting."

A breeze stirred the tree, and dried leaves floated down onto the quilt. I picked them up one by one so that they wouldn't crumble on the strips of cloth, then dropped them onto the ground, thinking about Aunt Polly's words. Was Avoca a mercy? I didn't know yet. But sitting there in the drowsing sun, I realized that in some way, David had loved me, and I knew I had loved him, and that was enough. The rest of it—the hate and the guilt—I could let go.

Aunt Polly murmured, "Amen" as she sewed on in the light that filtered through the oak leaves and the Spanish moss. After a time, I picked up the second needle and began to weave it in and out of the quilt.

Epilogue

T HE OLD HOUSE LOOKED LIKE a dying thing in the early-winter gloom, and, indeed, in the little more than a year since I had first seen it, I had watched Avoca enter its death throes. A wild storm that lashed the house with wind and rain had sent the roof crashing through the second floor of Avoca. It landed on the spot where Amalia's bed had stood. Tramps built a blaze in the marble fireplace, and it roared up the clogged chimney and sent smoke billowing through the rooms. I had moved Amalia's statue from the Great Hall to the garden of the billiard house, and, true to the captain's threat, when the support that held the statue in place fell, the floor of the Great Hall sagged like a clothesline. Goats now wandered in and out of the house, and birds built nests in the empty rooms.

"It's like a great feudal estate," Caroline said, rolling

down the window of the REO for a better look. I had just picked her up at the station on her first visit to Natchez. "And creepy. I'm perfectly furious to see it."

"You'll ruin your clothes. We'll explore it tomorrow—the first floor, at any rate. There's no way to get to the second, because the staircase fell down."

"Are there ghosts?"

"There are always ghosts in Natchez."

"One of them must be your crazy old grandmother." Caroline added quickly, "Oh, I know, I won't say a thing about her indiscretion."

"It seems to be an open secret in Natchez." Although Mother knew nothing of what I'd discovered about Father, I had confided to Caroline that Amalia was not my aunt, but my grandmother, and that my father had been illegitimate. She had dismissed the revelation with a wave of her hand. "So what? My father's a bastard, too, although not in the technical sense."

Now Caroline said, "But you aren't sure who your grandfather was."

"Most people think he was Bayard Lott, the man who killed her."

"And you?"

I shrugged. "How would I know?" And the truth was I didn't. When I asked Aunt Polly if Ezra was my father's father, she replied, "No way could I know that. Even Miss Amalia don't know for sure. And no way do you need to know. It easier for you in that way." I mulled that over for a long time and decided she was right. What did it matter whether Ezra's blood or

327

Bayard Lott's ran in my veins? If it were Bayard's, I was the descendant of two old Natchez families. And if it were Ezra's, then my father was the son of two people who loved each other, no matter their color. I never asked Ezra about it, but he knew what Aunt Polly had told me, because things between us softened. We kept our distance, just as he and Amalia must have, but we treated each other with affection and kindness, as if we were family.

I put the old car back into gear and we bumped along the road to the billiard house. I had finished remodeling it in the spring, adding electricity and plumbing, a kitchen and a bathroom. Now I divided my time between Colorado and Mississippi. I had arrived back in Natchez just a few days earlier to make sure everything was in order for my friend when she visited for a few days on a trip to the East.

I parked beside the cottage and unlocked the front door. "You should have seen the original key—impressive but not very effective. Most of these old doors open with a screwdriver or a skeleton key. Ezra put in a good lock." He'd also cleared the underbrush around the building, opening up the long view across the meadow to the woods.

We left Caroline's luggage in the guest bedroom, which was bright with one of Amalia's quilts, and Caroline followed me down the hall into what had been the billiards room, now my living room. Buckland had taken the billiards table, but I'd kept the heavy old furniture, which had been reupholstered. I'd added floor lamps, a radio, draperies, a scrap picture of Avoca that I had made; my Natchez friends were demanding I make them similar pictures of their homes, which pleased me. The room had been designed to be both grand and cozy, although I wasn't sure it was either. It was comfortable, however.

Sitting down in one of the big chairs, I pulled out my hat pin, then removed my hat and fluffed up my hair. Caroline toured the room, exclaiming over the fireplace and the jib windows, the books and the odds and ends that I had salvaged from Avoca. She checked the hem of her dress in the petticoat mirror I'd saved from Avoca, then stopped for a moment in front of the framed "Wez Free" sampler that Aunt Polly had stitched long ago and given to me the day I moved into the billiard house. "The whole thing's swell, Nora." She sprawled on a chair, stretching out her long legs. "Would you ever move here for good?"

"I don't think so. It's too far from Mother and Henry."

"Be that as it may, what about this Holland fellow?"

"What about him?"

"Don't be coy, sweetie. I've known you forever."

I leaned my head back against the chair. "Okay. I honestly don't know, not that I haven't thought about it. We're taking it slow." Both Holland and I were wary of marriage, had talked only vaguely about it, but we had developed an affection for each other. "He's different from David." At the mention of David's name, I touched the aquamarine drop at my throat—the necklace that he had given me in Central City and that I had begun wearing again.

"Is that such a bad thing?"

I glanced at her to see if she were being sarcastic, but of course I had not told Caroline why I left David, and she had not figured it out. "I suppose not. You'll meet Holland tomorrow, when we go to Pickett's for dinner. You brought that slinky frock, didn't you? We want to show them how uptown two girls from Denver can be."

"Do they still wear hoopskirts?"

"Only on special occasions."

"What kind of a name is Pickett anywho?" Caroline put her feet on top of a footstool.

"Oh, all the women here are named after dead Civil War heroes. Except for Odalie, who's named for a Prussian goose, for all I know. She wears rings over her gloves, and her diamonds look like peach pits. They're almost as valuable. Not like this." I held out my hand so that Caroline could admire Amalia's champagne diamond. "Her family made their fortune in used motorcars in Jackson."

"Oh my, you've certainly gotten your snap back," Caroline observed. "I've missed it."

"Don't let Odalie bait you. She adores to do it," I continued.

Caroline frowned. "Why in the world invite her?"

"Oh, you don't understand Natchez women. They are slow to forgive hardness of heart and unkindness, but they tolerate it in someone who is amusing. And you

330

will adore Pickett. She is just like you—only with better manners."

Caroline swatted my hand, then kicked off her slippers and arched her back. "I'm tired, even though I went Pullman."

"Lucky you. The berths were all booked when I came, so I rode coach." When Caroline rolled her eyes, I added, "It was fun. I sat across from a man in overalls, whose hair looked like a stubble field, and I thought I ought to buy him breakfast in the diner, since he'd probably spent his last nickel on the ticket. But I didn't, because he pulled out a dinner pail. When he got off the train, he was met by a chauffeur. I spent the rest of the trip making up stories about him."

My friend looked at me curiously. "You really are back to normal."

"Applesauce," I protested mildly.

"Yes, you are. Like I said, you're snappier." She paused. "And you're not as sad." She reached for my hand and squeezed it. "I'm glad."

Caroline was right. I had not expected to be happy again, but I was. I did not want to discuss it, however, because it meant talking about David. I preferred to keep my thoughts of him for my quiet moments, when I could remember the better times. The other times . . . well, they were not so wretched now, more bittersweet. I was glad the conversation was interrupted by a tap on the front door, a sound so faint that Caroline didn't hear it. But I had grown used to listening for it, and I looked up when Ezra came into the room carrying a tray.

He set it on a table, and I saw that he already had put out the tea things. "Aunt Polly make you a ginger bread." He lifted the napkin over the cake so that we could admire it. "I fix the tea." He went into the kitchen and in a few minutes came back with a silver teapot. "It steep yet."

"This is Miss Caroline, Ezra," I said, then turned to my friend. "Without Ezra, I could not live here." I added, "Ezra and Aunt Polly. How is she today?" Like Avoca, the old black woman had deteriorated over the past year, and she'd been relieved when I told her that I would prepare my own meals at the billiard house. In fact, I sometimes cooked for Ezra and Aunt Polly. Still, when Mother and Henry or other guests visited, Aunt Polly sent up cake and biscuits and pots of stew, and when I gave my first dinner party, Aunt Polly made chicken shortcake.

"Best to be expected this time of year," Ezra replied. "She got dark shadows 'fore her eyes."

"Does she feel up to meeting Miss Caroline? We can walk down to the quarters later."

Ezra nodded. "Her head is tired, but the sight of you pleasure her. All her friends has left her, and you and me all she got left. You want you a fire?" When I nodded, Ezra struck a match and laid it on the kindling. The dew was still frozen on the grass outside, and the wind rattled dead leaves against the windows. The blaze took the edge off the chill. Ezra looked around the room to make sure everything was in place, then said, "By and by, I fotch you more wood. Aunt Polly say you come one of these week-a-days and help her finish her quilt 'fore Old Death put out his hand in the night for her." I had gotten in the habit of stitching with her one or two afternoons a week when I was in Natchez.

"I will, Ezra. Thank you."

"And thank your aunt for the ginger bread," Caroline added.

Ezra chuckled and sent me a sly glance. After he left, I said, "Aunt Polly's Ezra's mother. Old Negro women are called 'aunty' in the South. Shoot, at first I thought Aunt Polly was Ezra's wife."

"He's colored?"

"It takes only one drop."

Caroline got up and stood before the fire, rubbing her hands.

"They were both slaves," I said softly. "*Our* slaves."

Caroline's hands stopped moving. "Not *your* slaves. You didn't even know you had family here."

"I do now, and they're my charge. We take our responsibilities seriously."

Caroline turned and studied me to see if I were joking, but I was not. "What do you have to say about miscegenation? It's obvious Ezra wasn't sired by any colored man."

I remembered Pickett's answer to the same question, and I said, "We pretend it didn't happen. Pretending is one of the things we in the Old South do best."

" 'We'?" Caroline asked. "*We?* It sounds like you've become one of them." She looked at me expectantly, waiting for me to laugh.

I picked up a pillow fashioned from lace and scraps of silk that I'd found in Amalia's workbasket and plucked at a thread. "Of course not. It takes a lifetime to become a southerner."

Caroline turned back to the fire as the wood popped, sending up sparks like fireflies.

I went to the table where Ezra had set the ginger bread and put the pieces onto Amalia's Old Paris plates. Then I poured tea as I thought about Amalia and Ezra and Aunt Polly, and how my life forever would be intertwined with theirs. I handed Caroline a cup of tea and the ginger bread. "As we say, here's you your corner piece."

Caroline laughed and said, "I believe a corner piece of you really has become southern, kiddo—or at least it wants to."

I thought that over while I sat down and sipped my tea and tasted the cake, savoring the bite of ginger mingled with cinnamon. And I told Caroline, "That's not worth denying."

Center Point Publishing
600 Brooks Road ● PO Box 1
Thorndike ME 04986-0001 USA

(207) 568-3717

US & Canada:
1 800 929-9108